Praise for The Aftermath:

As a psychoanalyst for many years, I worked with countless PTSD victims. I highly recommend *The Aftermath* for those seeking to understand trauma and know more about its manifestations and repercussions. Coffin writes with a deep and compelling veracity.

—Lore Reich Rubin,
Author of *Memories of a Chaotic World*

Coffin has written a deeply engaging novel of the struggle of a trauma survivor that makes the reader question what survival really means. We are carried into the near-madness of PTSD and the search for resolution. The tale of how, and whether, resolution occurs, written in Coffin's evocative style, makes for compelling reading. *The Aftermath* is not so much read as experienced.

—Rebecca Meredith,
Author of *Last of the Pascagoula*

Coffin brings to the page a very real conflict faced by many people. She shows how the struggle to survive, to heal, exacts itself morally and physically on a person. Her resolution brings a contemporary edge to the narrative. The action resolves in a surprising and yet perhaps inevitable outcome that needs to be heard and considered by the contemporary world. This is a book of suspense to savor. *The Aftermath* testifies to the struggle of all of us to be whole.

—Dustin Pickering,
Author of *A Matter of Degrees*,
Founder of Transcendent Zero Press

"In rich, nuanced prose, Coffin weaves a wide-ranging story. We experience a young woman's initial devastation and dependency, then move with her beyond that, to a denouement which is both unexpected and convincing. *The Aftermath* is an exploration of love far beyond its physical manifestations. Consensual and non-consensual sex are here, as well as homosexuality and bi-sexuality– and an utterly "straight" knight. In the hands of a seasoned fiction writer, we are carried forward by the compelling narrative of a woman learning to be brave.

—Laureen Nussbaum, Author of *Shedding Our Stars*

Praise for Coffin's short fictions:

"Lyn Coffin's *Falling off the Scaffold* has, in a sense, no characters at all, only the projected personae of two people unknown to each other; yet it respects the contours of reality and gives us, in a most unusual form, a story about illusion and self-deception, timely in its related ness to current thinking about male-female roles...."

—Joyce Carol Oates, Editor *Best American Short Stories* 1979

"Sexy, smartly engaging and quirkily off-beat, (Coffin's fictions) are a delight to read and ponder."

—Judith Roche,
National Book Award-Winning Author of *Wisdom of the Body*.

"Like Oates, like Updike, Coffin gives us characters we recognize, in spaces that are familiar– a coffee shop, a bar. She masterfully reveals the small yet extraordinary moments which eventually become irrevocable fate. Fiction worth re-reading: witty, wise, deeply imagined."

—Jed Myers, Author of *Watching the Perseids*

"Coffin's fiction shows evidence of an original and delightful intelligence. Her lively and memorable characters speak as if they are possess by forces slightly beyond their control, in voices brimming with wit, intelligence, cunning, and love. The structure of her stories unfolds with such grace that one forgets the skill it takes to produce such 'effortless' architecture."

—Alice Fulton,
Winner, American Academy of Arts and
Letters Award in Literature

"(Lyn) depicts an array of strong voices. The infusion of poetry and drama in her prose expands our strict genre definitions.... Readers who take time to savor the multiple layers will be richly rewarded."

—Marilyn Stablein,
Author of *Climate of Extremes: Landscape and Imagination*

"Perhaps the inevitable allusion is Scheherazade who spins out her fictions in order to survive... Diversity is the name of Coffin's game... the kaleidoscope of voices holds us spellbound. That's what it all comes back to– the timbre of speech, the astonishing succession of tropes that capture our attentions. And what a pleasure it is to read an author with such mastery over metaphors. The writing sparkles with them...."

—Laurence Goldstein, Editor, Michigan Quarterly Review

"Lyn Coffin writes with heart of longing and searching– for place, for connection, for love. Coffin's fictions cross boundaries; they are funny, ominous and heartbreakingly true."

—Ethan Yarborough,
publisher IronTwine Press

THE AFTERMATH

The Aftermath

A novel
by

LYN COFFIN

Adelaide Books
New York / Lisbon
2020

THE AFTERMATH
A novel
By Lyn Coffin

Copyright © by Lyn Coffin
Cover design © 2020 Adelaide Books

Published by Adelaide Books, New York / Lisbon
adelaidebooks.org
Editor-in-Chief
Stevan V. Nikolic

For any information, please address Adelaide Books
at info@adelaidebooks.org
or write to:
Adelaide Books
244 Fifth Ave. Suite D27
New York, NY, 10001

ISBN: 978-1-953510-57-0

Printed in the United States of America

For Robert, Jim, and the real Adam Ferrier

"It passed through and gave back no words for that which
happened; yet it passed through this happening...."

—Paul Celan

"But Lot's wife was turned into a pillar of salt."

—Genesis: 19:25

Contents

The Thing That Happened

It was New Year's Eve. 1999 was about to become 2000, but the Hotel Carrigan was deserted. The only thing moving in the lobby was the tinsel on the artificial Christmas tree. The manager had left hours ago, muttering darkly about bankruptcy. Café Carrigan was empty and officially closed. The other waitress had left a little early, saying she really wanted to be with her family.

Susan was putting new salt in old shakers. Since childhood, there had never been anything she really wanted. There was something wrong with that, she thought.

A man paused in the doorway, then stepped from the lobby into the café.

He was wearing a plaid sports coat and jeans. He was carrying white roses, holding them away from his body with a kind of loving mistrust, as one might carry a baby without a diaper.

He stood just inside the door and smiled at her. When she got closer, he apologized.

"I'm sorry to bother you," he said. His smile was boyish, his teeth were straight; he seemed sober. "If you don't mind—I'd like to give you these flowers."

"Why?" She remembered her New Year's resolution to be more trusting, and corrected herself. "I mean, thank you," she said. "They're very nice, and very- unexpected."

The man laughed. "My date stood me up," he said, handing her the flowers. They had not really been arranged, but were thrust together in a bunch, wrapped with newspaper. She cradled them in her arms.

"If I were a painter," the man said, "I'd do a painting called 'Young Woman with Flowers.' The flowers would be roses, like these. The woman would look like you, with big almond eyes, and dark wisps of hair corkscrewing down in front of her ears, no matter how she tried to pull them back."

"Thank you again, but we're still closed," Susan said, resisting the impulse to touch her hair. "Even if you have given me these lovely roses. The sign is right there."

"I'm sorry," he said. "I guess when I'm hungry, I go a little blind."

Susan considered him. He was too ill at ease and rueful to be threatening. He seemed to exude good intentions. His hapless expression was endearing. Her New Year's resolution was to trust people more, especially men.

There was a moment of awkward silence, like the weedy strip between railyard tracks. She lost her place. "I'm sorry," she said. "Did you say something?"

He squinched his mouth together. "Is there anything at all you could give me to eat?"

"Well," Susan said. "The cook is still back there. I could probably get one last meal out of him, if you're really hungry."

"I'm famished."

"It would have to be something standard. Like scrambled eggs and coffee."

"Scrambled eggs would be perfect," he said. "I don't need anything to drink, not even water."

Susan went out to the kitchen, and saw Joe sleeping in the alcove. He was snoring like a buzz saw.

Susan found a plastic vase stuck behind a pile of "sizzler platters," and put the flowers in that. Let sleeping cooks lie.

She made scrambled eggs and toast and went back out into the cafe. She put the plate down. "Happy New Year," she said.

"Would you sit with me? Are you old enough for me to buy you a drink?"

"I'm 22, but we don't sell drinks. Even if we did, we really are closed, I'm afraid."

The man stood and extended his hand. "I should have introduced myself. I'm Tat. I'm an Instantaneous Translator, an I.T. guy."

"Tat?" The phrase "tit for tat" vaulted unbidden into Susan's mind. It had been a long and unexciting day. Her imagination was threatening to go into overdrive. "Well, Tat, I'm Susan, a waitress. I'm not sure what an 'Instantaneous Translator' is."

"How do you do, Susan. Forget the job title, please. I was just trying to impress you, not that being a translator is so— whatever. Sorry. As for my name, it's a little odd, I know.... Never mind. Please accept this in satisfaction of my debt to you."

Tat inserted his thumb and index finger into the breast pocket of his sport coat and handed her a crisp $50 bill.

Susan looked at the bill in her hand. "Don't you have anything smaller?"

"Fortunately, I don't." Tat sat down again, speared eggs with his fork and stuck them in his mouth.

Susan waited a moment while he finished chewing. "I have no way of giving you change," she said.

Tat smiled up at her. "I have no reason to expect any."

Susan put the $50 in her uniform skirt pocket. "Thank you," she said.

"You're more than welcome.... So, could I persuade you, please, come across the way to the hotel bar for just one drink with a Georgian home boy?"

"I don't know you," Susan said.

"Right," Tat said. "And I don't want to pressure you. But if you could just this one time take pity on a stranger, alone on New Year's Eve, in a lonely city by a lonely lake. I mean, the bar is, what, 50 feet away, right here in the hotel. It would be a real act of kindness on your part." He spoke between bites of food. His tone conveyed no belief whatsoever in the possibility of anything's happening. He sounded completely harmless, sure he would fail. He epitomized the word 'feckless.'

"All right," said Susan. "Just one very short, quick, symbolic drink."

They went into the small hotel bar. Bruce, the normal bartender, wasn't there. "I'm just a part-time fill-in," the new guy told them. There was some kind of party going on at the end of the room, so they took a table near the front.

Tat ordered a bottle of champagne, pretzels and potato chips for him, cheddar cheese goldfish for her. The bartender brought these to the table and Tat popped the champagne cork: it went all the way up to the ceiling and made a little mark. Susan offered her empty glass to Tat, who said it looked spotty. He took both their glasses and the champagne bottle back to the bar. The bartender slid two new glasses off the ceiling rack and wiped them with a white towel. Across the narrow room, Tat asked Susan if she'd like a sugar cube in her champagne. Susan said she didn't think so.

"Oh, come on," Tat said. "Somebody told me that was the Mchigan way."

"You're only supposed to do that if the champagne is cheap or sour or something," Susan said. Tat nodded. The bartender poured champagne into both glasses and Tat tried a little sip of one. Then he frowned and nodded. "I'm sorry," he said. "But I'm afraid this qualifies under both counts. Besides, it's funner and fizzier with sugar. Watch." He dropped a cube into each of the glasses and grinned at her when they both foamed over.

Tat came back to the table with a full glass in each hand, the bottle under his arm. He proposed a toast to the New Year. He seemed a little nervous. He drained his glass and encouraged Susan to do the same. They drank. Tat poured both of them more champagne. It didn't foam over this time. Tat made a little speech about what it was like to be a Georgian home boy, and have people feel they were superior to you just because they spoke clearer or faster.

"This is really strong champagne," Susan said. "Thank you, but I really should be going."

Tat was pouring more champagne. She seemed to be in a moving car, and it was hard to see through the glass. The party had gotten smaller. The bartender had disappeared.

"It's those cheddar cheese fish," a man's voice said slowly. "They make everything taste weird." She could almost see the fish, dissolving as they swam. A big silver ball moved slowly down a spike high above Times Square where she first thought it was raining because everything looked blurry. Then she realized she was standing still but moving. She was moving through time as if in a parade. People were lining the streets. They were cheering but they didn't make a sound. She was in the elevator. The operator was out of uniform, and out of focus. His wrists stuck out.

There was a fireplace in the upper room they reached. There was wood in the fireplace, and the wood was already burning. How had that happened? There was a mattress on the floor. Did she need to use the bathroom? No, she could hold it. She sat on the mattress: exhaustion washed over her like a wave. They were at war. They were in a bunker. She'd been in a bunker her whole life.

Someone would have to pay. Where was her purse? There it was.

There were pillows everywhere, like clouds shot out of the sky.

Someone was tugging off her clothing. She was a child again. It was time for the whispering and closets with coats overhead. She needed to do what she shouldn't, because she had to.

Still, in the middle of pillows there was something waiting. Something like terror. And the terror was like lightning and by the light of the lightning, she could see she was naked and she was the only one. The switch confused her. She wondered about the champagne. There had been salty champagne. No wonder she was thirsty.

A voice said lie down on the wood. She was in a boat now, sailing out to sea. She was not in control. No one was in control. The water knew what it was doing.

The boat was sinking. Saltwater was pouring in, flooding her.

There was no room for anything personal. Wingless angels were dancing, dancing on pins and needles. Pins and needles. Sharp. Sharp.

A country had its legs open, forced into yawning. Someone was bent. Fingers were scrabbling in hair she didn't have.

A plane high overhead droned like a voice. It was noise. It meant nothing.

It would feel good. What would happen would not hurt, though birds dangled from the sky like coats.

Back and front, dry fans whirring, helicopters on their way.

Somewhere there was a desk she needed to get under.

There it was. A plastic night stick poked its head between metal teeth.

She was alone in a house at night. Men were at the back door, and she ran with the children to the kitchen and they pushed back, all of them, pushed against the door, digging in their heels, and even as they felt the door give way behind them, they heard the front door open.

If there was someone in charge, it wasn't someone you could reach: when it came to it, you had to let go, forgetting what came next.

Small animals ran for cover on a stubbled field. It was open season in a storm.

There were shots.

Animals were pushing at her, hard nosings, over and over. They would bite her if she didn't play dead.

The animals were blind and wet and teeth and fur and hands and mouths and things too fierce to mention.

If they bit her, she would not feel it. She would not feel it.

The animals had gone. There was just a bristling field, where storms happened.

There was an eye that closed.

And the animals pushed back, coming at the tree from hot, sticking, dry, muddy, front, back — double entrances in trouble of earth stabbed by forked tongues and lightning, and pain rounded Spain and ran zigzag in all the dark directions.

Anywhere it wanted. Anywhere at all.

Pain. Pain. Pain. Pain.

Chapter 1

Riding a Strange Horse

I stood, pulling myself up on a beam of sunlight, using it like a handrail. There was a door in my head, and someone was trying to knock it down.

Bam. Bam. Bam.

I hurt.

I was wearing my gold uniform top but I had buttoned it wrong. I left rebuttoning for later. The misbuttoning went with the jeans being too long. I rolled them up. Up and up. I had big flannel cuffs now. The flannel was red, with big whip-lashes of green and black across it. It looked hot and cold at once.

I needed to get home. Where was my skirt? They made you pay for the uniforms.

There was a $50 bill face up on the floor beside a small black cloth purse.

I hurt at the root of me.

I checked. The purse was mine. I recognized my picture on the driver's license. I was squinting. I tried to put the $50 in the purse. It must have fallen out. Money belonged in a purse. I belonged at home, in a place I wasn't living anymore.

The purse didn't want to open, but I made it. I put the money where it was safe. The purse didn't want to close, but it did.

What had happened?

No, that way was blocked.

How had I gotten here?

That could be figured out.. I worked at the hotel. But employees weren't supposed to go up to guest rooms. I could be fired. I didn't need the job, but it wasn't like me to go directly against the rules. But there had been a man, champagne....

I heard my mother's voice: "Don't look back," she was saying. "People who look back turn to pillars of salt." I was a woman unencumbered by a past. Last night was as far from me as the dark side of the moon. It was safer that way.

"Forgive and forget," mother had instructed me. But all you had to do was forget, and the forgiveness took care of itself.

There were bed covers mounded up on one side of the mattress. If there was someone under them, the someone wasn't moving. I hesitated, then pulled off the covers.

Nothing.

My head was knocking again. More like pounding.

There was a real someone, knocking. They were at the room door.

I needed them to go away. I needed them to go away so *I* could go away.

I walked to the door over a floor that tilted. I remembered to put the chain on. Then I opened the door. A man in white was standing in the hall. He looked familiar. "Do you need a doctor?" he asked.

"Do I look that bad?" I asked. Jokes were good. If you could joke, people thought you were okay. People would let you go.

The man in the white coat laughed, showing his teeth. I closed the door a little farther.

"Some tall guy was going down in the elevator when I was coming up for a delivery. He said there was a woman in here who needed a doctor."

I tried to focus. I felt dizzy. The power of suggestion. Someone had given up on the door in my head. They were banging on an anvil now.

"Are you a doctor?"

The man in white laughed again— loudly. "No, ma'am," he said. He was really only a boy. I thought for a minute of just closing the door. But, no, then he would call someone. They would batter down the door. They would break the chain.

"I thought you were a doctor," I admitted. "You're dressed in white. And you said you were here for a delivery."

"That's true," he said, and laughed again. But now it seemed to me his laughter was forced. I'd let the conversation go on too long. He was darting glances past me, into the room.

"I'm just delivering a pizza." He opened the box, as if in proof. The pizza looked too big for the box. It was pockmarked with pepperoni.

"Nobody ordered this," I said.

"Do you want it anyway?"

"No."

"Do you want me to call a doctor?"

"No."

He cocked his head. I must have spoken too loudly. He looked as though he suspected something.

"I'm the only one here," I said. "And I don't need anybody else. I just need to go home."

I half expected him to tell me to wait where I was. "Okay," he said cheerfully. "Just call across the street if you need a pizza or anything. I'll make sure it's hot."

"I will," I said. "Thank you." I closed the door on his smile and chained it. I counted to twenty and opened the door on the chain as quietly as I could. I half-expected him not to have moved, but he was gone.

I found my shoes and put them on. I opened the door, and I stepped out into the corridor, and I closed the door behind me, and I walked down the corridor, and I pushed the elevator button. It came and the doors opened, and I rode down to the ground floor, and I walked through the lobby on thick crimson. I was glad I recognized the lobby. It looked like a stage set, with ornate, overstuffed chairs no one ever sat in, and gilt-edged books no one ever read because their pages had been glued together. I was the only person going anywhere. I remembered to turn left to go outside, and I pushed the big glass circle door around like a clock until I was outside in a world newly-lit by sparkling snow, walking back to my apartment.

The world had changed, along with the year. I was happy to be going home, even to an apartment I didn't really have any more. Everything I owned was in boxes. I would have a home later today, which is what tomorrow had turned into. I would have a home with David and Raitlin.

I was tired, and the sidewalk was slippery. All the trees and bushes had turned white. The snow that was still falling was an after-thought, an unnecessary extravagance.

Mine were the first footsteps in the snow, though it must be late in the morning, since the sun was high over the trees. "Don't drink till the sun is over the yard arm"– my father's favorite laughless joke. Why was I thinking about my father? I'd had too much to drink last night. I had a hangover to beat all hangovers.

The stiff fabric of the jeans rubbed against my skin and the place where my legs came together. It was like a dry blue tongue. It hurt but thinking about where you hurt just made the hurt worse, and there was nothing to be done about it, anyway.

I started to fall but caught myself. I cursed myself for drinking whatever it had been. Champagne, probably. They should call champagne the Midas drink. But if a drink turned everything to gold, you'd die pretty quick. I had christened a ship with champagne once. It wasn't a real ship, just a little tugboat or something, which was why they asked a high school kid to do a woman's job. I'd been picked because someone felt sorry for me. They told me it would be very bad luck if the champagne bottle didn't break on the first swing.

I was passing some of those trees that looked down instead of up. What did they call those? *Weeping*, that was it. They looked like women with long hair and long arms and long legs. Marionette dancers with their strings cut. Old dancers: their hair had turned white. My feet were cold. My body ached with a vengeance. Juneau Street was taking a long time.

What had I been thinking about? Oh, yes. The christening champagne bottle had been wrapped in ribbons. Red, white, and blue. I cocked my arm sideways and gave it my best shot. The bottle exploded. Afterward, they said it was a special bottle, filed down all around the inside to make the green glass walls especially thin. To avoid bad luck. They told me, too, there was a crowd of sailors one floor down, under the party, under the christening party, and at the very moment someone gave the signal and I swung, a sailor had swung, too. To avoid bad luck.

It was a lot of work avoiding bad luck.

I sat down on a bench that presented itself. The bench was white. That was to fool you, so you wouldn't know if there was snow on it or not. There was. There were holes in the wrought iron seat, but the snow hadn't fallen through.

I should have driven to work. But there was never any parking when I drove to work. They wouldn't let you park in the hotel's parking structure. Well, they would. But not for free.

I got up and tried to walk, but it was harder. There was a story I had read in grade school, about a guy with a few matches and he hadn't been able to start a fire and he had died in the snow. I was like that guy. Only I didn't have any matches. That was how it was. You gave up smoking to save your life, but then you didn't have matches or a light, and you died of frostbite and when they did an autopsy, your lungs were white.

Down at the end of the block, a car was coming. It was a chariot, really. It was white, too, like the snow, like the bench, like the world. It was going in the right direction. It had a little bubble on top. It was probably a cab. Other cars didn't have those bubbles on them, did they? A cab would be good if I had money. Did I have money? Yes. At least $50. I stepped as close as I could to the curb without falling off and raised my hand to hail the driver.

It wasn't a cab, though. It said, "Ann Arbor Police Department" on the side. The police car stopped. The driver got out and came around the front of the car. He stood looking at me, not unkindly. He was dressed in blue. Maybe that was to match his eyes, which were bluer than other blues. In a world where delivery boys looked like doctors, what did policemen look like? Was he really a policeman?

He was carrying a gun. Guns were another way people tried to avoid bad luck. Maybe it was wrong to try too hard to avoid bad luck. Maybe when you did that, the luck got worse. Guns were scary, but the policeman seemed nice. There had been a nice policeman when I was young. He put handcuffs on all of us and laughed when he slid our hands out. "There's no catching you small fry," he'd say to us. "I'm going to have to throw you back."

My mouth was like a drawer of jumbled clothing. I rummaged around in it until I found my voice like a pair of underwear. No, not underwear. I wasn't wearing underwear. Like socks.

"You're a policeman, aren't you?" I said. My voice wasn't slurry at all. More like fuzzy. Fuzzy wuzzy was a bear.

"Yes," the man said. "I'm Officer Ferrier of the Ann Arbor Police Department. Are you all right?"

His voice was odd, full of starts and stops, like one of those tapes that people make to speed up and slow down because it's funny and different.

He handed me a stiff little piece of paper.

"Are you giving me a ticket?" I asked, too smart to answer his question directly. "I thought you were a cab. I didn't see your uniform at first, through the glass."

Officer Ferrier of the Ann Arbor Police Department smiled. He had the mixed up hair that people called "salt and pepper." His face was bulldog saggy. But when he smiled, he looked nice. He had wonderful eyes, bluer than sea or sky, or anything I could think of that was blue. He looked like someone you could go home with safely. Not that I was any judge.

"Have you done anything I should take you in for?" Officer Ferrier asked.

"I think I'm hung over," I said. "This is only my second time, though. I was only five the first time. It was after Thanksgiving and I threw up, and the school nurse said, 'I think someone's had a little too much turkey, don't you?' and I said, 'No. I think someone's had a little too much champagne.' It tasted good, but there was sugar… I don't know why I'm talking so much."

Officer Ferrier smiled, but his smile was wrapped around questions. "It's New Year's," he said. "You look really cold."

His smile reminded me of Humphrey Bogart. He should never have let Ingrid fly away. He should have handcuffed her to him when they were in Paris.

I was in the back seat now. I was coming home from the ball in a police car. My fairy godmother would be nonplussed. I was holding something. A business card. It was white with blue letters. "Officer Adam Ferrier," it said. He was looking at me in the rearview mirror. "Is there anything you want to tell me?" Officer Ferrier asked.

"No," I said. "Not at the moment." Had there been an accident? I hurt, but I couldn't remember. I had a card in my hand. I put the card in my purse.

The police car stopped, and Officer Ferrier opened the door.

We were in front of my apartment building. There were lions on either side of the cracked marble stairs. They'd been worn down in the middle by the traffic of lifetimes. The building bricks were the color of old mustard. They said at college only virgins could hear the marble lions roar. I hadn't heard them, but that made sense.

I looked at Officer Ferrier. I suddenly understood why he was wearing a uniform—so you could tell him from the others.

"You haven't been following me, have you?" I asked. He looked hurt, and I rushed to do damage control. "No, of course not. My friend's friend, who's kind of old, says I have trust issues, but he's a little suspicious, and he doesn't really know me. If I have such big trust issues, I don't think I'd be moving in with two guys, do you? The house used to belong to somebody with a lot of Harleys. It has a long driveway for testing motorcycles. It's not the money thing, either, the move, because my father died and left me enough money to keep going. I'll be there tomorrow. But I don't know how you know where I live today."

The officer smiled again, but the blue of his eyes clouded over, and he looked sad. He looked perpetually sad, actually. I wanted to make him a cup of tea. I would make him a cup of tea and put two squares of a Hershey bar in the saucer. Or maybe marshmallows. No, marshmallows were for hot chocolate.

"You gave me your address so I could drive you home."

"That was smart of me," I said. "Do you want to come up for a drink? I don't mean a *drink* drink. A cup of peppermint tea? With Hershey squares in the saucer? I hate peppermint, but it's good for what ails you. It's a very useful drink, and I think that's important. It's more important to be useful than beautiful, I think. I plan to drink a lot of peppermint tea today."

"I'm on duty," the man in blue told me. But he smiled again, which is what I'd wanted, I decided—what I'd wanted all along. "Are you sure you're all right?" he said. That was funny. It was exactly what I wanted to ask *him*.

"I'll be fine once I have a bath and don't look back," I said, trying to put some energy, some conviction into my words, for his sake. I wanted him to believe me, and people always believed you more if you put emphasis on your words. As a child who mumbled and looked at the floor a lot, I hadn't understood that. Too bad. If I hadn't always talked in a monotone, somebody might have believed me, and everything would have been different.

The officer was waiting. He looked worried. I tried to think why I might not be fine. But that was a blind alley that ran smack into a wall. The bricks in the alley were the color of dried blood. I felt like throwing up. I'd had too much to drink.

Way too much. I hurt. I should have known better. I was either hung over or hung out to dry.

"I'll be okay now that I'm home," I said. "Everything's in boxes, but I can take a bath and lie down." He was still waiting. He seemed like someone who could wait for a long time without losing patience. What had my grandmother said? 'In a crisis, be polite.' This seemed like a crisis, somehow, even though nothing was happening. "Would you like to come in?" I asked politely. Then I surprised myself by hoping he'd say yes.

The officer didn't smile. "Not now," he said. "You've got my card in your purse," he said. "If you need help, give me a call."

Somebody needed to do something. I decided to take whatever animal it was by the horns. "Could I ask you why you're waiting?" I asked.

The officer nodded. "I'm waiting to see you go in," he said. I understood. He had a problem trusting people, too. He didn't trust me. I had told him this was where I lived, but I had also said I was moving. Maybe he thought I didn't look like the kind of person to live here, in this large mustard-colored building with black bars on the windows, guarded by apparently toothless lions. I *wasn't* really the kind of person to live here. Mostly old folks lived here. But I was moving. I had told him that, hadn't I? He should have believed me, but people in his line of work were probably trained to be suspicious. People in his line of work were probably *naturally* suspicious.

My apartment key was in my purse. It was all by itself. "I don't have a key to the outside door," I told the officer. "I think I already turned it in."

"The door is open," he said.

"How do you know?"

"I just tried it. What about your apartment door?"

"What about it?"

"Will you be able to get in your apartment without a key?" The officer was standing with his feet apart. He looked planted in the sidewalk, or at least taped to it. When he started to walk, he would pick up giant hunks of concrete and carry them with him. Cement shoes. Wasn't that what they said about the dead gangsters they threw in the river? That was ridiculous. Nobody threw dead gangsters in the Huron River. It wasn't deep enough..

A key. He had asked me about a key. "I have an apartment key," I told the officer. "You don't have to be suspicious. See? Here it is. I painted it red with nail polish. I have an inner key, but not an outer key, somehow. No, wait. Even the outer key is here. It's just on a separate ring, for some reason.... I didn't turn it in at all. I'll be fine. Who wouldn't be fine with two keys?"

Officer Ferrier frowned. "You go on up," he said. "I'll wait down here. When you're in your apartment, I want you to wave and let me know you're all right. Okay?"

"Waving is definitely okay," I told him.

The elevator in the lobby was waiting for me like an open mouth. I took the stairs because they could be done one by one. Stairs let you change your mind at any point. You didn't have to commit yourself.

My apartment door didn't want to accept the key. At first, I thought they'd already changed the lock. Finally, it opened.

I put the key back in my purse, but didn't even try to close it, and stepped inside. I locked the door behind me.

The room was empty except for my boxes, and David's bird tracks picture, which was lying on the floor unswaddled and unpacked.

I had the feeling I was missing something, but I often had that feeling. That feeling was an integral part of who I was: it was *necessary*. I closed the door of the apartment behind me and dumped the contents of my purse on a box. Pen. Wallet with a clutch of plastic cards and some small bills. My driver's license. A small red plastic comb. Officer Ferrier's card. Some change. A $50 bill.

But I was not wearing underwear and the jeans I had on weren't mine. They could never have been mine. They were much too long. They were lined with flannel.

There was something I was supposed to do. I couldn't remember what it was. I went to the window and looked out. It was starting to snow again—big, wet flakes. David said where he came from in Texas, a blizzard was where the snow didn't melt before it hit the ground.

Down on the street, a man dressed in blue stood by a white car. Officer Ferrier. I had forgotten about him. After a moment, he looked up. I waved. He waved back. He stood for a moment by his car. I wondered if he was waiting for me to buzz him up. Then he got in his car and drove off.

I was a little disappointed, but I told myself it was just as well. He looked like a nice guy, though.

I started to shiver.

My coat. That's what was missing. I had left work. I had walked home in the snow without my coat or my hat or my mittens. My grandmother's ghost would be very disapproving.

No wonder I was shivering.

I went into the bathroom. I ran the water for a hot bath. Then I sat on the toilet for a long time, breathing in the steam, and waiting to pee.

The bath was almost full before I was able to do anything. My pee came in a painful thread, at first, and then a stinging stream.

They said astronauts had such good filtering devices, they could drink their urine.

When I was finished peeing, I stood up. The thought of anything of substance against any part of me was unthinkable. Maybe I could dry myself off with the hair dryer. But I didn't know where it was. I shook myself, then turned off the bath water.

I stood just inside the bathroom door and took off my clothing. I put the gold top in the wastebasket.... What would I say if they asked? I would think of something. My fingers were thick and clumsy with cold. "Happy New Year," I told the face in the mirror over the sink, when I was finally naked.

The face in the mirror swung forward, offering the same advice she always did: "Don't look back."

"You're the one looking back," I told her.

Looking past the face, deep into the slantwise mirror, I caught a glimpse of my small, knotty pine dresser. Next to it, shoulder to shoulder like stalwart comrades at arms, stood my three moving boxes. One was marked SHOES and CLOTHING; the second, BOOKS; the third, MORE BOOKS [PLUS HAIR DRYER]. Someone had wanted the hair dryer.

I stepped in the bathtub. Good. But the heat of the water made red stockings on my legs. and when I started to lower myself, the water scalded me. I howled. I sat on the edge of the tub and ran cold water. When the water was the same temperature as I was, I eased myself in, and leaned back against the white tiles, liking the feel of that against my head and shoulders. But my right hand kept creeping along the wall, forward and back, completely independent of me, dragging my right arm with it. It occurred to me that I might be on the verge of a breakdown. The thought was a little alarming.

I was cold. I was freezing, actually. But I couldn't stand the heat.

I didn't have the heart to thoroughly clean myself. I just lay there and felt warmth come crawling back to me like an animal who'd done wrong and was afraid you wouldn't forgive it.

When the water got cold, I stood, pulling myself up by the towel rack. Half of the towel rack came out of the wall and the towel fell into the bathtub and got wet. I stepped gingerly out of the tub and used a washcloth to dry off.

I pulled my last unpacked T-shirt and my last pair of un-packed slacks out of the knotty pine dresser and put them on. Luckily, they were soft. Then I kicked the jeans that lay discarded by the tub until they were out in the living room.

Let sleeping dogs lie. Only they didn't look like a dog as much as the discarded skin of a huge blue snake.

I steered my way across the now trackless living room, avoiding the jeans, and crawled into bed, under the single sheet. I closed my eyes. A white shirt, well-starched, dangled over my mother's red shoes. An umbrella, black and leaning. Fear, then pain.

It wasn't until I reached to pull down the window shade by my bed that I saw it. Scrawled on my right palm in marker, savage in its thickness, was a red "G." There was nothing on the other palm.

What did "G" stand for, "God?"

How did it get there?

I was exhausted, but I had to get the "G" off. The letter made my palm burn. I'd been caught red-handed. **A** was adul-tery. What was "G"? "G" movies were "General," as in "Public."

I spit into my hands, and rubbed them together, hard. Maybe I would start a fire. I rubbed some more. Spit. Rub. Spit. Rub. My whole palm was faintly red. The "G" was a little dimmer. There had been that story in high school about a

38

scientist who found a potion to eliminate his wife's ugly birthmark, killing her in the process.

High school had been full of stories with unhappy endings.

Now I licked my palm, remembering happy hours tucked into difficult days, hours of cherry popsicles and stick out your tongue. My palm tasted brackish and salty, like bad champagne.

I got up and went to the bathroom. I was having trouble moving. I arrived at the bathroom. Leaning on the sink with one hand, I opened the cabinet, but there was nothing behind the mirror anymore. All traces of me were gone. I thought for a moment I was going to fall over. Using the edge of the sink counter, I lowered myself to the floor. I remembered something: I opened up the cabinet under the sink. There was a can of Comet. I reached in and shook the Comet on my palm. As a first grader, I'd swallowed bunches of this once, trying to clean myself from the inside out.

I poured some Comet on my palms and tried to spit on the heap of blue sand. My mouth was dry. I pivoted and pulled myself over to the bathtub. The faucet was trickling as always. You could never shut those things completely off. That was good, this time. I let a few drops fall into my palm, and I made a witch's paste. A blue paste to rub out a red spot.

I rubbed and rubbed and the G got fainter and my hands were blue and smelled as though I were living underwater in a world of chlorine. I rubbed and rubbed and the G faded until it was only a hint, a suggestion. "For now we see through a glass, darkly. But then face to face." The psychic had grabbed my hand and I had said No, but David and Raitlin laughed and pushed me forward, and the psychic looked sad and shook her head and gave me a hug and wouldn't take any money and closed her booth right after that.

I made it back to the bedroom, but for a moment, I couldn't make myself touch the bed. The covers were all mounded up and it was as though someone were under there. Someone unable to move. I pulled the covers off and, like the space behind the mirror, there was nothing there. Nothing at all.

I fell asleep, trying to block out the dream I didn't want by remembering experiments in color. They wrote the word "Yellow" in blue marker, and they asked people to say the color of the writing. And people had trouble saying the color instead of the name. If "Green" was written in red, you would say green, because that's what the word told you.

The dream happened anyway. A man and I were riding somewhere fast, side by side, and I didn't know where he was taking me, except away from home. It was a cold fall day; the trees we were riding under had no leaves. They were like thin, black skeletons, waving stubby arms stiffly, as if signaling us to stop. I was riding bareback, on a strange horse, holding a baby in the crook of one arm. I was naked and so was the baby. We were both covered with white. I was having trouble reining in my horse with one hand. I could feel the horse's hair (and under that, its bones) pressing up sharply, between my legs. I must have been holding the baby too tightly, because it squirted out of my grasp and fell into a ditch of dirty water. I stopped my horse and slid to the ground. The man stopped, too. I began to tell the man that what had happened wasn't my fault. I was shivering because I didn't have any clothes to wear, I said. The horse was hard to ride. The man was going too fast. I didn't know the way. The baby had been squirming. After I explained myself, I picked up the baby. The baby was cold and gray, and the blue tracings on its limbs, like rivers on a map, let me know it was dead. The baby's squirting out of my arms and landing in a ditch, the water, the man, the horse, the weather—none of those had killed the baby. What had killed the baby were my explanations.

I decided in the dream I would call Officer Ferrier and turn myself in. If I did time, I might feel better.

Chapter 2

Polar Bear in a Snowstorm

I woke up. It was late afternoon. Most of a day had gone by without my seeing it, like a televised parade. Someone was at the door. Tap. Tap. Tap.

I opened the door, and there they were. Raitlin's thinning gray-black hair was combed back along the sides of his head. Standing there in the corridor, leaning against the wall in jeans and a black turtleneck, he looked like a middle-aged James Dean. But David had such an angelic face, whoever stood next to him looked troubled in comparison.

Some men were too beefy to be handsome; David wasn't beefy enough. David was tall, blond, and blue-eyed, but thin and hungry and vulnerable-looking. Raitlin called him "the perpetual boy." When the two of them stepped into the room, a rush of fresh air came in with them. It felt good.

David was good at giving people openings. "Are you okay?" he asked. "You look terrible."

Someone else would have said something about last night, but I didn't. I didn't really remember. Someone else might have confided her suspicions. But that someone else wouldn't have survived my childhood. I grew up denying my suspicions to *myself*, let alone anyone else. My father and mother had trained me well. I was to blame for what men did to me. No, not to *me*. I was to blame for what men did to my *body*. Pain was best forgotten, and my fault. I could ignore the seeping rawness between my legs.

There was a silence like a big worn spot in a carpet—a place where the underside of things showed through.

When I told David not to be mean, he looked stricken. "I'm not being mean, just truthful."

"Sometimes I get those two confused," I said.

"Your apartment is beautiful in its apparent absence of furniture," Raitlin said. "It's like an abstract painting— 'Boxes in a Box.' Have you been living out of cardboard all semester?"

"I recycled everything back to the Salvation Army," I said. "All except my futon. The landlady asked for that."

"Ah," Raitlin said. "I was wondering how we were going to incorporate you. Now that I see how insubstantial you are, I am considerably relieved."

"You don't sound relieved," I said. "You sound a little critical."

"Not at all. I admire people who live their lives unencumbered by a past concretized in personal effects. My wife was like that."

"I didn't know you had a wife and I don't understand what you just said," I told him. "Besides that, I'm feeling too awful to try."

David and Raitlin accepted that at face value. They let me sit on the floor and watch as they carried my two boxes out of my apartment and down to Raitlin's waiting U-Haul.

The only things left were my overnight bag, and the framed photograph David had given me to mark our moving in with Raitlin. "I wanted to put it in last," I told him.

"Sure you didn't just forget it?"

"How could I? It's the most precious thing I own."

"Right now, it looks like practically the *only* thing you own," Raitlin said.

"I can put the picture in the MORE BOOKS box," I said. "It should be fine if I put it on top."

"Where's the newspaper?" David asked, looking around hopelessly at the empty room.

"I forgot to pick one up," I said. It moved me oddly to think of people wrapping up their most precious possessions in last year's headlines.

"I'm not worried about the picture," David said. "But if we stick it in that box and this glass shatters, you'll be picking glass shards out of poetry for weeks." He put his arm lightly around my shoulders. I flinched when he touched me.

"Hung over?" he asked, in the tone people use when emerging from church.

"I think so. Yes."

"Well, you're forgiven for starting off the New Year so irritably, then."

We stood looking down at the picture together without speaking. The last rays of sunlight fell on us. It was a tender moment, until Raitlin stuck his head out of the bathroom and said not to expect him to emerge any time soon. Then he retreated again.

The picture was a white square, with some squiggly things on the sides, and some strange little markings near the middle that looked like a series of strange dots and dashes—telegraph markings, perhaps. They were in the shape of a chevron, a thin "V."

"I'm sorry, David." I wanted him to know I was sorry for all the ways I screwed up our friendship, all the doors I shut between us, all the fantasies I concocted about making love with him, which, at their best, got in the way of reality.

"Are you nervous about moving in with Rait?" David asked softly. "You shouldn't be. I told you. Underneath all his mordant wit is sentiment. He's a gentleman, Susan. The last of a dying breed."

He was offering me Raitlin as a way out of a conversation we weren't up to having, a conversation about us. David wasn't fond of "us" conversations in the best of times. We had that in common. "I just don't see why a retired professor would want us around," I said. "I mistrust the altruism of people I don't know."

"So pay him more rent."

"That wouldn't change anything."

"Sure, it would. The higher the rent, the lower the altruism."

"Are you serious?"

"Raitlin's just lonely, Susan. He's been rattling around in that big house ever since his wife died."

"What did she die of?"

"I'm not sure. Actually, maybe she didn't die. Maybe they're divorced or something. Raitlin just said she was 'out of the picture.'"

"I kind of wish I'd spent a little more time with him."

"What do you mean? You've spent a lot of time with him the past couple of months."

"No. The *three* of us have spent time together. I've hardly been alone with Raitlin at all."

David cocked his head at me. He looked silly and birdlike, now. A wren on a railing. He made me want to laugh. I couldn't quite achieve it. "Do you *want* to be alone with Raitlin?"

"It's just kind of weird, that's all, his taking us in, two for the price of one. He doesn't think we're a couple, does he?"

David's laugh was an insult. "Not at all. There's nothing you need to worry about, period." Before I could tell him that wasn't true, there was *always* something you needed to worry about, he shifted the topic back to the picture.

"Do you know what it's *of,* this picture you like so much?" David asked.

"Do I have to?"

"Of course not. A lot of people do, though—They have to know what something is before they commit themselves to liking it."

"Animal tracks in the snow, maybe?" I said. It was the first thing that came to me. I hadn't known it was "of" anything: that was part of what I'd liked about it. I liked pictures that turned realities into abstractions: they were less demanding.

"Animal tracks? Really?" David seemed honestly astonished. Of course, he fell into astonishment easily, the way I fell into despair.

"It's a polar bear in a snowstorm," Raitlin called from the bathroom. How much had he heard?

"Why don't you tell me?" I said. "I don't feel very perceptive today."

"Try to see it," David told me.

I knew what he meant, but it was an odd request, I thought. Trying to see what you hadn't was like trying to remember what you'd forgotten. I wasn't good at it. Still, I tried and got nowhere. The picture had solidified into snow for me—snow with squiggles on the edges, and funny little wedge-shaped tracks near the center. The squiggles didn't mean anything, unless they were branches in the snow. That was it: they were branches.

But if they were branches, and they *were,* they were upside down. The points of them were less in focus than the thicker parts, whereas if they were buried in snow—

46

Suddenly the picture flipped over—It wasn't a picture of someone looking *down*, at tracks and branches in the snow. Not at all. The branches extended upward, not downward.

Once I saw the truth clearly, I couldn't unsee it.

The picture was of a white winter sky: David had taken the photograph straight up. And those little telegraphic marks were not the tracks of a small, frightened animal, but a high-flying "v" of Canadian geese, a ragged, off-sided formation, high over the squiggly, raggedy-looking tree branches at the edges of the shot.

David was waiting patiently.

"Okay. I get it," I said. "They're geese." Now that I could see what it was, I liked it even more. The sky was lying on the floor.

David nodded. "It's a meager migration."

Raitlin came out of the bathroom. "Speaking of meager migrations, I think I dropped the car keys on my way up."

"What do keys have to do with migrations?" I asked.

Raitlin laughed. "I've just never met anybody with fewer possessions than you—other than street people. If you want to take the bed after all, I could probably find somewhere to store it."

"No, that's okay," I said. "I already gave it to the landlady. I think she's planning to rent this place out as semi-furnished now."

"It's a good thing to divest of things," David told Raitlin. "You should try it... What's that saying? 'Half the possessions and twice the money?'"

"That's for traveling, Davey. Not moving. Anyway– I'll be back before you can say 'sesquipedalian.'"

And he was gone.

I turned to David. "Raitlin's in love with you," I said. "Everyone's in love with you." I meant it lightly, as a kind of compliment, or joke. But the truth doesn't lend itself to humor.

David frowned. "What are you talking about?"

There was only the word "exit" written on a wall: I walked toward it. "People can't help falling in love with you, David. You're the easiest person to fall in love with I know."

"You're talking rot," he said.

"Isn't it true, though? Aren't people always falling in love with you?"

He jerked his whole body around, turning on me. "What are you saying?"

"I don't know. That you're very lovable."

"I don't think that's what you're saying at all, and, if it is, I don't think it's true. I'm unobjectionable and unthreatening and a whole bunch of other 'uns' like 'unexciting'. If I were a color, I'd be beige. People don't fall in love with beige. They depend on it. They incorporate it. They put it in public rooms and forget about it. I'm like a—What's that red mark on your hand?"

He meant the "G."

I looked down at my hand. I started trying to remember. But it was the picture in reverse: the harder I tried, the fuzzier everything got. The geese flew off soundlessly, headed north in winter.

I tried again. "There was a guy last night," I said. "Champagne. I think I drank too much, and when I woke up—" *Bam. Bam. Bam.*"—I don't know much more. This morning, there was this G."

"It's on your hand, Susan."

"I can see that, David."

"Who put it there?"

"I don't remember. I know *I* didn't."

"How do you know that?"

"I just do. It's probably a joke or something. A joke so private I have no idea what it means."

The more I forgot, the more manageable the past became, and truth was a mountain I didn't have the heart to climb:

Raitlin's reappearance saved me. "It was in my other pocket all along. Ain't it grand how you can *not have* something you never lost?" He brandished the key, which had a long piece of bright yellow plastic attached to it.

"That's nonsense," David said, shaking his head, managing to include both of us in the statement.

"So, it's nonsense." Raitlin shrugged. "I was running out of excuses to give you two alone time.... There are limits to how long a man can stay in a bathroom without magazines or excess t.p., you know."

David just shook his head again. He and Raitlin picked up the last box and I led the way to the door.

"It's a funny thing about firsts and lasts, you know," Raitlin said, between theatrical grunts and groans. "You know it's the first of anything before it happens. But you don't know it's the last until the fat lady warbles your swan song."

"Please, don't try to be clever, Raitlin," David said. "Susan isn't feeling well."

They maneuvered the box out the door, and I closed it. "Well," I said. "I just closed this door for the last time."

"Wait a minute." David signaled to Raitlin, and they put the box down. "Did you put the picture in here, Susan?"

"I thought *you* had."

He opened the door.

"See what I mean?" Raitlin said, mocking me with cheerfulness.

David went back in. I followed him, feeling abject. The picture was still lying on the floor by the window. The jeans were still by the bathroom doorway.

"This'll do," David said. He went over and got the jeans, then he picked up the picture and slid it as far as it would go into them. The picture stuck out of the top of the flannel-lined jeans as though someone had begun making a scarecrow. David folded the legs over to make a kind of package. It made me feel faint to watch the legs go up and over the picture.

He handed me the jeans-wrapped picture.

"Come on, children. Time's a-wasting," Raitlin said from the hall. He was sitting on the floor, leaning against the box he had just been carrying.

"Hush," David said. But he was talking to Raitlin.

"I don't want to bring the jeans," I said. "They're too big. They don't fit me."

"They'll fit somebody," David said. "They're bound to come in handy."

"Don't nay say David," Raitlin advised me. "He's a pack rat, but he's practical."

David put his arm, very gently, around my shoulders, and guided me out of the apartment. It was a good thing, too: I could hardly see.

Raitlin closed the door. "Let's hope this is the last time," he said.

We descended to the street in an odd little parade. Raitlin went first, backing down the stairs, dwarfed by the box; David was next, holding his end of the box up so high it sometimes seemed in danger of knocking Raitlin over. I went last– my overnight bag over one shoulder, the picture like a stiff baby, lying across my outstretched arms.

Outside, it was almost dark.

When the box and the picture had been stowed in the Rent-A-Trailer, and the door locked shut, I asked Raitlin if I could drive. Raitlin's car was a new red Lexus. It smelled like a fortune cookie. I saw myself at the wheel, confidently and symbolically steering the three of us into our new life.

"Be my guest, little darling," Raitlin said.

Guest, I thought. *Guest starts with a "G."*

"Do you think you're up to it?" David asked.

"What?"

"You don't look much like a designated driver to me."

"I'm fine."

"How about if you drive another time, honey?" Raitlin asked.

"That would be good," I said. He had put "honey" at the end of his question, like a marshmallow at the end of a stick, and I found that terribly endearing. Raitlin was sarcastic, but he meant well. And he was right about last times—you could never tell.

At the first stoplight, I put down the passenger visor and looked at David in its little mirror. He looked like a teddy bear, bright-eyed and anxious. He gave me a quizzical "Are we all right?" frown. I smiled at him. "I'm fine!" I said. He smiled back, "Well, good, then!" I laughed a little. He laughed a little longer. In a moment, we were laughing at our laughing. I waited for Raitlin to ask what we were laughing about, but he was smarter than that. In another moment, he joined in.

We drove by a group of women clustered near a streetlamp. They all seemed to be wearing black.

"If black means death, what does white mean?" David asked.

"Fear," Raitlin said. "Red means anger, and white means fear."

"No," I said. "White means purity or something."

"What was it you said before, Rait?" David asked. "A polar bear in a snowstorm?"

"Yes," I said. "He's wearing a red scarf, tight at the throat." I could feel it, as I said it. Scratchy red wool pulled tighter and tighter.

"Right," said Raitlin. "And he's probably holding a thick black Coke."

Raitlin and David kept making up color characteristics for the polar bear in the snowstorm, but I was cold and tired, and had to stop playing. "Does a 'ferrier' mean somebody who carries something?" I asked.

"No. A ferrier's an iron worker," Raitlin answered. "Why?"

"I met one," I said. "'Ferrier' sounds comforting, I think, even though it's kind of a cold word."

When we got to the house, darkness was in full swing. Raitlin asked if I would need anything out of the boxes and I said no, I had everything I needed in my overnight bag. Nobody admitted to being hungry, so we just stood in the kitchen for a bit, nibbling pieces of cold pizza; then we went to bed.

I had never been in the house at night before. In the daytime, it seemed friendly. But at that night, there was something about the largeness of the rooms, or their odd shapes, that gave me a funny feeling. No matter how many lights I turned on, darkness seemed to collect in the corners. I kept thinking we were being watched.

I got ready for bed quickly, and slid in between the stiff, cold sheets. I lay unmoving while digital minute after digital minute clicked by, but I couldn't sleep.

When I closed my eyes, I felt as though I couldn't breathe.

When I opened my eyes and stared up at the ceiling, I had the shivery feeling I wasn't alone. Knotholes in the heavy beams running across my ceiling glared at me like animals. I wondered what would happen if a beam fell on me.

Eventually, I got up and started walking through the house. My body was rusty, like a hinge, and it hurt to move.

Raitlin said his house was a merging of English Tudor and American Ranch, "a more uneasy marriage than most." It looked as though someone had built a mansion, and then pushed the lower half below ground, where it became the large rec rooms he never used. Having all the living quarters on one level was, Raitlin said, one of the house's selling points. "Living on more than one level is fun, but this is less confusing."

The floor in most of the house was made of huge, irregular pieces of slate with gray cement between them. The colors of the stone were lovely—wine, ice-blue, ocean-green. There were no rugs in the whole house except small, bristly Navajo scatter rugs, placed like stepping stones next to each of the beds and in front of the sinks. The walls were solid wood, different for each room, leading David to say the house had been patchworked together like a quilt. The front hall was elm, the dining room was oak, the living room was cedar, the breakfast nook, maple. The wood on the outside of the house was cypress. According to Raitlin, cypress logs could lie in a swamp for a lifetime and never get waterlogged. He said they were his role models.

I walked barefoot over the big stone slabs, liking the cold lick of slate against my soles. "G" was for "ghost." But I was not in pain now. I didn't need to feel or remember.

Both Raitlin and David had their doors open— "ears cocked for intruders," Raitlin had said—and I stood by turns in their doorways. My cold presence was unimportant to the sleepers and did not awaken them: this realization was as close to reassurance as I could get.

I was standing just outside Raitlin's room when a moonbeam suddenly lit up his face. I froze, but even Nature's spotlight did not awaken him. His bed was at right angles to the door; he lay on his side, facing the door. In the moonlight, for an instant, I saw his face clearly: his mouth was slightly open; his face as grave and lost and defenseless as a child's.

I wondered how David looked when he slept, but it was dark in David's room: he was just a shape under wraps. Never mind. He rarely looked the way he *was*. When he was embarrassed, he looked as if he'd been running. If he'd been running, he looked feverish. If he were feverish, he looked happy.

I wanted to crawl into bed with him, under his cloudy white comforter.

I went back to bed, put a small pillow under my head, and arranged the two big ones so they lay next to me, almost like a person. Several times, I caught myself falling asleep, and woke up with a start.

Finally, I let myself go.

Chapter 3

Hanging Fish

The next day, I woke up feeling gray and smeary. I had difficulty doing much of anything.

I heard my father's angry voice buzzing around in my head: the fear it inspired was like a knife in my pocket. "Just keep walking, one foot in front of the other," my mother said, and I easily translated this into what it *meant*, which was that it was Monday and I needed to call in sick.

I made my way down the corridor and into Raitlin's living room. It took me a moment to locate the phone, disguised as a decoy duck. To make a call, you lifted off the duck's back and head, and spoke into the equivalent of wooden brains. My mother would have loved it.

I got the number of the Carrigan from information and was reassured that the operator could hear me and I was apparently making sense. In another lifetime, I had thought it was funny the way they answered the phone, "The Carrigan Hotel wishes you good morning." But now the greeting provided reassurance.

The person at the desk didn't seem to know who I was, that I had been off yesterday and now was too sick to come in; when that had been established, she didn't seem to believe I was the person I said I was. I could understand that: *I* didn't believe I was the person I said I was, either. After several match-spurts of conversation, I was put on hold. In this limbo, I heard odd static and muffled voices in the background. Finally, a man came on, his voice like a car running out of gas. "Hello?" he said. "This is D.J. How may I help you?" I said I was sick and couldn't come in and D.J. said not to worry about coming in. D.J. told me to take all the time I needed to get better. I broke down and cried at this in a tiny but gushing thaw, mistaking D.J.'s words for crusts of compassion.

D.J.'s voice turned dark and embarrassed. I didn't understand, he said. My services were no longer required. The woman I'd replaced, who had been out on pregnancy leave, had returned suddenly. She was, after all, more experienced than I was, and had a long history with the Carrigan. There was an echo on the line by then, and "history with the Carrigan" was a small snake in the shell of my ear.

"Her baby's not due until February," I said.

"Exactly."

I asked to speak with the manager and was informed by D.J. that he *was*. He was the new "acting" manager, and it was his "unfortunate duty" to thank me for my services and let me know they were no longer required. I would get a check in the mail. I pointed out that I'd been hired "for the duration," but then I had the good sense to hang up before there was time for him to argue with me.

I had forgotten to ask about my coat. Never mind. I would get a new coat, a red one, so people could see me coming.

Silence established itself at the heart of my being and grew like enthusiasm for a bad idea.

Raitlin and David appeared shortly after that, and we had breakfast. We drank and ate normal things, like orange juice and coffee and cereal out of small boxes; we made nothing-special conversation. The three of us brought in my moving boxes from the U-Haul, then Raitlin went off to do research at the library and David went to return the U-Haul and do work in the lab. They didn't come back until dinner time.

At some point during the day, it became apparent that I was go-to-bed sick.

I made it a point to do everything in snatches. My breath came in snatches. I slept and ate in snatches. That was good strategy: it forced the depression to come in snatches as well. I had to deal with it, but I made it come crawling, hat in hand.

The following weeks were as pathless as the ocean, dotted with little islands of normality. Raitlin was at the middle of some of these, talking. We needed to become friends, he said, for David's sake.

There were other noteworthy moments, sunny and wide. Heartland moments. In one of these, David sat an arm's length away from my bed, tearing a grilled cheese sandwich into pieces, arranging the pieces in a rough circle on the plate. He leaned forward to hand the plate to me, then immediately leaned back. "Have just a morsel," he was saying; the word was so appetizing, I did. "It's good to see you eat something," David said. He smiled like an angel. "You're welcome to these morsels."

"Why are you sitting so far away?" I asked.

"I'm afraid of coughing," David said.

"Mine or yours?"

David laughed. He seemed to find me immensely entertaining this morning. "Mine."

"Well, you're not coughing now."

David nodded. He scooched his chair closer to the bed and reached out to me slowly. I watched his hand coming, and I wasn't afraid. It came to rest on my forehead. Something was warm and something was cold. "Am I freezing you?" I asked. He smiled again.

"You're spiking a fever," he said, and I saw my grandmother's aloe, a spiky green spider: you cut it, and it bled sticky green, and after you wounded it, it was your friend, and would help you get better in all the places that was possible.

"You're going to recover, you know," David said softly, in a voice like summer rain.

"Recover what?" I asked.

Everything I said made him smile. "Yourself," he told me.

I wasn't sure this was the good thing he clearly thought it was. I started to explain, but David was gone.

There was a small knocking. Raitlin stuck his head in the door. "Anything I can get you?" he said.

"No, thanks," I said.

"Sure?" Raitlin was waiting.

I closed my eyes and opened them, but he was still there, waiting. "I don't want to be any trouble."

"You're not *any* trouble," Raitlin said. I was about to disagree when he added, "You're *our* trouble."

That made some sense to me. "In that case, I don't need anything," I told him, and fell back to sleep.

I woke up to find David holding my hand. "You're holding my hand," I said, and immediately felt stupid. People didn't like it when you pointed out the obvious, and small realities were always obvious.

But David smiled. "It's only fair," he said. "You're holding mine, too."

I looked down at our two hands, hanging in space by the side of my bed. I let go. Then I looked at the two hands, still there in the same space, but now, not touching. "My hand looks rough and red next to yours," I said.

"I wish I had your hands," David said.

"Why?" I asked. "Your hands are beautiful."

"Maybe, but yours are strong."

Sunlight filled the room, warm and indiscriminate, like charity made visible.

"You're nursing me back to health, aren't you?" I said.

David smiled. "That's the general idea."

"It's working. I can see it. I'm riding this donkey and you've managed to lead it back to Health, which is a city on a hill, a kind of high-minded Mecca."

"Hush," David said. He had a rabbit in his lap and was stroking her. No, not stroking. He was *grooming* the rabbit with a square of red plaid flannel.

"David?"

"Yes?"

"Where'd you get that?"

"This is Sappho. She's Raitlin's rabbit, believe it or not."

I had meant the cloth, which was scary, somehow. The flannel was red, with big whiplashes of green and black across it. It looked hot and cold at once. There was a pull in that cloth. Someone was dragging a horse to water. I should call Officer Ferrier and report the incident.

"That cloth doesn't look very clean," I said finally.

"That's okay," David said. I must have looked my question, because he went on. "It's the oil. Unwashed clothing has oils that help make Sappho's fur shiny."

As usual, the correct response was beyond me. "Maybe you're allergic," I said.

"To you?"

"Ha ha. To Sappho. Or flannel. Maybe that's why you were coughing."

"I'm not coughing any more, though," David said. "All this bedrest you've been getting here has been really good for me."

Sappho sat in David's lap without being held, her lop ears dangling past his knees, her wet nose twitching. A wet nose was a sign of health in dogs, I thought. Perhaps it was a sign of sickness in a rabbit.

I loved watching David with Sappho. I was almost jealous, watching his long-fingered hands move over the rabbit's pale brown fur, over and over again, soft and sure and *dedicated.* I liked watching David do almost anything and listening to his lullaby voice.

"Can I hold her?" I asked.

"You can try," David said. I struggled to a sitting position, and David handed over the rabbit like a furry football. But the minute she felt my hands on her, Sappho struggled wildly, wriggled out of my hands, and zig-zagged around the bed for a moment, before David scooped her up again. She quieted instantly.

"Never mind," I said. "I should have known better."

"You were probably just holding her too tightly," David said.

That didn't make any sense. It seemed to me I hadn't been holding Sappho tightly enough, or she wouldn't have gotten away. "Never mind," I said. "She's happy where she is."

"When are you the happiest?" David asked.

David didn't believe in trick questions: I told him I felt happiest when I felt either beautiful or useful. I had never felt both at once.

"But how do you know if you're happy?" David asked. His questions were balloons he set adrift.

"There are signs," I said. "I'm not exactly sure what they are, but...."

David eased Sappho out of his lap and down onto the floor. The rabbit sat as though stunned. "I think I'm happy now," he said.

"Well, I'm glad," I said. "You don't look happy, though. You look guilty."

"Not surprising," David said.

"What? Happy and guilty go hand in hand with you?"

"No, but— taking care of you is what makes me feel happy."

"Making you guilty of what? Kindness?"

"No, but don't you see, I can only take care of people if they're sick, if they need taking care of, so it's like my happiness is built on their sickness. What kind of a person takes pleasure in someone else's suffering?"

"David," I said. "Don't be an idiot. You're a wonderful nurse. I feel a lot better now, thanks to you."

David smiled broadly. "I guess I'm not such a bad guy," he said. "I was happy taking care of you, but I'm happier that you're feeling better.... I can't wait for you to get to know Raitlin, Suse. He's easier to take on his own turf. And the turf itself is wonderful—the house, I mean. If you had to get fired, you chose the best time to do it."

He was heading into dangerous territory. "I'm actually feeling better than better," I said.

"What could be better than better?" David asked, grinning.

"Being hungry."

"And you're hungry?"

"I'm starved."

Dinner was steaks for Raitlin and David and a big porta-bella for me, cooked on the grill; baked potatoes, green beans with almonds, a salad with lemon zest in the dressing. Raitlin carved the meat into long slices: juices oozed into troughs cut in the silver platter. The meat was overwhelming present, in sight and smell; I remembered reading about an Irish family during a famine, hanging a fish over the tables, looking at it as it dangled there on a string—eating potatoes, but looking at the fish, tasting it raw and briny in their imaginations.

After dinner, we went into the living room and clustered around the empty fireplace. Without logs, it looked like a big stone mouth. A maw, almost. I wondered how many motorcycles could fit in the fireplace. Two, I decided. Raitlin had informed us over dinner that the house was haunted by motorcycles. It had been built in 1939 by Davidson, of Harley-Davidson fame: the side garage had been used to design and repair motorcycles, the long driveway had been used to test them. Raitlin claimed that if one were both quiet and awake in "the cut-throat hours of the morning," one could hear motorcycles "clearing their throats like mechanical panthers."

I watched Raitlin watching David, who was occupied in looking out the plate glass window. The two of them seemed to change shape and color when they were around each other. Raitlin grew larger and brighter, with softer edges. David darkened and intensified.

"See these red flowers?" Raitlin asked David. "They're geraniums. And those darker, bruised looking tatterdemalions are geraniums"—he pointed. "And these pinkly elegant floral felines, surprise, are also geraniums. And, yes, my friend, even those monstrous, tropical-looking purple things by the breakfast table, that seem to me each morning to lean ever more intimately over your fine, wheat-blond hair, as if tomorrow, surely, they would have you lovingly in their clutches—Even *they* are geraniums. An aberrant variety, but still geraniums. Do you notice the way they all crane toward the window—at least when you don't present yourself at the table, and confuse them?"

"All flowers do that, though, don't they?" I asked. "Isn't it in the nature of flowers to turn toward the light?"

Nothing delighted Raitlin more than a rhetorical question. "Of course!" he said, in his Grand Inquisitor manner. "But these geraniums once grew *away* from the light."

David turned and looked at the older man. The way the lamp light fell on his face reminded me of the Romance comic books I had devoured the summer of my sixth grade.

"My girl friend, fiancée, wife, whatever– she trained them to do it," Raitlin said. "The geraniums. She spent hours in here fussing over the things, calling for floral clay and 'frogs' for the seedlings. I couldn't fathom it."

"I think I'm allergic to geraniums," David said.

Raitlin looked as though he'd been struck.

"Of course, I'm probably allergic to lots of things," David said. "It doesn't matter anyway. The doctor said what he gave me would clear up whatever I had. Allergies, that is."

"Didn't I tell you?" I said. "I told you you had allergies. At least, I meant to."

Moments later, Raitlin left. He seemed discouraged. I could read it in his eyes and the way he said, "Kisses," when he walked out, instead of, "See you, Sue." "Sue" was Raitlin's idea of a joke.

Weeks passed in which all I seemed to do was arrange and rearrange my meager possessions. No matter where I put the clothes, they seemed out of place. No matter where I put the books, they looked pretentious and ill at ease. There were low shelves along the inner wall: I put folded sweaters on these, grouped by color. My room looked like a store. I put the folded sweaters on the high shelves in my walk-in closet, and books on the low shelves. I had too many books to fit comfortably on the shelves. When I jammed them in, my room looked like an elementary school library. I ended up putting the books on the high shelves on one side of the closet, and the sweaters on the other. I stood back and considered. After some thought, I put my shoes and boots on the low shelves. Now my room looked a little like a shoe store, but I didn't care. The arrangement was practical. It suited me.

I put David's picture on the long outer wall of my room, white on white. The world outside the long window was chronically cold and muffled. The snow came, and went away, and came back again. Raitlin was like that, too, coming and going— "for necessities," he always said. Raitlin was working on a book about Oscar Wilde, tentatively entitled, <u>Oscar Wilde, Sunny Side Up</u>. Raitlin was fond of saying Oscar was basically a clever scribbler burdened with a talent for perversity, "not unlike myself."

Sometimes David and Raitlin went off together: Raitlin to the library, David to the product design lab, though it was his winter break. David had graduated from Stanford a year ago; his goal now was to make it as a "free agent." Every few weeks, he had a different "revolutionary" product. When I was depressed, I saw myself as one in a long product line, midway between a new "doggie pooper-scooper" and breath mints on a roll.

One evening in the middle of February, David came and sat beside me on the couch. "Why don't we ever talk these days? Don't you trust me anymore?" David seemed genuinely hurt.

I trust you more than I trust myself, I wanted to say. *But that's not saying a lot.* "Of course, I trust you," I said. "I've just been sick. I'm paranoid when I'm sick. You know that."

"But you've been talking to Raitlin. I hear the two of you from down the hall. You sound a lot freer with him, somehow. You seem to talk about things that matter, but you're perpetually laughing."

I felt absurdly complimented by this misstatement. Raitlin's plentiful witticisms were often clever but seldom hilarious, and I wasn't the sort of person to be "perpetually laughing" with anyone. It was true that I felt freer around Raitlin than I did around David: I always felt constrained around people who really cared for me. "You wanted Raitlin and me to get to know each other, David. I'm making an effort."

David didn't say anything.

"What do you mean by 'things that matter,' anyway?" I asked.

"Tell me about your father."

I laughed. There was an unpleasant echo in my body when I laughed, a discordant jangling, a responsive ache. "Why bring him up?" I asked—but I thought I knew the answer. "My father and mother divorced when I was twelve. 'He was a devoted man', my mother used to say. 'Devoted and responsible.' I guess he was. Publicly devoted, privately something different. "

"I remind you of him, don't I? Of your father?" David said after a moment. "That's why you don't like me sometimes, isn't it?"

The deep blue aura I had felt surrounding me shrank to Saran wrap. "Don't like you, David? I don't know what you're talking about," I said. I saw my voice as a full cup of hot coffee. I carried it slowly and steadily as I dared. "Why would you think I dislike you?"

I was overwhelmed with all I was intent on not saying. If he thought I disliked him, even occasionally, even a little, why did he think I'd agreed to live here? He couldn't think it was because of Raitlin: Raitlin was the reason I almost *hadn't* moved here. There was nothing about Raitlin as observed that made me nervous, it was the realization that he only allowed me to see a little of him. Raitlin was like someone who always keeps the same half of his face turned to you; after a while, you can't help wondering if the other half is scarred.

"You told me your father was blond and tall like me," David said.

"But he was strange and scary and given to violence. You're like some kind of plant, all. thin and waving, and he was a boot, grinding things underfoot like used up cigarettes." I did not say this.

"That's part of why I felt—I don't know—guilty, taking care of you," David said. "I thought I was being like your father, sort of oppressing you, without meaning to." He stood, towering over me. "I shouldn't be talking like this. You're probably still—not completely well."

He put his hand on my head, and let it rest there a moment like a big butterfly. "It was nice feeling close to you," he said. "I guess I'm finding that hard to give up. Like smoking."

"What are you talking about?" I was stung by the implication he didn't feel close to me anymore, but David misunderstood.

"I wasn't always smokeless," he said. "In my teens, I wanted to join this marijuana group. They gave me two packs of cigarettes and told me to come back when I knew how to inhale. They said to imagine I was underwater and I had to breathe through the cigarette like a hose."

"How'd you do?"

"I came back a pack later, sick but successful."

I imagined David under water, sucking on a black hose.

"How did your mother die?" David asked. He was vulnerable—frail, even—but he had the habit of directness. He was a moth, going for the jugular.

"It was an accident."

"Car?"

"No. She fell off a cliff in England. Not far from Dover."

"Do you think it was– deliberate?"

"I don't know. Nobody ever figured it out. She could have been pushed. She could have jumped. In the absence of any real knowledge, people said she fell…. I miss her a lot sometimes."

David nodded. "I miss my dad a lot, too. And I'm still angry at him for getting drunk and driving. It's as though it happened last week…. Other people seem able to—I don't know—get over deaths. As though they were bridges or something. I guess, with me, the bridges are all washed out."

I wanted to ask him what he missed most about his dad. I wanted all of a sudden to tell him about the little lines mom got between her eyebrows when she laughed, and how her forehead was the only one I'd ever seen that could stay smooth when she frowned. I wanted to tell him about how the little finger of her left hand stuck out ridiculously from the other fingers whenever she picked up a cup. I wanted to recite for him our vaudeville act— 'Where'd you get that wound? I got it in the war. What war was that? The boudoir'—I wanted to try and tell him how mom's long soft black hair felt between my fingers, how she had a collection of duck jokes and laughed herself speechless telling them, how she looked at me with a tenderness that made me ache whenever she gave me a gift, but baked a blackbird of guilt into every pie.

I wanted to say that, way down in a place words couldn't go, I knew my mother was dead because she'd made the terrible mistake of loving me. I wanted to ask if he would be brave and strong and kind enough to love me and survive.

But David left before I could think of more things I wanted to say and couldn't. He left abruptly, covering ground like a mixed metaphor in that way he had, his legs seeming to belong to a different body than his arms did, his stride both quick and awkward.

Chapter 4

The Color of Butterfly Wings

I followed David down the corridor to his room. I wouldn't have done that with anyone else, with any other man, that is, but I kept telling myself, "We're friends. We're friends," as though it were a mantra that made everything all right. I was only steps behind him, but when I got to the room, he was already lying on his bed staring up at the ceiling. His body looked rigid, his eyes were wide open. He was the last person I would have chosen to talk about death with now: he looked almost dead himself.

"Can I come in?" I said. I always asked that. Normally, it was a formality, a not-quite joke. This time, I really felt I needed permission.

"Sure," David said. I stepped into the room. "Close the door, will you?" David said. I did.

"Can I sit on the bed?" I asked. The only chair in the room was the desk chair, and it was piled high with books.

"Please."

I sat down on the bed.

David put his hands behind his head. "You don't like it when people say 'please' as an invitation, do you, Susan?" It was not a question.

"Not especially." I could feel the warmth of him behind me, the gentle slope he made in the bed. "Are you okay?"

I waited for him to say something, but he was silent. I thought of getting up and going back to my room. But he was hurt, and I was responsible. He had taken care of me in one way or another ever since we'd come to Raitlin's, and the moment I felt halfway normal, halfway healthy, anyway, I had gone right back to hurting him. It must be a habit, some-how—a pattern. The silence was like a thin wall separating us. Thin as it was, I wished it gone. I needed to keep men at arm's length because they were dangerous. But David was different. He was safe, for one thing. He was more fragile than I was. More feminine. I opened the steamer trunk at the back of my mind. Sure enough, it was all but empty. There was a small hope at the bottom. Hope like a little yellow flashlight. I picked it up. I wanted to lie down beside David, to be com-panionable there in the gathering dark.

The silence grew heavy. I turned to him. "Would you mind if I lie beside you?" I asked. "Please?" The final word felt awkward when I uttered it, an orphaned afterthought. But it echoed pleasantly in the silence, round and full as a whole note.

David looked at me, eyes shining. "Of course," he said. But he said it with an exclamation point attached. "I *want* you to lie with me," he said. "I was almost *willing* you to do it. But I was afraid to ask."

I stretched out next to David.

"Would you take off your shoes?" David said.

I kicked my shoes off. They fell, hitting the floor with a surprisingly solid sound.

I lay next to David in silence in the darkened room, length on length. Far off, on the other side of the world, we could hear Raitlin in the kitchen, banging pans and arguing with the radio. I could feel the warmth of David all along my side.

David.

I lifted myself up a little, and turned over on my side, pulling on his arm to make him do the same. We were face to face. His face looked enormous up close. I was afraid of what I might see in his eyes, but I looked anyway. They were nothing like indomitable, but they were kind, and clear. "Why were you afraid to ask me to lie down with you?"

"I'm afraid to ask you anything," David said. He spoke slowly and quietly, as if to a child.

"Why?" I asked. "I do almost everything you ask. I'm hardly ever mad at you."

"I don't want to scare you any more than I have to," David said.

"You don't scare me."

"Then why do you flinch?"

"What?"

"Any time I reach out to you, or make any advance at all, you flinch."

"I don't flinch."

"You do."

"So how come I'm lying beside you in the dark then, David? Huh?"

"Because it was your idea."

The words were like nets. They were supposed to catch me when I fell, but they were lying on the ground, and I got tangled in them. I couldn't breathe. "I think you're afraid of me," I said. "Otherwise, I think you'd– you know— kiss me."

"Do you want me to kiss you?"

I heard sirens in the distance. The confused alarms of struggle and flight. "Don't ask me, David," I said. Did he hear the begging in my voice? I wondered. What was I begging for? I had thought this, only this, was what I had wanted, wanted full out, from the beginning. And now that my wish stood in the doorway of my life—exactly now, I felt an impulse to turn away from it. I was afraid, and I didn't know of what.

He moved a little closer to me. Too close. Instinctively, I moved away. "See?" he said, but he smiled. "You do it," he said. "Let me be the one to hold still." I hesitated, and then inched closer. Now we were touching all along our bodies, breast to chest, belly to belly.

"Would you kiss me now?" he said, "You have my total attention, and permission."

"You're not supposed to-" I began. David closed his eyes. I kissed him.

It was a strange and wonderful and extended thing, that kiss. It was like a conversation. It was like two hands playing the piano, or one hand, clapping.

The kiss trailed off. I lay still for a moment. When I was aware of myself as a separate entity again, I realized I had closed my eyes. All I could hear was David's ragged breathing. I opened my eyes and found David looking at me intently. "Will you teach me how to make love to you?" he asked.

"I'm not very experienced," I said. "There was one boy in high school, but he never really-" The pain in his eyes stopped me.

"Don't tell me about that now," he said.

"But what about you?" I asked. "Haven't you—I mean, you must have had a lot more experience than—"

"I've never been with a woman," David said.

I considered this. "David?" I said after a moment. "I don't think I can do this. I mean, I can do it, but I can't be *responsible*

71

for it. Remember New Year's Day, and how you helped me move here? You asked me what was wrong, and I—"

David rolled onto his stomach. "Do you have to tell me this now?" he asked, not looking at me.

"It's just that I have a history of bad experiences."

"Are you saying you're afraid to make love with me?"

"No," I said. "I'm saying maybe you should be afraid to make love with *me*. What are *you* saying?"

David spoke as though he were sleepwalking. "I'm saying I've never been with a woman, and I want to be with you now, to make love with you. I think you want that, too. But every time I reach for you, you withdraw or flinch or something."

"I don't know how not to, David."

David reached out his hand. I knew it was coming. That didn't seem to matter. At the last minute, I jerked away.

David nodded. "I don't know how to get past that…. You flinch even when I'm focused on not alarming you. It's hard to reach out to someone and have them respond by recoiling. I don't know why you're so afraid of me, but it seems clear you are. That makes me afraid of myself. To be honest, it also is part of why I want to make love to you. I wish I could carry both of us past that part where you flinch. We would probably be better friends then, too."

I felt my cheeks. They were blazing hot. "David," I said. "I think we should forget trying to make love. At least for now. I'm in no mood or—or—*position*—to try to reassure you."

A light went on. Literally. He rolled back toward me, on his side now. He looked at me. The only emotion I could identify in his blue, blue eyes was concern. "I don't want you to reassure me. At least not in the way you seem to mean. What do you think I want you to reassure me *about?*"

"I don't know," I said, and the phrase, honestly spoken, did not bring me its usual small release. "About your manhood or something?"

David rolled onto his back, away from me, and put his far arm across his face. I thought he was crying and moved to comfort him. But when I pulled the arm away, he was laughing. Strange little wheezes were coming from deep in his throat, but there was no doubt about his amusement.

"*With*," David said, between silent paroxysms.

I felt annoyed. David seemed to have retreated into a world of private, even unconnected amusement. "With what?" I said, hating myself for asking.

"I'm laughing with, not at you."

"You can't," I said. "I'm not laughing."

He turned toward me again, without moving. "Are you sure?" he asked. And I found myself laughing, too, though none of my annoyance had gone away.

"Stop it," I said.

"Stop what?"

"Stop being so damn irrepressible." And I laughed again.

"My '*manhood*'?" David said, laughing harder. "What Victorian novel did that come out of?"

"Why are you being so *idiotic*?" I loved the way the term felt leaving my lips; endearment or insult, it rolled away from my mouth like the stone from a tomb. "I'm attracted to you, David. Obviously. The point is, I've had terrible experiences with—you know, men, for lack of a better term—and I really don't feel *uncontaminated* enough to get into all of this with you, now."

"I'm different, though."

"How different?"

"My sexuality is a complete scramble, for one thing.... I might be gay. I might be bisexual. I might be *a*sexual, as far

73

as that goes. I might be a lot of things. What I technically *am*, though, is, sad to tell, a virgin."

"Well, that 'technically' makes me curious," I said. "But, as for the rest, I don't see that your virginity has much to do with anything."

"Give me a break," David tossed his hair out of his eyes. "You're supposed to be complimented."

I let the silence hang between us like a row of damp towels before I answered. "What about you and Raitlin?"

David spoke so slowly, he almost had a drawl. "That's our business. It's not relevant."

"I think it's relevant."

"You think wrong."

"I was just—I don't know.... Do you want to know what I feel, David? What I really feel?"

There was no hesitation. "Yes," David said. "I do."

"Well, you're right. I have thought a lot about- fantasized about- making love with you. And I want to. But now, at this moment, I feel sullied. I know it's a stupid, archaic, Victorian novel epithet, but that's what I feel. Worse than sullied. I feel *stupid.*"

I lapsed into silence. Why had I come into David's room, anyway?

"How does my being a virgin make you feel sullied?" David asked.

"It doesn't. Your being a virgin doesn't make me feel any-thing."

An image of Officer Ferrier sprang unbidden to my mind. Why was I never attracted to a man like that? One look at him, and you knew *he* wasn't sexually scrambled. But it was supposed to be a myth that you could tell by looking. Besides, I *had* been attracted to him.

"Are you crying?" David said after a moment.

"No," I said. "Actually, I was thinking of another man."

"Great.... Are you saying that because you feel sullied, you don't want to—or *can't*— make love with me?"

"Jesus, David. You sound as though 'making love' is research for a laboratory experiment."

"Yeah? Well, you sound like you're afraid of me."

"That's ridiculous. You scare me less than anybody else I know."

He rolled back, raised a little on his left elbow, and looked down at me. He was about to say something important. *I love you*, even.

"You're right to be afraid of me," David said. "Psychologically speaking, I'm not—in the best of shape." He rolled back away from me, and tapped the touch-sensitive lamp again, sliding us back into darkness.

"Don't do that," I said. "I want to see you."

The light came on again.

"Please turn this way," I said.

He rolled back to me.

"What do you mean? Aren't you healthy?"

David kept his eyes open but would not meet my gaze. "There were opportunities, you know. But I told myself sex didn't interest me. I should have known that was too convenient to be honest." I could tell he wasn't finished and made myself wait. "I like you, Susan," he said. "I like you a lot. Sometimes, when you're being really finicky and irritable about things, I wonder *why* I like you, but I always remember pretty quick. Huh. When I was eleven, some of my buddies and I got drunk. We started talking about what we were afraid of—you know, about sex. Some kids were afraid they wouldn't be able to do it at all. One kid said he thought about things women

75

might have hidden inside them. Cameras. Knives. That sort of thing. Another was scared witless of germs. I didn't say it, but I was afraid of all of it. Everything. I don't even know why I'm telling you all this, except—You make me feel I'm the one to be afraid of, and that—reassures me, or gives me—I don't know— power over you. And somehow that's exciting. And I hate that it's exciting. Jesus."

"Yes," I said.

"What do you mean 'yes'?"

"I mean I think I understand, even if it's like a butterfly in my mind."

"What in god's name are you talking about?"

"I think I understand what you just said. But it's this delicate connection in my mind. If I try to articulate what I think I see, it'll come apart in my hands."

"Since when do butterflies come apart?" David said.

"When you touch a butterfly's wing, the color can come off on your finger, and sometimes the butterfly dies."

"I didn't know that," David said. "I've never been much of a butterfly-toucher."

"I don't care," I said, punctuating my words, for some reason, by drumming on his chest with my fists. "It's true, anyway."

David began drumming on *my* chest. I pushed away hard, so he began to tickle me. The best retaliation for that seemed to be to unbutton his shirt, so I did. Then he unbuttoned my shirt. I took off his belt. I didn't have a belt, so for retaliation, David unbuttoned the top button on my pants. After a moment, he unzipped them, then he unzipped his jeans. It was like the punch line to a joke.

We started laughing and kept laughing as we took off our clothes. The more clothes we took off, the funnier it seemed.

Finally, we were both naked, wrestling together on top of the covers.

We stopped laughing and wrestling at the same time. David looked about twelve years old, and scared.

I didn't know what to do. He lay on his side unmoving. He was fully erect.

It was embarrassing.

"Some kind of a sexual *scramble* you are," I said.

"I'm a cold scramble," David said.

"Get under the covers, you idiot," I said. The word rescued me again, giving me a sudden spark of something like hope.

We lay on our backs under the covers, which were loose, and light, and slightly tented over David's still erect penis. We lay not speaking, hardly touching.

"Susan?" David said. He sounded far away.

"Yes?"

"This is horribly embarrassing."

"I know." I giggled. Suddenly, he was my friend again, the person with whom I could afford to be honest.

"What a ridiculous pair we are," I said. "We're hopeless, you know that? This is supposed to be the big moment, when the love trembling in our hearts bursts into flowers, and cellos play and fireworks explode above us in the dark February sky.... Instead of which, here we are, naked, embarrassed, and not touching. And to make it worse– do you know what day it is?"

"It's the 14th. But how does that make it worse?"

David laughed a laugh that ended in what sounded like a painful cough. "It's Valentine's Day," he said.

We laughed again. But when we finished laughing, we were still lying on our backs together, not quite touching, in a room that was now totally dark.

Out of curiosity or affection, I reached out for David. His penis was both stiff and soft, a contradiction in terms. I began to stroke him. I didn't really want to, but I couldn't think how to withdraw my hand, without making it seem like a recoil or rejection.

"Don't do that," David said. "I'm not really excited, now."

His penis had been going down. When he said this, it went up again. Now I didn't want to stop. "You *seem* excited."

"That's *aroused*, not excited. I just want to be inside you, that's all. I want to hide myself in you. I want to know what it feels like to be swallowed up by a woman, to be in the dark place where children come from. I want to go in and come out again, unhurt." His penis went down a little.

"So, be inside me," I told him. His penis went up.

"Are you sure?"

"No," I said. "I'm not sure of anything, but it seems like the thing to try."

"I know." David rolled over and touched me lightly between the legs. "You're wet," he said.

"Well, that's your fault." I started to giggle.

David drew back. "What are you laughing at?"

"Not at, *with*. I'm laughing with you because your penis is nuzzling me. He went down and up and down and now's he up again and nuzzling. I think he's bipolar."

"He's a bipolar polar bear," David said. Then he started to laugh, too. He put his hand on my right breast, and for a moment, I felt silly. Images of reciting the pledge of allegiance filled my head, even as my heart began to beat irregularly. It was a struggling bird, and would die, clutched in the hand of its would-be rescuer.

I pushed David away, onto his back. "You're doing too much," I said.

"I'm not doing anything."

"I know. It's just—your penis...."

He clicked off the light. "What's it doing now?"

"Don't you know?"

"Am I my penis's keeper?"

I pummeled him in response. "It's only continuing to express its nature, as far as that goes," I admitted. "But its nature is apparently to be either stiff or droopy. I mean– the whole time we've been talking and just lying here, and it's still– *excited*."

"Whether it's stiff or droopy is not my fault," David said. "I have nothing to do with it."

I laughed. "If I didn't love you so much, I'd walk out right now," I said.

David froze. I could feel that I'd said something wrong.

"Do you really think you love me?" he asked.

"Well, I love you as a friend. And I trust you," I said. "And I want you inside me."

His question had opened a gap between us; partly to cover it up, I knelt over David, then lowered myself onto him. A vision of New Year's and the glittering Times Square ball slowly descending flashed like a light bulb. The crowd roared.... No. It was okay. He wasn't moving at all. I was doing this. I was a boat, drifting—letting myself be lifted and lowered by gentle waves.

David cried out.

I stopped short. "What?"

David looked up at me. I couldn't see his eyes, but I knew they were open. "You seem to be swallowing me," he said.

"Is that okay?"

"Keep going," he said. "I'll let you know."

I moved all the way down and rested there a moment. "David?" I said. "You don't have a condom, do you?" I noticed the lateness of my noticing. It was sort of late to be speaking up now, wasn't it? Not if I got right off. Was I going to get right off? No. Why? Didn't I care? What if David made me pregnant? What if? Was that what I wanted? David and I–?

"You don't have to worry. I'll explain." David took a big breath. "Next time, I will, though," David said.

"I love the sound of that," I said. "The next time. The next time...."

"I'm not saying— Oh, never mind." His tone was as dry as stale biscotti. "We could go get one." It was more a question than a suggestion.

"Next time," I said. I began to move on him again, slowly. We didn't seem to be having sex, really. Sex was all about hard and out of control and sensations overwhelming you like a flood to which you surrendered. And here I was, on David, feeling a little silly, but strangely comfortable. I was in a rowboat, and the rowboat was filled with a great catch of fish—white and black and brown fish. No. They weren't fish. They were —shoes.

What were shoes doing on a boat? But it wasn't a boat anymore; it was a closet. I was in a closet. Oh. Now I got it. Shoes came in pairs. And not just shoes. Boots. Galoshes. My mother's umbrella was in the corner– a propped up raven, with folded wings.

Go away, raven. When are you invited back? Nevermore. Nevermore.

I began to move up and down, gently. And I was a little girl riding the merry-go-round. Music was playing and my mother stood watching me and she was smiling and I felt so wonderful and safe I could even take one hand off the reins and wave bravely into the dazzling sunlight, first to my mother, and then to everyone, everyone who was watching and would be waiting for me at the end of the ride.

But I couldn't take my hands off the reins. My hands were paralyzed. They were wooden talons grabbing wooden spheres. I couldn't let go. I couldn't hold on.

David began to moan, and thrash. He was gasping for breath now, like a fish drowning in water. I slowed and stopped. "Oh, no," David said. "Don't stop, please. Just keep...."

"David?" I said. "Are you–?"

"Susan..." David said. "Susan. Susan. Susan."

My whole body tingled now, in painful reassurance. I was a child, coming in from the cold, having dug myself out of a snow fort that collapsed, coming back to the world of cocoa and voices, dry warm hands, and wet boots hissing like snakes under a clanking radiator.

Just when the world was beginning to make sense, the carnival stopped, and there we both were, hanging high in the air, in a swinging bucket on a Ferris wheel that wasn't moving.

A brass ring, like a door knocker, dangled just beyond my reach. I leaned toward it— elbow locked, arm straight, fingers at attention. I could touch the ring now. It wasn't so much a ring as a ball. A claw and a ball. A ball and a chain. I had to hold on. I had to let go.

And then with a long, slide-descending sound, with a muffled-wail-squeal-shriek-frightened-smallanimal-noise, David began to collapse.

I could feel him growing small inside me. It was a kind of death, and I very much wanted him back, alive. I willed him to grow large again, and larger still. I needed further invasion. I wanted to be occupied.

But he was done. Finished. I was still in a rocking metal basket, but now I was being lowered into the cold, salt ocean. Disappointment deepened to something like despair. I gathered up the remnants of my courage like the shreds of a flag and looked at David.

He was smiling.

Slowly, I lifted up and off. Now, I was lying beside him again, feeling awkward. But this time he slid his arm under me and pulled me to him. "Susan," he said. "You probably already know this, but…."

I held my breath. Now, he really *was* going to say he loved me. That wouldn't mean it was true. Love was something you grew into, even if you were already best friends. But the fact he had said it would be a small black rock, keeping the door of the future from closing.

A hard knock at David's actual door made me jump.

"Are you all right, David?" Raitlin's voice was full of someone else's emergency.

"I'm fine," David said. Then he giggled, which made him cough, which made him put his hands over his mouth and giggle some more. "I'm fine," he said again.

"Be quiet, then," Raitlin said. And his footsteps made their way back down the hall, his slippers sounding like cards slowly shuffled. The thought of possible negative consequences with Raitlin raced into my head and raced out again. I didn't care. David had almost said he loved me. We'd had sex, more or less successfully. I remained unreleased, but I had a sense now of what freedom might feel like. I had not exhausted myself pushing for *less*. I knew for the first time what it was to want *more*.

I giggled.

"What?" David said, kissing the top of my head.

"You said you were fine."

"It's true," David said. "I'm better than fine."

"What could be better than fine?"

"You said being hungry was better."

"Are you hungry?"

"No."

"Good," I said. "Happy Valentine's Day."

We lay tangled together in the dark.

"David?"

I thought he said "Huh," but maybe what I heard was just a strong out-breath.

"I'm not sure what the signs are, but I think I'm happy," I said.

For answer, David began to snore. It was a pleasant snore, really. Quiet and steady, like a motor. It reminded me of something I couldn't quite remember. A memory stood at the edge of my vision, like a child in the doorway, beckoning. In the hell days, someone had come for me. Someone said to follow him, and went away, not looking back. . . .

—I couldn't look back: I was being ferried through the forest on a white stag. He was my indomitable friend and confidante. He stopped, and I slid off his back. For a heartbeat moment, everything was perfect. Then I heard shots from somewhere in the forest, and I was afraid. "Don't worry," the stag said, looking at me with his clear, blue eyes. "I'm an officer. I can't be killed." A shot rang out. The stag was hit. He didn't die, but his eyes glazed over: they scarred and blackened and turned into knots. The stag's face roughened and sank in a sea of bark. His glorious antlers turned to skeletal branches: he couldn't talk, he couldn't carry me through the forest; he couldn't help me. I carried the stag-tree to the edge of the forest and left it there—part of a long line of trees—bare-branched, rootless—alive without beauty, of absolutely no use.

When I woke up the next morning, David was gone. Before I could really register this, Raitlin poked his head in the door. "Hello, there," He didn't seem at all surprised to see me lying in David's bed. "Young Lochinvar's gone abroad early this morning. Let's the two of *us* have breakfast in the drawing room, shall *we?*"

I muttered something affirmative in reply. I got dressed in my own room and took my time with a shower. I didn't quite know what to say to Raitlin, without David there. Maybe I shouldn't say anything. Raitlin had probably figured the whole thing out already, anyway. Of course he had.

By the time I wandered out to the kitchen, Raitlin had gone as well. He left a little note behind: "Waited a.l.a.p. Try the coffee cake. –R."

I nibbled the coffee cake as recommended. It was all sugar and nuts: there was no coffee or cake to be tasted.

Raitlin and David were gone most of the day. I found a couple of romance novels nestled among newspapers in the recycle bin. I swept my floor and reread the novels before throwing them into the garbage.

I made myself a whole box of frozen French fries and ate them soaked in ketchup. I made myself tea, then threw it out, and drank most of a half-liter bottle of Coke I found in the fridge.

I was taking a bath early in the evening, when I heard the two of them come in. They were laughing about something. In a little while, I heard them out in the yard. I stood in the tub and peeked out through the curtains: they were throwing a football back and forth, with great hilarity and gusto.

A little while after that, I heard the front door slam, then steps.

There was a knock at the bathroom door.

"Susan?" said David. "Are you in there?"

"I won't be long."

"Dinner will be ready in about ten minutes," David said.

"David?" I said.

"What?"

"Are you okay?"

"I'm fine. More than fine. Happy, even."

"Could we talk for a minute?"

He opened the door and started to come in. Instinctively I grabbed the plastic shower curtain and pulled it around me. David looked baffled. "I thought you wanted to talk."

"I meant later, when it's convenient."

David nodded, and drew back. He closed the door. There was a moment or two of silence, then he knocked again. He stuck his head in. "How about now?"

"Silly. How about after dinner?"

"I'll check my social calendar," David said, withdrawing. His steps receded down the hall. He was gone again.

The two of us joked easily with each other through dinner, teasing Raitlin. "Quite the young couple, eh?" Raitlin growled. But he didn't glower the way he usually did when he resented being "odd man out."

The three of us sat around the dining room table like characters from a story, trying to pretend nothing had happened.

After dinner, Raitlin suggested we watch a cops and robbers show— "Triviality and violence," he said. "A marriage made in heaven. Speaking of which, did you see the cop car today, Davey?"

"Cop car?" I asked. I found myself remembering a craggy face, and a name like iron.

David shrugged. "I guess people in this neighborhood must be worried about break ins. The same cop drives by here every few days late in the afternoon, just when I'm getting home from work. He doesn't stop, he doesn't speed up. He just drifts by."

"What does he look like?" I asked. "Is he craggy?"

"'Craggy'? I guess so. Most policemen look craggy to me. The guy seems friendly enough. He waves to me, I wave back. Maybe next week we'll get to talking."

It seemed as good a segue point as anything. "Speaking of which, David, do you think you and I could talk now?" David got up slowly, telling Raitlin he'd be back soon. Raitlin didn't seem upset at this, quite the opposite, in fact: he said he would be "supportive" and do the dishes.

"Should we just stay here?" David asked me, when Raitlin had gone into the kitchen.

"How about your room?" I asked.

"Fine by me," David said. But he made no move to touch me on the long walk down the hall, and when we were in the room and I sat down on the bed, he pulled out his desk chair and sat backwards on that, so the rungs were between us.

"Is something wrong?" I asked.

David smiled, but shook his head. "No," he said. "I feel pretty happy, actually. Look– about last night…." He hesitated just a moment, as if waiting for me to deny anything had happened. I wanted to deny it, but I couldn't; last night was exactly what I wanted to talk about.

David shrugged. "Last night was great, Suse. And it helped me. I know how awful this sounds, but I'm really grateful to you."

I didn't know what to say, so I assumed a theatrical pose. "Oh, god," I said.

David looked wounded, but when I started to explain, he made shushing noises. "It was a first," he said. "A first and a last."

"What are you talking about?"

"I hate that you always say that."

I wanted to shake him like a rag doll. "And I hate that *you* always say stuff I don't understand."

"Look, Susan. If I make a comparison that I think will explain things, do you promise not to be offended?"

"Of course not. But don't let that stop you." I was reeling.

"Last night was like the time I went bowling."

Needless to say, this wasn't the conversation we were supposed to be having.

David was rejecting me. No, it was worse than that. Rejecting would have had some dignity, some tragedy to it. He was dismissing me. Dismissing last night. For me, it had been an earth-shattering event. For him, it had been gutter balls.

"I'm just a bowling ball around your neck, is that what you're trying to say?" The extraneous stupidity of the comment was intentional, but there was a bitter flavor to the words I hadn't intended. There was a smell in the air like burning leaves.

"Susan," David said, and it was the mildness of his reproach that stung me the most. "Last night was a thing apart for me. An introduction. An education, even. I'm glad it happened. At least I *was*. I felt close to you last night, and it helped me—I don't know—get my priorities straight. But I don't want to try to attach any other significance to it, okay? I don't want to look at it in some especially momentous way."

David wiped his forehead with one hand. He looked as though I were *interrogating* him or something. I hadn't asked him for all this explanation. All I had done was try to respond in kind to his bowling image.

"Look," he said. "I'm not good at this post-mortem stuff."

"*Post mortem*? Wonderful."

"See? That's what I mean. You pounce on the word as though I'd let something slip. But I didn't. Nothing died last night, and I wasn't trying to say it did. It wasn't a death or an aberration or a bowling ball in any sense."

"So what was it?"

"Last night," David said —already that phrase was a fingernail scraping a blackboard— "was like a sailboat ride, a once in a lifetime, won in a lottery, midnight sailboat ride. Now we're back at the dock, and you're trying to load up this beautiful little sailboat with a bunch of college footlockers. Do you see?"

"Yes," I said. "I see perfectly. I see all the little footlockers sinking to the murky bottom of the lake and making the fish goggle-eyed."

"I need to go help Raitlin," David got out of his chair and moved closer until he towered over me. If he had been anyone else, any other man I knew, I would have been afraid.

"Fine." I stood, too. We were only inches apart, but there was no give to David's face or his body. I edged around him, keeping my face turned toward him, and he pivoted in place, keeping his face turned towards me. I backed slowly to the door and hesitated, feeling behind me for the knob.

The cold round hardness of it in my hand reminded me of something; I couldn't remember what. A wooden ball, maybe. "Are you saying you want to be just friends, David?"

David's face twisted into clear distress. "Susan! Why are you doing this? We *are* friends, and there's no "just" about it. I'm saying I don't want to be lovers– or, if you have to have accuracy, I don't want to be lovers *again*."

I turned and fled to my room. I had made love with David, the man of my dreams, and the fact of our coming together had made no difference.

Nothing had changed.

In sleep, I was naked again, galloping on a horse. The weather was the same, and the ditch. But this time the man was floppy and naked, and the baby was stiff and blue. It was easier this time to carry the baby. Easier because it was dead.

Someone had killed the baby, but who? I wanted to stop and ask Officer Ferrier. I thought he would know because, in the dream, he was stiff and blue himself.

Chapter 5

Bringing Small Animals Home

Two months went by— relaxed on the surface, but with pockets of tension underneath. The weather was like that, too. It veered back and forth like a car about to crash. It went from snow flurries to spring thaws. Snowbanks melted to reveal crocuses, then snow fell and covered them up again. There was frost on shriveled magnolia buds. Nature seemed distraught.

Despite seesawing temperatures and divergent schedules, the three of us clung to our new but already "normal" routine, eating breakfast and dinner together. I often cooked the dinner, since I was home the most. I cooked vegetarian meals. Raitlin and David sometimes added "meat side dishes," like chops or steak.

After breakfast, David went to the product lab, and Raitlin went off to find what he called the "needle of normality in the Wildean haystack." Then I sat at the breakfast table and stared at the dirty dishes that had become mine to clean, and the cereal and orange juice boxes that had become mine to put away.

David and Raitlin seemed to talk more animatedly when they didn't know I could hear them. They laughed and scraped their chairs and pounded the table. But as soon as my presence dawned on them, their raucousness drained away. They made pleasant, even solicitous conversation, and were careful to include me, but they were clearly engaged in a mutual effort to be nice.

I wondered how I'd become the awkward *third* in the threesome.

I wondered how long I could stay who and where I was.

I found myself getting up later and later. I still made it to the breakfast table before Raitlin and David had to leave, but not in time to eat with them. That was just as well, since the sight of food in the morning made me feel sick. I was queasy for an hour or two, from the moment I got up until I'd had some tea and toast. Normally, I loved everything slathered with butter, but now I found myself preferring dry toast, or a little cereal.

I felt part of me split off from the rest. This part hovered above me like some kind of neutral angel, watching me closely, noting change after change, each of them small and pale and insignificant, mattering only in the aggregate, like a jar of pennies you collected over time. Even after you poured all the pennies into a money-counting machine, and the money counting machine gave you a $6 credit slip, you still didn't understand. It was only when the $6 credit slip bought you a bottle of coke and a box of crackers and a stick of cheddar cheese that you realized: they might be grubby pennies no one wanted but they were still money.

I didn't get my period at the end of February. I had thought I might get it in force, since my January period had been painful, strange, and short. But I didn't. That was nothing new. Any time I was under stress, my periods were apt to disappear, and I was definitely under stress. The long ago elementary school doctor had said, writing me a note to go home with, that I might, like some girls, "grow out of irregularity," but I hadn't.

I didn't get my period in March, either.

I woke up late on April 1ˢᵗ and lay in bed unmoving. Normally, I would have struggled up and out of bed. David and Raitlin would be long gone, but I was still part of the household: there was always something needful and domestic I could do to earn my keep. Last week had been "fix the knobs and latches" week. This week it was take off the old storm windows and replace them with old screens.

But today, it was as though I were glued to the bed: the white sheet was really a thin layer of glue, painted on by an evil magician. My mouth was full of saliva, and I really didn't want to be vertical. I turned my head, and there on the bedside was the almost-empty glass of last night's milk. I remembered a poem I'd read in grade school, about a white spider on a white flower wrapping up a dead white moth, and how the three whites meant either something or something else, and both of the somethings were bad.

In my case, it was the sheet and the milk and the mental glue. Turning as little as possible, I reached for the glass, and spat into it.

I stared sideways and down into the glass. The last of the milk and the saliva seemed somehow to go together. The saliva made white bubbles in the sloshing sea of milk, and I felt a wave of disgust. "I'm coming unglued," I told myself. This made me laugh out loud, but the laugh came out as a cackle.

I replaced the glass on the bedside table and lay back. The glue was gone: there were swan feathers. I was lying on a barge covered with swan feathers, floating out to sea. The sun slanted in the window at an odd angle. It must be very late. I lay unmoving. A breeze not so much blew as washed over me. Where were my covers? They had slid onto the floor.

It suddenly occurred to me that even when I was just lying in my own bed doing nothing, my life kept jogging on. *Now* was a harbor, a watery refuge from the sea. David was a boat that had drifted in, moored in the harbor for a night, then set sail again for wider waters.

And I'd had no period since our night together. It was as though my whole body were trying not to bleed.

Maybe stress wasn't the only factor in the withheld periods, the ache in my belly. Maybe my body wanted to be pregnant? Could that be part of what was going on inside?

Yes.

"Pregnant."

My mind caught on the word like a sleeve on a nail. I couldn't pull it free.

Pregnant, I thought.

Sex with David.

Missed period.

Pregnant.

My getting pregnant was as unlikely as my getting the lead in a Hollywood movie. But it was within the realm of possibility. Few things that could be imagined were out of that realm.

Although confusion has always been one of my major stocks in trade, I felt a new certainty. I went immediately past "go," past the "I really could be" to "I am."

It hit me like a bucket of water.

I was pregnant.

Another thought came fast in its wake. Maybe David and I could be partners, now. Allies, at least.

The fates, with their love of irony, had seen to that, hadn't they? They had grappled the two of us together, with hoops stronger than steel, or at least stronger than romance.

The image made me feel nauseated. I got up quickly, slid on my slippers, and flapped to the bathroom as quickly as possible. I made it just in time to throw up in the toilet.

I was kneeling by the porcelain bowl. A man I didn't know was standing over me. He handed me a towel. "Wipe yourself off." He was a man I recognized but couldn't name. He looked at me with a knotted face. "We're not going to say anything about this," he said.

I couldn't place the image. It probably wasn't a memory at all, but a terrible dream.

That night, the three of us had our first annual April Fools' dinner. We had been joking about the "dark and stormy night" outside. Raitlin was feeding me lines: he seemed to like being a straight man. That was a surprise. But, after all, why shouldn't he? He was very good at it.

David passed me the serving plate. The fish he had breaded and sautéed looked good, and smelled even better. "Go on," David said. "Have one."

Raitlin frowned. "Shame on you, David. You keep forgetting Susan is a vegetarian."

"She used to be a vegetarian," David said. "But she's been scarfing down the tuna fish at lunch. I think she's a fishetarian now."

I took the plate of fish back from David and helped myself to two small filets. They smelled of brine and sunken cargo, somehow, and the smell appealed to me.

"It depends how you define 'vegetarian'," Raitlin said. "Susie is entitled to that sobriquet, I'd say."

"I guess," David said. "Meaning she only eats meat that tastes good."

I swung to face him, but he was looking up at the ceiling.

"David?" I said, trying to keep my voice level. "What are you talking about?"

"I'm sorry. I haven't been feeling all that well. It's no excuse, but– there it is. The principles on which your vegetarianism is based do seem to be slipping a bit, that's all. "

"You're talking nonsense," I responded. "My 'vegetarianism', as you call it, is a *practice*. You make it sound like a *religion*." I cursed myself for being inarticulate, but Raitlin smiled as if I'd said something terribly clever.

"Here's a riddle for you, Susie Q," he told me. His voice was uncharacteristically gentle, almost loving; there was not growl or gravel to it at all. "If vegetarians eat only vegetables, what do humanitarians eat?" He reached over and with both hands, drew me and my chair over to him.

At first, I thought it was part of the stupid riddle. Raitlin half-closed his eyes and leaned forward, as if sleep-walking. He kissed me—first on one cheek, then the other, then on the top of my nose; he seemed to be headed for my mouth.

I jerked my head back.

Raitlin's eyes flew open. "Susie, I'm sorry! I only wanted to—"

"Never mind," I said. I wanted to cry. No. Crying was too small, too mean-spirited: I wanted to *wail.*

I pushed my chair away from Raitlin, away from the table. David was standing by the sink, with his back to us, but he had eyes in the back of his head. I couldn't forgive him his distance. He had put the two of us on opposite sides of the world. The one match left in my emotional matchbook was the match of annoyance; I lit a twig and threw it on the realizations I'd been gathering…. The whole unwieldy stack of wood burst into flames.

I looked down at my hands. That was what you were supposed to do in dreams, to remind yourself that you were beyond the province of reality: nothing really could hurt you; no matter how far you fell, you would never hit bottom, you would never die.

"I think I'm pregnant," I said. "I'm not positive, but my last period was in January and I seem to have morning sickness. I've been irregular my whole life, but this feels different. This feels *very* different."

They stared at me: David, head-swiveled, still at the sink, a brown apron tied backwards around him, his shoulders held high as though it were freezing; Raitlin in the "head of the table" chair. My back was to the wall. I could feel the cold of it like the breath of a corpse on the back of my neck. Minutes passed. The grandfather clock in the hall ticked ponderously away. Nobody said anything. It got to be a competition.

"'Get up and bar the door,'" Raitlin said finally.

David looked frightened. "I don't know what to say, Susan. Wow. That's—I don't know— Is it good news? Tell me what to say."

I stood, then couldn't figure out why, and sat down again. "It's yours, David. I was hoping it would be good news."

Raitlin reached behind him, grabbed a bottle of Wild Turkey, unscrewed the top, and took a big slug.

David came to the table, his hands dripping. "That's not possible. We only slept together once, and as far as I–"

I threw my voice at him like a javelin, aiming way above his head. "You're my only candidate."

"Do you want me to leave?" Raitlin asked, to no one in particular.

"Stay," I said. "You don't have to worry, David. I gather you want me to forget our whole interaction, and I accept that. There are *options* of course. I'll look into them." I liked the sound of what I had said. Everything was as cut and dried as dead flowers. Nothing to do but arrange them.

David sat down directly across from me. "Is there nobody else it could be, Susan?"

"No."

David flushed. "I was engaged in my twenties," he said. "We did tests. The tests were pretty definite. My sperm are inconsiderably few. The doctors seemed to think I would be unable to be a father."

"Well, good, then," I said. "It's obviously a false alarm."

"I'll make tea," Raitlin whispered. He sounded like a grandmother.

"Look, David. Given your inconsiderable sperm, I guess I'll wait a little longer before going to a doctor. If I don't get my period soon— I suppose I'll take a test. If the test is negative, I'm wrong, and something else is going on. I could be sick. I've heard that stops women in their monthly tracks sometimes. If the test is positive, then—well, I'll– decide then what to do."

David reached across the table. He took my right hand in his, lifted it to his lips, and kissed it.

"Your announcement is sort of out of the blue," he said.

"I'll remember that, David. The next time I get pregnant, I'll try to time it better."

He flinched at that and I felt not glad but *justified*.

Chapter 6

Rabbit in the Headlights

The day was cold and wet, and the wind was as fussy as a Nordic housekeeper, sweeping piles of wet leaves into corners of the garden. It felt like fall, but it was just spring, being coy. The leaves were the leftovers of last year's collection, and when I crouched down, I could see little spears of green coming up out of the crusted earth. Where the lawn had the good sense to stop, there were crocuses growing again, full out this time. Unstoppably. Purple and gold. The colors of royalty. They must be new ones, I thought. Snow had killed off all the early bloomers.

I was sitting on one of the two redwood chaises, moving my fingers lightly up and down on the arms, feeling for splinters. Raitlin sat nearer the table, hunched on one of the wrought iron chairs, not looking at me. He was drawing circles with his finger on the table, staring at the glass. "I hope you don't leave when the baby's born," Raitlin was saying. "Having a child around would be kind of great for the little *scenario* we have going here. I could even marry you, if that has any appeal."

I wasn't sure how we'd gotten onto this topic. "We're not sure there even is a baby," I pointed out. "But if there is– are you kidding?"

"Not that I'm aware of, no."

"That's really nice of you, Rait," I said. "I appreciate your good intentions. But I would think a baby would– I mean, you and David are kind of—" I stopped.

"Oh, now, this promises to be interesting. What are me and David, 'kind of'?"

"Well, you're just—like bookends or something." I said. "There's nothing wrong with that. But a baby's kind of a big interruption in everyone's lives, that's all. And men are traditionally not—thought of—as constituting the most reliable.... Oh, to hell with it. Thank you for your offer."

"I think David and I have proved ourselves to be quite domestic, really." Raitlin was smiling, but he sounded hurt. "I can't speak for you, of course, but David and I have never meant to crowd you out. When two people in a threesome have an odd or special relationship, it makes it difficult."

I didn't know which two people he was talking about, and, after a moment, I said as much.

"Well, I don't know that you and I have a relationship at all, yet, though I hope the passage of time will remedy that. And you and David—well.... To get back to the topic at hand, the fact that David and I have a really close connection might make it easier for us to—help you with the baby, don't you think?"

"If this is you trying to tell me you and David are— lovers, it's not necessary."

Raitlin laughed. "More than lovers," he said. "We're not just lovers, we're in love. We're not just in love. We love each other. Like from now to forever, sickness and health, and like that."

"Do you mind my asking when the two of you—realized— you felt the way you feel—about each other?"

Raitlin leaned forward. "Not long after your night to- gether, actually."

"So— you *knew?*"

"I knew before it happened," Raitlin said. "Might as well try to stop the rain." An uneasy silence spread above us like a black beach umbrella.

"You always have to allow for 'false positives'," I said after a moment. "I mean, with the pregnancy tests."

Raitlin nodded. "I knew what you meant," he said. "If it's positive, ask David to take a DNA test. That'll settle things pretty quickly."

"If I'm pregnant, it's David's," I said.

"May I tell you something without your taking off in some flight of—internal migration?" He really seemed to be strug- gling to communicate.

I told him I would do my best to stay put.

Raitlin nodded and something like the ghost of a smile passed over his face. For a moment, I could see what he must have looked like as a young man. Handsome, really. And some- thing more—spiritual. Saintly, almost.

"When Carolina and I had been married a handful of years," Raitlin said, "she had an abortion. She felt hideously guilty: pretty soon, she heard babies crying all over the place, even when there were no babies."

"Why are you telling me this?"

Raitlin unfolded his legs, and stood up. He had long legs, I realized. Long legs, on a short body. He grabbed a broom and started to sweep the flagstones. In a minute, he sighed, and the tension dropped out of his shoulders, though his blue eyes were still fixed. "I'm afraid you're going to have an abortion, and I don't think you should. I think it's—for lack of a better word, *wrong*." The tone of his voice reminded me of something on a plate with all the bones taken out, even the tiny ones.

"I know that a—a fetus—" he seemed to choke on the word— "isn't a baby—but…. I had this dream over and over, right before Carolina got her abortion, and for weeks afterward. In this dream, I was in an aquarium, looking at all these beautiful fish. Suddenly I realized one of the fish had a baby's face. Then I realized they *all* did. They all swam up to the glass, facing me, and they put their mouths on the glass. They started mouthing at me— little puckery kisses of 'help.' The pressure of all those mouths broke the glass, and the water and the baby-fish rushed out and over me in a great whoosh and I woke up gasping for breath. All of that, and as far as I know, it wasn't.

Raitlin began sweeping again. "I'm not ready to adopt a child," he said, after he had swept around both chaises. "That goes without saying. But I'm ready to adopt a *mother*, meaning you."

He wouldn't look at me. There was a silence that went deeper than "awkward."

"I think you might worry too much about the motivations behind other people's behaviors, Susie," Raitlin said finally, leaning against the wall. "And not enough about your own."

I wanted to object; instead, I found myself wondering if he were right.

Never mind that. Did he really think I would consider an abortion? This was, after all, David's child we were talking about. Of course, he couldn't be sure of that. But I had made it perfectly clear there was no one else. Either they thought I would consider aborting our baby, or they thought—I couldn't get it for a moment, then it swam into view. If they thought I was lying about there not being anyone else, then maybe they also thought I had slept with David to trick him into being a father.

Raitlin said he had seen my night with David coming before we had. Why hadn't he tried to stop it? Maybe he wanted a baby in the household to make up for Carolina's abortion, somehow? Maybe Raitlin had hoped for exactly what had happened: David had tried sex with a woman, with me, and the failure of that had sent him bounding into Raitlin's bed.

Raitlin pulled a white cloth out of his pocket. It looked like a linen handkerchief. He began to wipe the top of the glass table. The table was only peripherally dirty, and the cloth was dry, so not much dirt came off. Raitlin nodded as though someone had said something, and he started walking around the table, spitting at it. Over and over, he would spit, then consider, then spit again. It was almost as though he were painting with saliva. He seemed to be in a kind of trance, or dance. The way he moved was so slow and deliberate, it didn't occur to me to feel queasy until after Raitlin stopped spitting.

Now, when Raitlin wiped the table, long dirty streaks came off on the cloth. He held it up for me to see. "When I was about your age," he said slowly, "I tried to kill myself in Chicago by jumping out of a twelve-story window."

"Oh, my God."

"Exactly. Your God sent an open-backed truck around the corner at exactly the right or wrong moment, and when, I jumped, I fell onto that truck. The truck was full of mattresses, as it turned out, and when I came to fifteen minutes or so later, I was in a warehouse on a pile of mattresses, unhurt, but terribly embarrassed. I decided God was making fun of me. But Carolina saw it differently. She saw me as, I don't know, blessed, and married me within the month. —A chaste marriage, she called it."

"You never made love to her?" I had a picture of the two of them, Raitlin and Carolina, living together in this house, laying out the stones of the floor, training flowers to turn inward. They were best friends, telling each other about their romantic escapades, lying together at night; there were no rockets of passion, no breathtaking flights that soared to the stars and ended up on the bottom of the ocean.

Raitlin laughed and sat down on the other chaise. Where did that idea come from, I wonder? Of course, I made love to her. What else is a man to do with you women? He can talk to her and get in a shouting match or make love to her and hope she'll fall asleep."

I leaned forward. I had been sitting wrong on the chaise. My back felt as if it had been branded by the taut weave of the fabric.

I stood. I felt defeated by him, by Raitlin, who he was, and what he stood for. I felt defeated by his stories, by having to listen to tales of abortions and fetuses —ugly words, both of them. Botched abortions. Fetid fetuses.

I was about to go inside when David entered the enclosure. It was wonderful to see him. He was such a long, clean drink of water, such a breath of clear, cold, invigorating air, I had one of those ridiculous moments when a cliché comes true: I was suddenly, undeniably, weak in the knees. I sat down in the chaise again.

David walked swiftly over to me, and sat sideways at my feet, looking alternately from me to Raitlin. "I've been thinking, Susan," he said. "You need to go to a doctor."

"You're the one who's short of breath."

"You need to make sure you're pregnant. All of our—speculation—may be completely unnecessary." He must have seen something in my face: he flushed and fell back as if I'd struck him. I wanted to kiss him and make it better. "You should make sure as soon as possible, that's all I'm saying."

"I'm pregnant, David." It was the first time I'd said it baldly like that, out loud. I wanted to say it again, and again, like a chant. I wanted to build a fire and dance around the fire to the beat of a drum, with my fist raised in the air, and say it.

"I don't know about you two," Raitlin said, "but I need a drink." He went to the outdoor bar and busied himself behind the counter.

"So you took one of the tests?"

"No, but I'm certain anyway."

"When was the last time you had a period, again?"

"Don't do this, David."

David stood up. "You're right," he said. "You're right. I'm wrong. I'm sorry. I'll change." It was a "save your relationship" formula he had gotten from a talk show. He sounded really upset. Why? Or shouldn't I be worrying about "why"? Was this an example of what Raitlin had talked about? What was I supposed to be worrying about, instead of people's motivations? I couldn't remember.

"I can't force you to do or say anything. Nor would I want to. But I'd really appreciate it if you'd try to think when you had your last period."

"It was in January, okay? Somewhere toward the end of January."

"Are you sure?" David's eyes were still locked on me. *Look at Raitlin,* I wanted to say. *Look anywhere but at me.*

"Why haven't you tried any of those pregnancy tests you bought?" David asked.

"It's too early. I'm going to, though. Soon."

"It's not too early. Some tests you can do right after conception. That's what I've heard, anyway." David took both of my hands in his left hand and started stroking them with his right. "Okay. Here's another thing I've been wondering about.... If you're pregnant, will you keep the baby?"

His voice was really tender now. He might have been asking me to marry him.

"People don't make life-altering decisions about babies, just *snap* like that," I said. "They need *time*. Besides, I think *you* might have some input here."

"What I'm asking is– it's not really in your thinking to get an abortion, is it?"

I felt like a rabbit caught in the headlights, about to be run over. "No," I said finally. "I didn't know that until now. I mean, when I – made the offer, I assumed I could, that it was the right thing- or the less wrong thing to do under the unfortunate circumstances.... But I realize now I couldn't do that, really. No matter what. It's my baby, even if you don't— Even if you can't think of it as— If I'm pregnant, I'm going to keep the baby."

I heard odd sounds coming from behind the bar. Raitlin was not to be seen. I exchanged a look with David, and we went to investigate. Raitlin was crouched on the flagstones behind the bar, arms wrapped around his knees.

"What's the matter?" I asked.

Raitlin looked up. "Don't spoil it," he said. "I'm crying for the first time in a very long time. And I'm crying because I'm happy. And I'm happy because you're pregnant and you're going to keep the baby."

"Happy" was the last word I had expected to come out of his mouth. I looked at him. There was no trace of tears.

"We're going to have a baby," Raitlin whispered.

"What an actor," David said, his voice shaky.

Raitlin didn't bat an eye. "Well," he said, "for the first time in my life, I *feel* like crying and if I *did* cry, it *would* be for happiness. We're having a baby. So there."

I looked at David for support, but tears were were actually brimming in his eyes. I thought of saying he looked like the hero of a romance comic book. Surely, something of a sarcastic order was needed to get the three of us out of the emotional slough into which we'd fallen. But I couldn't bring myself to say anything. I was going to be a mother. I was going to be fierce and uncompromising—a very *different* mother than my own. Whether David would ever admit it or not, I was carrying his child.

Everything was different.

I wanted to laugh. My mother had never laughed. I wanted to cry. My mother had never cried. I would bring a baby into the world and I would nurture that baby and protect that baby. I would never turn away. I would never turn into my mother.

Raitlin poured us each a shot glass of whiskey—a full one, for him; a half-one, for David; a splash, for me. "I'll do my best to take good care of you and the baby," Raitlin said, speaking to the space between me and David. "Come hell or high water, even if it's not David's, even if it's not *yours*, I will."

I felt absurdly moved. "Hell or high water isn't much of a choice," I said.

"I love you both," David said, tears still in his eyes. "We'll get through this somehow."

"Well," I told him. "I just wish the two of you could lighten up a little. You make it sound as though having a baby is something out of the Brothers Grimm."

"Please go see a doctor," David said.

"I will," I promised. "But let me take a pregnancy test first, okay? Let me just wait a little longer."

Raitlin and David raised their glasses and drank. After a moment, I joined them; it seemed like only possible.

After this, though, I wouldn't drink again. No more alcohol until after the baby was born.

My baby.

Chapter 7

The Raccoon and the Dogs

It was a bright, warm April day. The willows by the creek bed at the back of the house had turned yellow. Their long yellow wands drooped over the water, and they swayed in the wind, like tall slender women, washing their hair.

Yesterday, I had begun what Raitlin called a "house-keeping attack" on the detached garage. Back behind a collection of old pots and pans, which the squirrels were using to store their nuts, I found what I took, in the gloom, to be a dead mouse. I steeled myself and slid a shovel under it; then I carried it out into the sunlight, meaning to dump it in the garbage. But when I carried it out into the light, I could see it wasn't brown and dead, but black and pulsing. What I had on my hands wasn't a dead mouse at all, but a dormant bat. As if in confirmation, the bat extended one enormous black wing; I dropped the shovel. Several of the squirrels in the vicinity began to close in: I picked up the shovel and waved it at them. "Leave him alone!" I told them. I was afraid to try picking the bat up again, for fear of hurting it, but I didn't want to leave it there on the pavement, black on black, at the mercy of the sun and squirrels. Eventually, I got an empty bushel basket from the garage, and turned it upside down over him. He could crawl out when he was ready, I thought. Until then, he was safe.

Earlier this morning, I had gone to check on the bushel basket, and was delighted to discover the bat had vanished. But something about the whole incident, and the earlier discovery of a nest of carpenter ants—an infestation, Raitlin said, necessitating professionals—made me feel I had come to the end of my domestic renovation rope. I loved tackling screens and managing hardware, all the nuts and the bolts and the screws of things. But nature's brigades of the small and the furious were altogether too much for me.

I was telling David that I looked forward to getting back on the work horse.

David looked at me. "It was strange that your last job ended so abruptly. Don't you kind of wonder why?" He seemed to be weighing his words out like produce. Brussels sprouts, maybe, or green beans.

"Okay, David. Just say what you're saying." I kept looking straight ahead: the back wall of the garden was inlaid with tile pentagons. The sharp angles of the five-sided figures were a nice masculine contrast to the feminine fleurs de lis of the chaise. Masculine and feminine. I understood now why so many languages saw gender everywhere.

"Let me apologize in advance for the rudeness of this, but I don't understand why you went up to some guy's room on New Year's Eve."

"What?"

"You went up to some guy's room, even though you knew you weren't supposed to."

David was attacking me now, but somehow, he was the one who was cornered. I remembered being on the beach with my father when I was little. Animal tracks, a lot of them, had been stamped on the spring beach, swirling in the sand in front of one corner of the high retaining wall. I asked my father what had happened. He stooped and looked carefully at the tracks before answering. "Well," he said finally. "It looks like a raccoon was backed into this corner by five or six dogs." "Oh, the poor raccoon," I said. "No," my father answered. "The poor dogs."

"You went up to some guy's hotel room after having champagne with him in the bar. You spent the night at the hotel, probably because you were drunk. Maybe more than drunk. You might have been drugged. That's almost certainly why you were fired, but if it makes you feel better to deny reality, go ahead."

David stood. His cheeks were flushed a motley red, but the area around his eyes was dead white. He looked ridiculous. "You need to talk to Joe," he said.

I was saved from needing to respond by Raitlin, who entered with a loaded tea tray, whistling under his breath.

Raitlin set down the tray, and busied himself with cups and saucers, napkins and tiny spoons. All his attention was on the tray and he looked so focused on the choreographing of his own hands, so self-involved, one might have thought Raitlin believed himself to be alone.

"Joe?" I repeated stupidly.

David flushed. "I'm sorry. I don't feel well, but that's no excuse. I don't feel well, but that's no excuse. I don't know why I sound like this.... Joe, the off-hours cook at the Carrigan."

"You know Joe?" I asked.

"Don't you remember? He develops photos in the product design lab. He was the one who got you the job— It doesn't matter. The point is, I saw him at the lab yesterday and we got to talking and he says he woke up in the kitchen on New Year's Eve, and found you'd left some flowers for him."

"Why would I have left flowers for Joe?"

"I don't know. But he says you did. He woke up before midnight, found the flowers—"

I reached over and touched David's sleeve. "What kind of flowers?"

"Roses, I think. Why? What does that matter?"

I saw white roses in a bulky bouquet, carried vertically, away from someone's body, held mistrustfully, as one might hold a baby without a diaper. "I don't know. It probably doesn't. But I remember something about flowers. It might lead to my remembering something else."

"Joe says he went looking for you to say thanks. He says he was just in time to see you get into an elevator with some guy who was presumably staying at the hotel."

I remembered something about translation. Instantaneous translation. "A translator?" I said.

"So you do remember?"

"No. Well, not exactly. It's just I can kind of hear a voice, a kind of drawl. It might be relevant or–"

"What were you wearing?"

"What do you mean? I was on duty that night. I was wearing my uniform."

Raitlin paused in his laying out of the tea things and stared at me. "What are you staring at, Raitlin?" I said.

Raitlin began pouring tea. He started with the tea pot right over the cup, then raised it higher and higher. He was like a child, really, daring the hot liquid to misbehave, making a daredevil operation out of the simplest of domestic acts. That was his way. Any time emotion reared its ugly head was a good time to serve a beverage.

"Joe saw me get into the elevator?"

David flushed. "Yes. He said he thought of reminding you that going upstairs could lose you your job, but decided it was New Year's Eve and you had the right to celebrate in your own way."

I tried to remember how we had gotten onto this obscure and dangerous topic. Oh, yes.

"That's not all," David said.

"Maybe it's enough, though," Raitlin unexpectedly put in. He handed me a cup of tea. It was peppermint tea, from the smell of it. I didn't like peppermint, but it was good for me. I took it gratefully. I dipped my spoon into the tea: the cup was small and I couldn't seem to bring the spoon up without losing all the tea in it.

"Here," Raitlin said. "Try this." He took the tiny spoon from me and bent the bowl of it up until it was at right angles to the handle. It looked ridiculous, but now I could lower and raise it without losing any liquid. I brought up a spoonful and was actually able to get a taste of tea. It was too hot and scalded my mouth. It was also unsweetened. To my surprise, I liked the pepperminty taste.

"I don't want to talk about this anymore," I said. "I want to relax and enjoy my tea."

David came and knelt on the floor in front of me again. He was always doing that. "You have to think about this," he said. "You have to try to figure out what happened. Otherwise—"

"Otherwise what?" I took another spoon of tea. Peppermint was good. A little medicinal tasting, but hadn't mother always said expecting something to taste good and be good for you at the same time was expecting too much?

"There's someone who could maybe help you," David said. "I did in fact get into conversation with the cop I mentioned."

"What cop? You never mentioned a cop."

"The cop that keeps driving past here. He said he'd be happy to talk with you. In fact, I –"

"What?"

"Nothing."

"What exactly did you tell him?"

"Nothing, really. I just thought– He seemed friendly and competent, somehow, like somebody who would know what to do in difficult situations. I just–" David stood and turned to Raitlin, as if in appeal.

"What do *you* want to talk about, Suse?" Raitlin asked. "With us, I mean. *Now.*" He had a nice voice, really. The voice of experience.

I started talking about the job I wanted to get, as a clerk in a hardware store. I could see myself, directing women customers to our newest gadget, a handy-dandy gizmo that would let them repair latches with one hand, and hold their babies with the other.

David interrupted me. "Don't you want to know why the Carrigan fired you?"

"I think you just told me," I said. "Anyway, Raitlin says I shouldn't worry so much about why people do things. I should worry about—something else. Besides, I wasn't fired. One of their full-time people wanted to come back unexpectedly, and they let me go."

"Look, David–" It was Raitlin again, warning David to let it go. Thank goodness for Raitlin, I thought. I had underestimated him. And he had offered to marry me. He had offered to take care of me. Maybe I should take him up on his offer.

We sat silently after that, until the knot of us unraveled.

I sat in the kitchen an hour or so later, nibbling crackers, and wondering which clothes I would still be able to wear once I started showing.

I rubbed my belly tentatively. Maybe the baby would be a boy, and look like David, and then he'd have to recognize the truth, and deal with it. Maybe the truth was easier to deal with if it looked like you.

But if I were pregnant, the baby needed a doctor. A clinic, at least. And if, somehow, I wasn't pregnant and had just stopped having my period– Well, in either event, I should already be receiving medical attention. "Medical attention" was a nice phrase- like a warm and fuzzy blanket. Some nice muted pastel color. Anything but plaid.

I decided to look up some names. That was not looking back. That was doing something positive. I went to get the phone book, but when I pulled out the drawer in the small table where it was usually kept, there was no phone book.

I stood in the center of the living room and all of a sudden, I started to cry. My legs buckled and I crumbled to a kneeling position on the floor. I was only like that a moment before arms slid under my arms and wrapped themselves around me: someone was kneeling behind me. I stiffened a moment, and then relaxed into the momentary warmth and comfort. I thought at first it was David. I willed it to be David. But it was Raitlin.

"I'm sorry," he whispered. "Truth is the one live round in a game of Russian roulette, and it won't help any of us do right by each other."

I leaned forward and threw up, splat, right on a beautiful wine-dark flagstone. I expected Raitlin to leave and he did, only to return almost immediately with a wet red-and-white-checked dishcloth. This, he applied tenderly to my forehead.

"What about the mess on the floor?" I said, weakly.

"Never mind that," Raitlin said. "The housekeeper— meaning me— can get that." He produced another rag and began to clean up the mess. The look and the smell of my own vomit made me start to feel queasy again.

"Go to bed, Susan," Raitlin said. "Get a good night's sleep. Tomorrow, you can solve all yesterday's riddles."

I went back to the little table and got out the phone book but couldn't remember who I was going to call.

There were shadows just over the crest of the hill. Everyone on the playground was playing war, apparently. They were all in a circle, throwing stones. I went to look. There was a snake in the middle of the circle—a big snake, coiled around itself. Every time a stone hit, the big tail lashed in pain. I stepped into the ring. "Stop throwing stones," I said. "The snake's not hurting anyone." The snake slithered over and wound itself around me. I could feel the strength in its coils: eventually, I was wearing the snake like a dress. "Thank you for helping me," the snake said. "You can talk!" I exclaimed. "Only by giving up power," the snake told me. With every word the snake said, I could feel it losing strength. The snake's grip weakened. It fell to the ground. I was naked. Everyone started to laugh.

It was morning. I was in bed. My bed. Birds were singing outside my window. I could smell spring in the breeze coming through the window. I knew what I had to do. I went to find David. He was on his way out the door, but he stopped short when he saw me.

"Are you okay?" he asked.

"I'm fine. No. Better than fine. I'm sorry."

David took a deep breath. There was a long silence. He took another deep breath. He seemed to be underwater, somehow, breathing through a straw. "I'll do the best I can, Susan. I—didn't expect this, obviously. And I don't know what it means, but—I'll help, in whatever way I can, no matter what. That's all I've got to offer you though. Help."

He meant he didn't love me. Not that way, at least.

"I appreciate that, David," I said, and cursed myself. He had said something from his heart. I'd said something stilted. I tried again. "Sometime in the future—maybe there could be something more, though, don't you think? Between us?"

David looked as though he were in pain. "I don't see what more there would be, Suse," he said. "Our friendship is already a lot. And there's Raitlin."

For the first time, it occurred to me that Raitlin had not been exaggerating his connection with David, that theirs was a bond I hadn't allowed for. "Are you and Raitlin–?" I began, but my mind balked on the approach, like a horse at a too-wide water jump. "How do you feel—" That was better. "How do you feel about Raitlin?"

"What?" David seemed genuinely astonished.

I felt painfully warm—as though I'd been out in the snow all day and had suddenly come in to sit by a fire. "I'm sorry," I said. "I didn't mean to offend you. I know you and he are—"

David laughed. "'Offend me'? You didn't offend me at all. I love Raitlin. I thought you knew that."

I fought the impulse to flee. David would never forgive me if I fled now. "Well, I mean– I guess I'm just really obtuse. But if you, you know, love Raitlin, then I don't understand why you, you know—had sex with me."

David looked at me: I pictured Hansel trying to retrace his steps: the breadcrumbs were there, but they were few and far between.

"I don't know, either," he said finally. "Clearly, I shouldn't have, but I only figured that out after I did it." Then he laughed. "He asked me the same thing. I honestly don't know. Maybe it was my "normal Christian" upbringing reasserting itself for the last time.... I– I don't know. It was wrong of me."

"Well," I said. "After all, it doesn't really matter. I mean, no harm was done. Quite the opposite, in fact.... On which note, I'm going to go check things out."

When I got to my room, I went to the dresser. I pulled out the bottom drawer. All six pregnancy test kits were still there.

I took one of the kits into the bathroom and opened it.

I peed, then withdrew my hand and looked. The paper was crossed by two parallel and slanted pink lines. Pink lines. Like a little girl's washed out valentine. I had felt sure all along, but somehow I hadn't expected technology to second the motion.

All six tests confirmed the fact– I was going to have a baby.

Chapter 8

The Baby Sardine

It was just a week later, but April's child had already succeeded in sticking her green lance right between the white ribs of March. Thoughts of the unstoppable future were making everyone nervous.

I was sitting in my favorite seat in front of the fireplace, writing. Raitlin was on the couch, reading a monograph on Wilde and pretending to be deaf.

"David?" I said.

"What?" David was sitting at Raitlin's desk across the room. He had bent the brass gooseneck lamp over so far, I was surprised he could see around it to draw. He sounded annoyed. He'd sounded annoyed for several days running. I thought I knew why. He was stifling disapproval. For David, what you didn't say could never be an expression of anger.

"I'm going to contact a doctor today. Will you be my ride?"

David stared. "Are you kidding?"

"Am I kidding, you haven't got time, or Am I kidding, of course you will?"

"Of course. Right now?" David said. I got up and walked over to the desk.

"I told you I was going to go," I said. I felt myself getting dizzy, as though I'd swallowed helium from the bottle of the laugh I had planned.

"Yes. But you didn't." David sounded really serious. His seriousness was a cork in the in the bottle.

But David wasn't finished. "I think there's really something wrong, Suse. "It's like you're pregnant in a dream. And you don't seem able to wake up, to actually do anything about it."

"I took the tests," I said.

"Okay. I guess I'm being unfair. But– your periods stopped a while ago, right, and you were pretty sure you were pregnant and it was a week ago you took the tests. It's not even just that. You've been talking about getting a job– but you haven't actually done anything about anything. Have you even gone out of the house?"

"I suppose you have a theory to explain such aberrant behavior," I said, trying for a tone of patronizing indulgence, and failing.

"Yes. I do. I think you may be suffering from Post-Traumatic Stress Disorder."

"Okay, fine," I said. "Give me the lecture."

David hesitated. "Let's please get you to a doctor, okay?"

"Okay, but you mean, let's get the *baby* to a doctor."

"I feel like a pumpkin," I said. I couldn't expect David to understand what I had only now realized. I had thought all along I was Cinderella, but I wasn't. I was just the fairy godmother. Not even that. I was just the carriage, the pumpkin carriage, taking Cinderella to the ball. I could try to be useful, I could try to be good. But my importance was secondary.

"So, where's your doctor's office?" David asked.

"I don't know. First, I have to decide who she is. Why?"

"It's just—it's that time, you know, and I thought I could combine two errands in one swell foop. That's all."

"What do you mean— 'that time'?" I asked. "Nobody told me anything about a time."

David stared at. "It's April 15ᵗʰ today, Susan. Tax time. Did you already file?"

"Yes," I said. "I filed on New Year's Eve, because I didn't have anything much to report."

"What about your W-2s?"

"What about them?"

"You have to file your W-2s with your taxes or they aren't any good," David said. "Some workaholic you are."

"I forgot," I said. I was back for a moment watching a brown envelope slide out of sight, proud that, for once, I had done something on time. Early, even. And then....

I had been in the lobby, and I had watched the envelope slide out of sight. I'd come right back, because what was her name—Janice—had gone home early, and Joe was in the kitchen, drunk or asleep or both. And a man had come in the cafe.

I saw him again.

The man was wearing jeans and a sport coat. He was from the south, he said. He had a strange name—Tat. That was it.

The past was unrolling in front of me, like a newspaper that was no longer needed to whack an unhousebroken dog.

"They found your underwear," David said.

"My underwear?"

"Oops," Raitlin said.

His voice made me jump. I'd forgotten he was there. I was mad at them for acting in concert. It felt good to feel something in stereo again.

"What do you mean, my 'underwear,' David?"

"Joe said they found your skirt and underpants in the laundry room. The underpants had blood on them, Suse."

"Maybe I was spotting."

"There was semen, too."

"Semen? What are you saying? How would Joe or anyone really know it was semen? Doesn't it take a lab or a detective or something to figure that out? Anyway, I think Joe has been watching too much television. And you are just– latching onto it as a way of I don't know what. But all of this is just the distant past. I'm going to be like Scarlet and think about it tomorrow. Meanwhile– what I need now is a doctor," I said.

I went to the phone stand and pulled out the drawer. The phone book was back where it was supposed to be. I opened the red section at random.

Suddenly, I was filled with a reluctance like dread. Surely, other women didn't get their doctors' names by skimming the red pages, pointing and dialing.

My baby had no father. Even if we did tests and they proved David *was*– he didn't want, really, to be involved. My baby had only me to depend on.

I heard a voice on the other end of nowhere: "Mary Mahoney Health Facility. How may I direct your call?"

"Hi. My name is Susan Manderley. I'd like to see a doctor as soon as possible," I said.

"Is this an emergency, Mrs. Manderley?" The voice was breathy and fast in a pleasant way, like a river moving at its own pace, quick and unhurried.

"Yes…. I think it is…. Well, no. But I'm pregnant. I've been pregnant– a while, and I'd really like a doctor to– talk to me."

"When was your last period?"

"Toward the end of January."

"And who have you been seeing?"

"I beg your pardon?"

The voice was slower now. This was not reassuring. "Have you been seen somewhere for prenatal care up to today?"

"Oh," I said. "I thought you meant.... Never mind. I haven't seen any doctor yet. That's why I hoped I could–"

"You're lucky, Mrs. Manderley. Doctor Oberdorster just had a cancellation today at 12:30. Can you make it in here by then?"

"Of course. I just.... Thank you."

The Mary Mahoney Health Facility was on the 7th floor, accessible only by a rickety-looking elevator whose door you had to close yourself.

The waiting room was new and clean and an oasis from the dingy hall—a pink and pale green haven. It was an odd color scheme, carried out even down to the smallest details—the writing board onto which the receptionist clipped my "Intake Form," the pen; even the magazine holders were staunchly pink and defiantly green.

There were three women already in the waiting area. A few minutes after the last of the them had been called, it was my turn. I stood, and David stood with me.

The summoning nurse smiled. "You'd probably be more comfortable waiting out here, sir," she said.

David sat as though someone had pushed him back into his seat. As I passed through the doorway into the inner sanctum, the nurse turned to me with a big, confidential smile. "Is that the dad?" she asked.

I hesitated. "Sort of," I said. I cursed myself, and waited for the interrogation, but it was not forthcoming.

"Pregnancy is sometimes hardest on the dads," said Nurse "Hi! I'm Elaine," busy scribbling something in her folder.

"Come on over and stand on the scale, Ms. Manderley," Elaine said. I did as instructed. "130," Nurse Elaine announced, in a "here's a prizewinner" tone.

"Wow," I said. "That's a lot."

She showed me to a little cubicle. A small table. Two small chairs. A small sink. A small desk. The bed, with a pink and green paper robe folded in a big square where the pillow ought to be, and metal stirrups sticking up at the end like feet.

"The doctor will be right in," Elaine said, and closed the door. I didn't want the doctor to come in and stand around with her clip board while I undressed, so I quickly unbuttoned my jeans—they were uncomfortable, anyway—and started to wiggle out of them.

The door clicked open. "Wow. You're a quick one," Elaine said. "And showing nicely, I see. I just came back to say you don't have to do that, to undress, if you don't want to."

"Won't the doctor want to examine me?"

Elaine laughed. "Yes," but we let new 'obis'—'obstetric in-takes'— stay clothed during the initial interview. It can be long, you know. Plus it's more comfortable meeting someone when you're not naked. After you and the doctor have exchanged a little information, *then* you can get undressed."

"I'm sorry," I said, trying unsuccessfully to rebutton my jeans. "I seem to be getting bigger by the moment."

Elaine laughed again. Her laugh had a kind of horsy sound to it, not obnoxious like a whinny. More like a whicker. It was a nice, dead on, hayseed kind of laugh. I liked Elaine.

"I'll tell the doctor you're here," Elaine said. "Sorry about the not knocking. I didn't think you'd had time—Never mind. I didn't think, period."

She left.

I was alone, still clothed, in a small but sunny room, dwarfed by the long, high examining table. On the window ledge farthest from the sink was a book-sized stand-up calendar. There was a funny three-colored drawing on the front that looked like a page torn from some mechanic's coloring book—a colorful reproduction of some plumbing fixture, perhaps. The title said, "Female Anatomy Calendar."

Inside the cover was a drawing of what at first looked like a dark bough, from which dangled a heavy red hive, the center of a small swarm of angry black bees. Fascinated, I put on my glasses, and the diagram and its word-bees immediately swam into focus.

There was a small knocking at the door, and it opened partly. A woman who looked about my age stuck her head in the door with a questioning look.

"May I come in?"

"Sure," said I. "You've caught me red-handed."

The woman stepped into the room and closed the door behind her. She was short, with bright green eyes, and red hair that was too flamboyant to have come out of a bottle. She looked like a leprechaun playing doctor. She was wearing bright green sneakers, dark, silky slacks and a white cotton lab coat. Around her neck was a pink and green stethoscope. She caught my glance and smiled. "I'm Dr. Ellen Oberdorster."

"Hi," I said. "I'm Susan Manderley, as in Scarlet's house."

"Scarlet's house?" said Dr. Oberdorster, looking doubtful. "Do you want to sit down?"

"On the table?"

"The chair is fine."

We both sat.

"You're young for a doctor," I said.

Dr. Oberdorster nodded. "You can call me Ellen if you want."

"Ellen was my mother's name," I said, "If it's okay, I'll call you Dr. O.?"

I looked down at my hands. My palms were still red. An image started to come back to me, something drifting up to the surface of a pond where a child had drowned. I stood on the bank with a dead branch, ready to scoop it out. Up and up it came—it was a big red, plastic "G," but when it hit the surface, it melted like hot wax, and liquefied into blood. The water turned red.

"My hands are red."

Dr. O. leaned over and patted me lightly on the tips of my fingers. "That's pretty much 'first pregnancy' in a nutshell," she confided.

I wiped my hands together. My palms were sweaty. I had an impulse to wipe them on Dr. O.'s lab coat, to see if the red would wipe off. "I don't know what I said…. You don't think the hands are because of our detergent? I do a lot of dish-washing."

"It's hormones," Dr. O. said flatly. "It'll go away soon after delivery."

"I beg your pardon, but are you sure I'm pregnant? Even without a test?"

Dr. O. consulted the form. "Doctors are never sure of anything unless they've got numbers or diagrams to point to, but it says here you ran a home test, and that was positive…. So let's see—" She consulted the form I had filled out in the waiting room. "You put down 'toward the end of January' as the date of your last period. Can you do any better than that?"

"I beg you pardon, but are you sure I'm pregnant? Even without a test?"

Dr. O. laughed. "Geez. I've never had another patient beg my pardon so much. I meant, can you be more specific about the beginning and ending date of your period?"

"I don't know. January 19th, or 20th, maybe, for the start, and January 23rd for the stop."

"But you say here your periods normally last a week."

"Normally, they do. But this one was really short. I think it maybe even ended before the 23rd. I don't know."

"All right. Let's say your last period started on January 18th. That would give us October 25th as your Estimated Due Date."

"I think conception was later than that," I said.

"Really?" Dr O put on a pair of wire-rimmed glasses and then looked at I over the top of them. She looked both amused, and comical. "When do you think it was?"

"February 14th."

"Could that be wishful thinking?"

"What do you mean?"

"Well, you know. A baby conceived on Valentine's Day— Sometimes people adjust the facts to fit a hope or a wish they have."

"I'm not adjusting anything," I said. "I'm positive it was then. It had to be."

"Well, if February 14 was the gestation date, then EDD would be November 7. Why don't you hop up on the table. Undo your zipper and let me palpate you."

I clambered awkwardly up onto the table and did as requested. Dr. O. came over and began a soft, blind and, at first, disconcertingly icy three-fingered probing of my abdomen: it was a little uncomfortable.

Dr. O. went over to the counter and came back holding what looked like a transistor radio in one hand. Attached to the front end of that was a cord, and at the end of the cord was a little, funny-looking microphone.

"Are you going to record me?" I asked.

Dr. O. smiled. "I want to listen to the baby's heartbeat."

"Wow," I said. "It must be about the smallest heart in the world."

Dr. O. just smiled, but it was an inclusive sort of smile, and I didn't feel embarrassed for having made such a strange comment.

"Should I get undressed now?" I said.

Dr. O. laughed. "Not yet," she said. "Just scooch your jeans and panties back down to your bikini line and roll up your shirt a little." She stopped and considered. "Would you like—ah, your friend or partner out there to be in on this?"

"You mean David? I—uh– Is there a problem?" I asked. Malformed babies started swimming around in a big aquarium, along with sea turtles and sharks.

"No. It's just—it's kind of neat to listen in. Helps 'support personnel' feel more a part of things. It's up to you, though. Everything's up to you."

"I—uh—Sure. I mean, I don't know if that's something he'd want, or not." I tried to remember what I knew of David. All I could think of was the baby's heart beating. Babies' hearts beat faster, didn't they? Like birds?

"Would you like me to go ask?" Dr. O. said. I must have nodded, because she put her gadget down on a chair and vanished. In a moment, she was back with David. David was gawky, and stumbled coming into the room.

"Hi, David," I said; then I felt silly.

"Hi."

David looked down at my belly, and then away.

I understood.

It looked so naked there, so bland and doughy.

People—men, anyway, looked at faces and then legs and breasts and asses and genitals. Nobody was interested in bellies.

Mine lay cold and exposed—almost baleful, as if it were all too aware of this fact.

Dr. O. squeezed a blob of clear jelly onto my belly button. The effect was of a little fountain. A riddle from grade school came back: "Deep in walls as white as milk, lined with skin as soft as silk, in a fountain crystal clear, a golden apple does appear. No doors are there to this stronghold, yet thieves break in and steal the gold." The answer was an egg.

I looked at David. He was sitting hunched over in his chair, watching the doctor.

I saw myself in a delivery truck, careening down the streets. It was raining, and I could hear the wind shield wipers making their rapid, side to side, shush-shush, shush-shush, shush-shush.

The doctor and David were staring at me. What was I not understanding?

Shush-shush. Shush-shush.

The doctor moved the microphone nose just a little to one side, and I could hear the wipers more clearly now. Shush-shush, shush-shush. Quick, but steady. Confident.

'David had tears in his eyes. The doctor's eyes were dry but big.

"It's always a miracle," Dr. O. said.

I understood. It was the baby's heart, beating loudly, for all the world to hear.

We were a tableau. I was lying down. *Hear no evil.* David was sitting. *See no evil.* Dr. O. was standing. *Speak no evil.* Shush-shush. Shush-shush. Shush-shush.

Wow. A baby. Our baby. A new life. Shush-shush. Shush-shush.

I felt so *grateful*, I started crying.

The doctor took her hand away. The sound stopped. David looked at me and grinned a congratulatory, conspiratorial grin, as though I had done something unexpectedly and incredibly right. I felt absurdly proud.

The doctor waved a hand between us. "Sorry to break up this motherly moment," she said. "I'm wondering if you could be mistaken about February 14 as the date of conception?"

"No," I said.

"Yes," David said.

Dr. O.'s look swung back and forth between us like a pendulum for a moment. Then she nodded. "Well. I want you to have an ultrasound, no matter what, partly just to make sure everything's developing the way it should."

"Is there something wrong?"

"Not at all. You're just very advanced, that's all. You're big, for one thing. And if that was—well, I'm sure that was a heartbeat. If you're right about February 14— Well, let's just get you ultrasounded, okay? Then we'll know everything, pretty much."

"Will you need me to get undressed for the ultrasound?" I asked.

Dr. O. smile was like a shadow. "No. I'll just need you to go to the room at the end of the hall. Elaine, our sonographer, will be with you shortly."

"Should I leave?" David asked.

"No," I said, then realized he had been asking the Dr.

Dr. O. smiled at David. "It's up to mom," she said. She turned to me. "It'll be basically the same thing all over again," she said. "But this time the jelly will be warm, and we'll get a picture to go with the sound." She turned back to David. "There's a quart pitcher at the nurse's station," she said. "If you wouldn't mind going and getting that and filling it at the cooler, I'd appreciate it.... Susan, your job is to drink water. We need your bladder as full as you can get it. My partner's out sick today, so you can just stay in here, if you like. After an hour and a half or so, we'll come and get you."

The doctor poked her head in and assessed the situation. "Okay, you two," she said. "I think it's time."

We went down the hall. I climbed into another bed and Nurse Elaine came in.

She sat down on a chair next to the bed with her back to me. I had trouble seeing the television screen. "I'm going to scan both longitudinally and transversely in sections," Elaine said. "That way, I'll be able to get an entire picture of the contents of your uterus." She looked up and to her left, as she said this, looking at David as though he were the one with the uterus.

There was silence in the room. I craned my head around, but I couldn't see David anywhere. "Eureka," Elaine said. "There's the baby." She spoke with cheerful enthusiasm but moved her wand very carefully as though she were coloring and needed to stay within the lines. "Now, we'll just grade your placenta, here... Good.... A plus, in fact."

"Is there another one?" I asked. "Another baby? I mean, I feel pretty big– for not being very far along, and I just–"

Elaine leaned closer to the screen and scratched her head a moment. "As a matter of fact- No. No twins for you this time. I'll give you your first snapshot in a moment, though," she said.

Dr. O. came into the room. She and Elaine muttered and nodded together.

"Okay," Dr. O. said, turning and patting me on the arm. "You can go and get dressed."

It was then I realized David was standing on the other side of me, and he was holding my hand.

I got down from the table with difficulty and waddled off to the bathroom. When I came back out of the bathroom, everyone was gone.

I found the three of them in the original examining room. When I opened the door, the three turned as one and looked at me with the deer-in-the-headlights look I associated with demonstrable guilt.

"What?" I said. Clearly, something was going on.

"Excuse me, Dr. O," Elaine said, brushing past me in the doorway. "I've got to go mind the store."

"Come on in, Susan," Dr. O. spoke in a tone that seemed to match her pink and green stethoscope.

"Is something wrong? I couldn't see anything but shadows."

"Not at all. I've got good news and other good news. The baby is fine. That's the main thing. It's a little soon to say boy or girl, but we can do that next time and tell you or not tell you, as you like. Be sure to make an appointment in four weeks, okay?"

"What's the other good news?" I asked. I felt suspicious of Dr. O. for the first time, and ashamed of myself for feeling suspicious.

"You're farther along than we thought. Your EDD isn't October or November, but late September— any time from the 20th on. You're already in your second trimester."

"Wait," I said. "I thought you said November 7."

Dr. O. looked at me and nodded. David had turned and was looking out the window. "There was apparently—a miscalculation—as far as the date of gestation," she said. "This baby was conceived a lot earlier than Valentine's Day. If you have to have a holiday, I'd say more like Christmas or New Year's."

I hesitated. Wanting to be sensible and feeling as if I had a choice about what to do, I looked at the doctor, meaning to ask how sure she was. But I couldn't find my voice. Dr. O. set an office visit for four weeks ahead and handed the slip to David.

I made "thank you" sounds and let David steer me out of the office.

Chapter 9

Unsatisfied Wolves

I think I was more or less *status quo* going down in the elevator, and walking to the car, and even in the car.

But then the car got stuck in a traffic jam on Jefferson, and David had me slide, with difficulty, over into the driver's seat, while he ran into the main post office with his and Raitlin's tax forms.

The minute he did that, people started coming to the passenger side window, and knocking on it. It was open at the top, and one eager young man even stuck his hand in the opening. And another young man and then a girl and an old man joined the young man, and they all stuck their hands in and then I realized they were dropping papers and leaflets into the car.

In my head, I saw a hand at the window-sill, one hand groping for—what? A brass ring…. No…. A yellow pull-cord. The circle dangled just out of reach. In a moment, my mother's fingers would have it, and the shade would be bad the way it always was and fly *up* when you pulled down. Someone had told me not to move a muscle, not to make noise. His hand was over my mouth. My heart was pounding. I was breathing too loud. I wanted to scream but was too afraid to move or make a sound.

By the time David came back to the car, the crowd had moved on.

I couldn't say anything. The car was shaking.

I had been raped on New Year's Eve and I hadn't remembered and now I was pregnant with the child of that rape.

The door I'd had my shoulder against since childhood sprang open.

And there he was. The wolf had huffed and puffed and blown out the back of the closet. There was a hole there in the bricks, a secret door. There was a world in back of the real world. It was the world where stories hurt, where wolves were not satisfied with swallowing up grandmother, but lay in wait to devour Little Red Riding Hood– white roses, wicker basket and all.

I was crying– carefully.

I hated myself for crying.

We drove home. By the time we reached the long, curving driveway, I was someone I hadn't been for a long, long time.

Before I had been *myself*, living in a well-made house with well-made strangers, strong enough to keep the door shut, no matter who or what knocked.

Now the house was gone. Nothing remained of it but brick wreckage. Someone had huffed and puffed and blown my house down. That was frightening enough.

What made it scarier was, the person standing in the middle of that brick wreckage was not me at all, but a character named "Susan."

She was alone. She was unprotected. She was *me*.

David came into the bedroom without knocking and sat on my desk chair and asked if he could get me anything, but I sent him away. "I don't want you to see me like this," I told him. He said he had seen women cry before.

"Not like this," I said.

"Oh, I think so," David said. I knew what he was thinking—He was thinking quantity of tears, he was thinking amount. That was why I sent him away. I was thinking motivation.

It was one of the few times in my life when I knew exactly what I was crying about. My tears came from the anger of the powerless.

"Tit for Tat, Tit for Tat," hammered away at my brain like a woodpecker on a dead tree. I had a headache.

That bastard had raped me on New Year's Eve, and I didn't remember it and I was pregnant because of it.

David was right: the alcohol wasn't enough to explain it. I must have been drugged. There must have been something in the champagne. All I had to go by were lightning flashes and half a name.

No. There was more. There was the red "G" on my palm. The jeans I'd come home wearing that weren't mine. David had cut those jeans up into squares for grooming Sappho.

But I had been raped on January 1st, and this was April whatever it was. April 15th. Tax time.

I had been drugged and raped. And now I was pregnant. I should do something. What? I should get DNA testing. I would take control and find the creep who did this to me.

I took Raitlin's kitsch "girls and kittens" calendar down from the bathroom wall and counted the interval—15 weeks since IT had happened. IT. Tat had said he was an IT guy.

And if I went to the police tomorrow, what then? They would want to know why I hadn't reported the rape for 105

135

days— Because I didn't remember what happened, I'd say. Because I was drugged.

I would not say, because I'd been *raised*, even *trained*, to repress my memories of rape.

But even in my new state, I didn't remember much. I had no real information to give anyone. Joe could testify, maybe. But what could he testify to? That I'd gone upstairs with a man.

I would go to a hypnotist. No, a hypnotherapist. You could recover memories.

Even if I went down to the Carrigan tomorrow, and Tat was still there—months later– even so it would just be my word against his.

And of course he wouldn't be there. He was from out of town. He'd said he came from—Georgia. "A Georgia home boy," he'd said.

But he hadn't had a drawl. He'd sounded Northern, hadn't he? At least Midwestern.

I should have been suspicious right then and there.

Why hadn't I been suspicious?

He'd given me a bunch of white roses and warned me about the thorns.

And money. He'd given me $50 and I'd gone off with him up to his room. No, the bar. And we had funny champagne. Salty.

He must have put the drug in that.

An *Expert*, that's what I needed.

I'd already gone to a doctor. Yes, but that was a doctor for the baby. My baby. My baby's father was a rapist. *"We aren't going to tell your mother about any of this."* There was a closet with shoes, and my mother's black umbrella leaning against the wall. I was kneeling on shoes. They made my knees hurt. My dress was torn. One of the buttons had come off. It was blue and had a face on it. I recognized the face. It was Mickey Mouse. My knees were knobby. My father was leaning over me. That was the trouble with Memory Lane. It led to a closet where bad things happened.

The police would never believe me. *He* would, though. What was his name? Officer

Ferrier. I'd go in and ask for him. But I'd seen him right after it happened and I hadn't said anything. If I'd told him what had happened, right then, there might have been proof of what happened. I could have had an abortion. But I hadn't. I'd mumbled something about having too much to drink.

It wasn't my fault. I'd been drugged. But it *was* my fault. I was the sort of person who didn't go with a stranger to his room or even to a bar. Unless the bar was across the hall and the stranger gave me money and flowers and a line.

David had talked to a cop who said he could help me. How much had David told him? How much was there to tell? Why had he done that anyway? He had talked to Joe. He had suspected what had really happened. But instead of telling me his suspicions, he had talked to a cop.

I came to myself, lying on my bed, ice queen in a coma, and people came to visit from the nightmares of my childhood, ugly and deformed. They came on leg stubs, and crawling on their bellies, burned and disfigured, maimed and twisted, with open mouths and gaping sores. They brought images and thrust them at me, terrifying and horrible. I had seen them all before. But this time, at the end, there was a Shush Shush, and someone put a baby in my arms. A baby born in a manger, swaddled in white. A real baby. My baby.

Then I saw myself committing hari kari with a spoon— digging into my belly with a huge spoon, and scooping the fetid fetus out of me, like brown rot from a slovenly peach. I saw myself sticking a vacuum down my throat and sucking everything up out of me, then popping the fetus out of its plastic covering like a gigantic pill out of cellophane wrap. I saw myself gnawing on my own entrails like ropes. I saw myself dropping depth charges down the hole of my mouth, and surf boiling up in my throat, thick with bloody debris. I saw myself taking a bath and dialing the temperature up and up until the fetus I was holding turned into greasy, bloated fat and drifted like a dead fish among a fleet of nodding yellow ducks with red on their beaks like blood. And at the end of all of it, there was a sound like a Shush Shush, and someone put a baby in my arms. A baby born in a manger, swaddled in white. A real baby. My baby.

I saw myself on an operating table and a doctor wearing an evening coat and gloves reached up inside me, and pulled out a round, black bomb, still ticking.

I not so much fell as *dove* into sleep.

The next day, and the next, and the next day after that, I had no appetite, appetite, but I coaxed myself to eat. I watched game shows on television. I took long not hot baths. And I realized something. I really, really wanted it. Yes, it had come to me wrapped in horror. But it was a baby. Babies and children were not guilty of what was done to them. And it was mine. I was still fighting my unconscious. But now I fought it as a clear and present danger to my unborn child. I was determined to take good care of it. For the baby's sake, I would learn to be careful. I would learn to be responsible.

But it was his baby, too. A rapist's baby. If it was a he, maybe the he would grow up to be like his– But I would be his mother, and with my good mothering, he would grow up to– What? He would grow up without a father and one day he would demand the truth and he would look at me and he would be– what? unbelieving. He would want to contact his father and his father– That wasn't his father. That was a monster. He should be killed, the rapist. He should be caught and killed and...

I sat outdoors and watched Sappho hop around in the daffodils and crocuses and grape hyacinths, which looked like baby hyacinths, but weren't.

And I *plotted.*

I didn't feel angry anymore, or scared, or worried, or hopeful. The big feelings were safely beyond my scope. All I felt was determination. I could check out David's cop and if he didn't seem the right person, I could ask if he knew Officer Ferrier. How many Officer Ferriers could there be?

I called David at the lab. Was he going to be home at the usual time? What about Raitlin? Had he seen the drifting cop recently? Could he tell me again what he had told the cop?

David said he was going to be late, he was busy at the lab designing a bike stand and couldn't talk very long. Raitlin had gone to a cafe and was presumably hard at work on Oscar Wilde. He, David, hadn't seen the drifting cop for a few days. He had told the cop a friend of his had been the unsuspecting victim of a crime and asked if she wanted to talk to him, would he advise her?

I decided to find out whatever I could from the police, without tipping my hand. I would loiter around at the end of the driveway, as if waiting for David. If the cop showed up, I would initiate conversation. I would ask for his help in tracking Tat down. When I found the bastard, I would decide what the baby needed me to do.

Wait- Wait- Wait- then Pounce. But people who pounced weren't protected.

I steeped in concentrated inaction until David came in from the lab—early, as it turned out: the bike stand was finally finished. I suggested we could maybe go down to the end of the driveway at the drive-by cop's normal time (4:30) and see if the drifting cop showed up. David said he thought that would be a really good idea, but as soon as I suggested it, I regretted having done so. Still, I felt it was too late to back out, so at 4:20 we trudged down the driveway and stood around in the weeds at the side of the road and waited until 5:20 and no car at all came down the pike.

As we trudged back up the quarter-mile driveway, I thought to ask David the officer's name. "His first name is Adam," he said. "I don't think I ever knew his last name."

"It doesn't matter anyway," I said. "If I want to talk to a policeman, I know someone I could ask."

We left it at that.

When we got back to the house, I asked David if he would read to me. He readily assented. I thought dreamily of Winnie the Pooh— "The more it snows, Tiddily Pom, The more it snows, Tiddily Pom, The more it goes—Tiddily Pom, on snowing. And nobody knows—Tiddily Pom, And nobody knows—Tiddily Pom, How cold my toes—Tiddily Pom, Are growing...."

David and I were in the little walled garden. He had bought a dog-eared copy of <u>The Expectations of Expecting</u> in a thrift store. I would have much preferred Pooh, or any other children's book, but he was so excited about his purchase, I didn't have the heart to stop him. Besides, for the most part, especially on sunny afternoons, his voice was like a drone in my ear, a pleasant bumbling like the buzzing of stingless bees.

"David?" I said. "Sorry to interrupt, but what time is it, exactly?"

"It's 5:02 in the afternoon, Central Standard Time, April 23," David said.

And exactly at that moment that his voice was buzzing around me, burdened with the black nectar of meaningless numbers, I felt a white butterfly land for a moment on a wide, green leaf heart. Its wings were like flower petals, breathing. I had such a clear picture of the white butterfly, it took me a moment to I realize I hadn't seen it; I had felt it inside, deep down.

I had felt something which was me and not me, something definite but tentative, at 5:02 in the afternoon, Central Standard Time, April 23rd.

"David," I said. "Read me about quickening."

"What's quickening?"

"It's in the index."

I heard the pages rustling. David's voice began again. "'Quickening,'" he said. "'Page 159....' Here.... "'That first momentous sensation of life, or 'quickening', can occur anywhere between the 14ᵗʰ and 26ᵗʰ weeks.... A hundred pregnant women may describe it in a hundred different ways. Perhaps the most common descriptions are 'a fluttering in the abdomen' and 'butterflies in the stomach.'"

"Mine was butterflies," I said. "Well, one white butterfly, anyway, with wings like flower petals that were breathing."

I had tried to keep the lid down, but it was too late. All the big, bad emotions came flying out like red bricks and black bats and black and blue brickbats. And at the bottom of the barrel was a small white something with bedraggled wings. Once its feathers were dry, I thought, it would certainly fly again.

It was amazing how a few nudges from inside could shake everything into clarity. There was no point now in going to the police and filing charges—Months had gone by. Whatever meager evidence there had been was almost certainly destroyed. Even Officer Ferrier was unlikely to believe my tale of drugs and rape and repressed memory. If he did, he would probably tell me I had no basis for filing charges: it would be my word against Tat's, if that was his real name, if he could even be found. I didn't want him found, anyway. If he were found, I would have to deal with him. He might ask for custody—at least visitation right. There was a horde of unthinkable thoughts.

I had to be careful. If he were to find out about the baby—wasn't it a horrible outside possibility he might demand rights? That was unspeakable. Unthinkable.

Chapter 10

Teddy Bears Wearing Black

I woke up with the flu. For two weeks, the farthest I traveled was from the bedroom to the kitchen, and back again.

I had brought up every doubt in the book, every negative feeling but they couldn't seem to stop, or even *impede* my determination to do *something*. Whatever I had to do, moreover, I had to do in person. I couldn't very well *call in* a belated rape. I was spiking a fever—the visions dancing in my head had nothing to do with sugar plums: I saw Hallmark cards on a rack, in a section marked "Belated Rape."

"So sorry I missed your rape," it would say. There would be teddy bears wearing black.

Raitlin, who had finally surfaced as an active member of our threesome again (looking, he himself acknowledged, like the cat who swallowed "several hopes with feathers"), seemed interested in hearing about my pregnancy so I found myself talking to him a lot. "It's as though my hearing has split into two strands," I told him after breakfast on day at the beginning of May. "My 'inner' hearing has gotten really sharp. Sometimes I think I can hear the baby burping, or even just breathing. But my 'outer' hearing has suffered as a result. Sometimes I don't hear anything you or David are telling me, because I'm too focused on what the baby is saying. Does that make any sense?"

Raitlin nodded and said that it did, but then added, "No one could blame you for not paying attention to us anyway, David and me, we've gotten so ingrown.... Speaking of which, there's someone I'd like you to meet..."

"Smoothly done, Rait," said a woman's voice from behind me. I turned carefully in my chair—in the old days, I might have swung around—and saw an attractive, middle-aged woman—bleach-blonde and a little chunky—standing in the kitchen doorway. "I knocked but nobody answered," the woman said. "So I used my key."

"I'm Susan," I said.

"Hi, Susan. Raitlin's told me a lot about you. I gather the reverse of that proposition is untrue, however. I'm Carolina."

"I thought you were—Uh—living somewhere else— like California maybe," I said, California being the farthest place I could think of from Ann Arbor.

Carolina laughed a light, shallow laugh, a laugh that made me think of brooks and streams: She was clearly the sort of woman who laughed a lot, who felt comfortable laughing. She had an easy air about her that made me like her at once. There was a kind of mannishness to her that I found refreshing; come to think of it, Carolina's mannishness balanced out Raitlin's feminine ways and features. They were exactly the same height, and could have been brother and sister, or bookends. Carolina's gray-blonde hair came to a kind of duck-tail point in the back. She was wearing no makeup, and she didn't just walk, she *strode* into the room.

"I'll leave you two to talk," Raitlin said, standing hesitantly, as though he expected any moment to be shoved back into place.

"Do you have topics in mind for us?" Carolina said.

"No," Raitlin said. "Women don't need topics, anyway. They talk much more comfortably without them."" He started to leave the room, then turned back. "I'm glad you're here, Caro," he said. "You know you're welcome to stay."

"Raitlin?" I said. "Carolina's here to see *you*."

But Raitlin was gone.

"That's not actually true," Carolina said. "Do you mind if I have some of this coffee?" She sniffed suspiciously at the brown murk in the bottom of the glass coffee pot. I wanted to laugh but was afraid of how my laugh would sound in my own ears, so I stifled it. "I gather Raitlin's coffee was always bad," I said to Carolina. "Here, I'll make a new pot."

"I'd rather have tea," Carolina said. "Chamomile, if you've got it." She saved me the trouble of rummaging in the cupboard by doing it herself and pulling out a single untagged teabag. "A little dusty," Carolina said, and blew on it.

"I'm not sure that's chamomile."

Carolina sniffed the bag. "It is, though," she told me. She offered to "do the making," which I accepted. We both ended up having tea from the single teabag and sitting on the little screened-in porch off the kitchen. It was shady on the porch, and quiet.

"My," said Carolina, looking up to where the grape-vines were making their erratic but dogged way across the screen above us. "It's hard to believe I planted these vines just a couple of short decades ago." She looked at me. "So Raitlin didn't say anything about the possibility of my– uh– dropping in?"

"No," I said. "Actually, I—Maybe I wasn't paying close enough attention or something, but I actually thought you were—you know, dead."

Carolina laughed so hard she slid into a coughing fit. She leaned back in her chair and gestured for me to come over and pat her on the back. I did as I had been silently requested to do but was apparently too delicate in my ministrations. Carolina kept gesturing with one hand for "more" and "harder," until finally I let loose with a good whack that almost unseated her. Carolina stopped coughing and sat up straight. She took a deep breath, held it, then relaxed back into her wicker chair, waving me back to my seat.

"Raitlin and I have been writing each other sporadically since we split up, but it was never important until he wrote me a month or so ago, asking me to come and stay for a while."

"Huh. He never mentioned it."

"Not surprising. He believes in letting things evolve... He suggested we might want to get divorced in person.' Though nowadays it's easy to do divorce, like everything, long distance."

"So you're still his wife?"

Carolina nodded.

"I'm sorry. I just– I'm surprised you weren't divorced a while ago."

Carolina seemed genuinely perplexed. "We never saw the reason, I guess. Separation, yes. Divorce, no. Still, all the cards are in place, if we decide to go ahead with it."

"He and I have worked out the details— you know, who gets the marble gewgaws, and that kind of thing. All we need now is a judge's signature, and Raitlin will be able to get married and waltz off into the sunset."

I found myself unable to meet Carolina's gaze. I looked down at my belly, and put my hands there, as if the baby were kicking. First things first, after all. "I don't know what to say," I said. "I mean, here and there over the last few months, Raitlin's mentioned our getting married but it was always in *passing*. I never really thought he was serious."

"What? Oh, you mean because of the *baby*," Carolina said. I found the emphasis on the final word more than a little insulting.

"Well, that—and other things," I said. "Is it so obvious? Am I that big already?"

Carolina shook her head and poured herself a second cup of not-exactly-chamomile tea. How could she have drunk her first cup so fast, I wondered. The tea was still really hot.

"Well, I think I'd have guessed you were pregnant even if Raitlin hadn't told me. But that's because I'm trained to notice the signs.

"And I didn't mean to insult you. I can certainly understand Rait's having flirted with the idea of marrying you."

Now it was the tense that caught at my attention. "You don't think he really wants to get married, then?

Carolina shushed me with a look that suggested I was being weighed in the balance and found waiting. Her mouth twisted itself into a little moue. "I think Raitlin wants to marry *David*," she said. "They can't legally, of course. But– you know...."

"Oh." I nodded, feeling a perfect idiot. "Well, I guess that makes sense, given how they feel about each other. I just never thought of—their making it *official* is all."

I struggled to shut the door on pictures of Raitlin and David in a church. Raitlin was waiting at the altar, wearing a suit. David came down the aisle in a white dress– What was the matter with me? I had known for a long time that they loved each other. Why should the mention of their marrying unloose these silly images? It was good when people who loved each other consecrated their feelings with a marriage. Wasn't it?

Carolina smiled—a sad, weather-beaten kind of smile. "Don't beat yourself up about it," she said. "I never thought things would go this way, either. Even when he told me about David, I never dreamt—Well, good for him, anyway. right? It's never too late for a little dignity in life, that's what I always say."

I wanted to ask her what dignity had to do with anything, but my mouth seemed to be frozen. Maybe ice-mouth was a symptom of the second trimester: I'd have to look it up.

Carolina nodded, as if reading my mind. "That's the other reason I've come," she said.

"I beg your pardon?"

Carolina laughed. "You're the other reason I've come. That's what I was leading up to."

"Me?" I said. "What do you mean?"

Carolina thought a moment before answering this time. "I don't know how you feel about it, but I'm a great believer in what my high school history teacher used to call manifest destiny. Of course, he meant our country's 'realizing westward' and all of that nonsense. What *I* mean by it is that I believe everyone's life is set up to follow a kind of pattern or game plan, and a little thought can reveal what it is. We don't have to follow it, of course, but, in general, things work out better for us—and we're happier—if we do."

I drained the last of my cup and reached for the teapot. "And I'm part of your pattern somehow?" I tilted the pot, but nothing came out.

"It's empty," Carolina said. "Here, have mine." She pushed her tea cup across the table. I was about to refuse it, but I decided that wouldn't be polite. Besides, I was drinking tea for two. I took a swallow or two of tea, and nearly gagged. There was no sugar, just the leafy herb taste of the chamomile and something bitterly medicinal. "I put Echinacea in my cup," Carolina said, laughing. "I never drink tea without it these days. It's really good for you."

"It must be," I said, adding a generous spoonful of sugar. Now the taste was earthy but endearing, in a weird sort of way.

"Anyway," said Carolina. "I'm sure Raitlin has told you about the baby I aborted. I was never able to get pregnant after that. The doctors couldn't find anything wrong with me, you know. They were mystified, but it made perfect sense to me."

"What did?"

"It made perfect sense to me that I couldn't conceive. It was my body's revenge."

Carolina took a deep breath and shook her head like a dog shaking off water. "Sorry. That was a stupid thing to say, under the circumstances. The point is, I don't think my body trusted me after I attacked it. I started going around to different groups, reading everything I could get my hands on about abortion and pregnancy and eventually I became a doula—a midwife with an attitude."

I felt what I can only describe as a sudden rush of trust in Carolina. I began hinting around about something bad that had happened on New Year's and how I had plans to take steps to "handle the matter."

But Carolina was having none of it. "Don't look back," she told me confidently. "Looking back turns people into pillars of salt. You need to look forward. For the baby's sake."

"Yes," I said. "I see what you mean." It wasn't a lie. I did see what she meant. Her response was the same as my mother's had been, lifetimes ago, when I tried to tell her about my father and the closet.

Eventually David, and then Raitlin himself, manifested themselves (from different directions), and the four of us went out for dinner to Riverbrook Restaurant, just across from Estabrook Park. When we came in, "Hi! My name is Barb!" grabbed up four menus and showed us to what she called a "quiet little booth in the corner;" though the big room was dotted with people, most of them were alone.

"Well, how are the parents and grandparents doing to-night?" Barb asked, as Carolina slid into the booth ahead of me. The four of us looked at each other and started to laugh.

At that moment, there was a loud crash outside, and all five of us, including Barb, joined the crowd at the bank of windows on the west. An older car had broadsided the first in a row of cars parked at right angles to the building. That car had slid over, but not far enough to hit any other cars. Someone's horn blared for a minute as if insisting something important had happened, then abruptly lapsed back into silence. The car that had been hit had bent around the nose of the intruding car in a way that made me think of a big metallic hammerhead shark.

I looked through the plate glass window, and something about the way the light was dying outside, or the swirling chiaroscuro of emergency movements made it feel as though we were watching a silent film.

"Come on, folks," a small, dark, sweaty man with a big food-spotted apron came up to us window-watchers and made shooing motions with his hands. "Back to your tables, please. The show's over." And everyone else moved obediently back to their booths and stayed there, even when it turned out the show wasn't really over, because an ambulance and two police cars showed up, and lights began chasing each other around the walls of the restaurant.

I lingered at the window.

And there he was—Officer Ferrier. I had promised myself to go and find him and ask him for help, and I hadn't, and he had come to me.

It was already almost dark out, and people were running around in a confused state, but he stood still, there at the center of it, my knight in shining squad car armor.

I know the world doesn't work this way, but I couldn't help feeling he was a gift to me. I hadn't gone after him; the fates had brought him to *me*.

Without saying a word to my three dinner companions, I did a pregnant woman's version of bolting out the door, forgetting even to grab my coat, though the night was chilly.

But he wasn't there.

I was breathtakingly disappointed, and very cold, but hung back for a moment anyway on the outskirts of a small babble of people and watched as two young guys in white put an elderly man on a pallet and rolled him past the gawkers, stopping in front of *me* while they waited for the ambulance to back up. He looked like my father. Like an older, wizened version of my father. For one heart-stopping moment, I thought it *was* my father. He had the same long face, the same prominent nose, the thin mouth, the narrow, wide-set eyes.

His thick black hair with the silver streaks had thinned and paled to a wiry gray, as he had often predicted it would. He was very proud of those silver streaks. He liked me to comb them "into prominence," which, as a young girl, I heard as "into promises."

"How can hair turn into promises, daddy?" I used to ask him. And he would laugh the way adults do when you've said something stupid they've decided to label cute.

I would sit behind him on the big living room chair with wings. And comb, and comb. "It never gets any longer, daddy," I would say. "My hair does, but your hair doesn't." And he would laugh again. He always laughed at me when he couldn't see my face.

And if it were my father, what would I do? I would step forward and accuse him. Now that he was weak and in pain, and needed me, I would spit on him. **No.** I would kiss him. And he would smile, thinking all was forgiven. But it would be a mafia kiss, and the hit man would step forward from the shadows and put a bullet behind one ear. There would be no mess. He always hated mess. There was no need for that, though. The mafia man didn't actually have to pull the trigger. My father just had to know he was there and would *pull the trigger* if I wanted him to."

The man smiled at me. There was nothing of my father's recklessness or charm in that smile. It was a wistful ghost of a smile. I must have been glaring at him: he looked startled by me. But there was a blissful absence of recognition.

I smiled back, in reassurance.

The ambulance was in place, and the two men in white loaded him into it. Then they jumped in after him. As he leaned out to close the doors, the one closest to me stuck his head out, and repeated what the guy in the greasy apron had said. "That's it, folks. The show's over." Then the doors clicked shut, and the ambulance left, its siren off, but its light spinning.

"How can a heart attack be minor?" someone asked as the little knotted gathering began to dissolve.

"When they put him on the gurney, he was saying he didn't think his insurance would cover any ambulances," came the response. "If your biggest worry is money, I'd say you're in pretty good shape."

That would be my father, too.

I was suddenly overwhelmed with something very like grief. Someone I didn't know, someone who'd probably never hurt a fly in his life, had had a heart attack, and I'd glared at him because he looked like my father.

Somebody tapped me on the shoulder.

I whirled around.

"Oooh. Sorry. That was stupid of me." Officer Ferrier stepped back, out of arm's reach, as though he were afraid I meant to strike him.

"Hello!" I said, a little too loudly.

"I'm sorry," he said again. "I should have come around. You probably don't even—"

"Officer Ferrier, right?" I said.

He smiled at me, and there it was again—the not-quite miraculous surprise of having something you wanted to happen actually *happen*. His face, his blue eyes, his smile—they were all exactly as I remembered them. *Exactly*. I suddenly felt very grateful. In a moment, if I weren't careful, I would embarrass us both by crying. I needed something dry and accountable to focus on. I had been called on the carpet, and the carpet had a bare spot, and the dark pine floor was showing through. I could see its black knots, like fists or roses.

I brought myself back to the cold, drizzling present with an effort. I was in the middle of trying to figure out how to re-introduce myself when Officer Ferrier said, "So, how's the New Year's mystery woman?"

"You remember me?"

"I remember everybody," Officer Ferrier said. "It's my business to remember everybody."

"Really?" I said, shivering.

"No. Not at all. My short-term memory is really terrible. But I remember you quite vividly."

I felt a strong need to enlist him in my support. The strength of that need drove me to honesty. "Do you think you could—help me, maybe?"

The smile broadened, the way I knew it would— into a not-quite-slapdash grin. "At your service," he said. "And I *mean* that. Only, can you tell me what it is *inside*? You look hungry, and you're shivering. Plus you're busy having dinner with your friends. But maybe you'll let me buy you dinner some other time."

Something about the jumble of his sentences reassured me. This was not a prepared speech. He was floundering, too. We were alike in that. Except, how had he known–?

"How did you know I was having dinner with my friends?"

It seemed an innocent question, but he flushed as though I'd touched some vital nerve.

"Oops. Some policeman I am. I'm not normally like this. I mean, I normally am very- I wasn't supposed to say anything but your friend asked me to swing by here. I–"

"David? David asked you to come here tonight?" Officer Ferrier nodded. I couldn't put the puzzle pieces together. "But there was an accident–"

"Oh, yes. That was real enough. Unplanned. But I was here when the accident happened, on my way to coming inside, to see if I could sort of run into you by chance, and...." He stopped.

"I've been wanting to see you and I couldn't quite summon up the nerve, but I was going to tell you when we got together- if you agreed- about David's asking me. I know he has your best interests at heart and I do, too, but I can understand if you're a little put out by the whole–" His voice trailed off.

"You came here to see me?" I said, feeling silly for asking.

"Yes. Well, I mean, I came here to see if you wanted to see me.... I mean, I thought your friend's plan or idea was okay because it would give you a chance to say just a "hi" and brush me off, you know, without it being awkward for you."

"And you're the cop that's been cruising by our place every day?"

He flushed. "Not every day. Now and then. I guess I was kind of hoping for a glimpse of you. You know- you'd be going to the mailbox or something and you'd see me and then you'd either stop to talk and remember me or you wouldn't and then I'd give up my little–"

"Little–?"

"Little fantasy or whatever it was- **is**- about our getting together for a talk. Dinner. Coffee."

"Well, that actually all sounds good to me. I've been thinking of calling you."

His cheeks flushed crimson. I pretended I didn't notice. "But my friends are, in fact, waiting, but I suppose you could come in and meet them unless– Aren't you on duty, though?"

"For all *intensive* purposes," he said.

I couldn't believe it. "What did you say?"

He grinned ruefully. "Sorry. That's how I learned the phrase, and it always made more sense than—"

"No," I said. "I just— That's how I say it, too."

"Really?" He seemed inordinately pleased. Maybe he wouldn't be so pleased if he knew

I had an agenda.

"Could we get together tomorrow?" I asked. "I mean, I know that's awfully soon."

He nodded, as if it were the most reasonable thing in the world to be put on the spot by a shivering pregnant woman he had spoken to for five or ten minutes five months ago. Maybe David had said something that–

"What did David tell you about me, exactly?" I tried to sound lawyerly.

"Nothing, really. Just that he had a friend, Susan, and she might need some help from someone who knew the law and so on. I said I thought I might know you but that's all I told him, and we both let the subject drop at that point."

So he didn't know I was pregnant. Better to talk about that in person.

"Tomorrow's not soon at all," he said. "I'd really like to help you, but I'm going out of town for a seminar. I'm taking an FBI class on Mass Disasters— Never mind, you don't want to know. The point is, I'll be out of town until almost June."

He looked so sad and sympathetic, he might have been telling me my dog had been run over.

I just nodded. I was afraid to say anything, for fear our whole tenuous connection would fray to miscellaneous threads right here and now. But even with his hat on crooked, and his generally *rumpled* demeanor, there was something about Officer Ferrier that gave me confidence—confidence in him, of course, and confidence in myself. Confidence in FBI classes. Even confidence in Riverbrook Restaurant.... Some people radiate optimism or understanding; he radiated confidence. I hated to think what I was radiating: "Attention. Attention. If you are a normal man, run for your normal life before I mess it up."

He frowned. "I really wish you'd go inside, but never mind that. Um—my name is Adam, by the way." He put out his hand, and I shook it. His hand was enormous, but I could hardly feel any pressure at all. He was a retriever, holding an unbroken egg in his mouth.

"I could fix you up with someone else, if you like. For help, I mean. If you can't wait.... I'll understand, believe me."

He made it sound like a date with escape hatches; he seemed to think it was some kind of privilege to be able to help me out.

"That's okay," I said. "I've waited this long. I can wait another few weeks. It'll give me a chance to do some research, anyway."

"Okay," he said, his grin back in place. "How about you and I get together exactly three weeks from now—June 1st, 6 p.m."

"You got it," I said, and kicked myself inwardly, wondering what on earth it was that I supposed he had got. "Where do you want to meet?"

"How about here?"

"Here would be fine."

Suddenly, Raitlin was at my side, trying his best to look genial. "Good evening, officer," he said. "What's the trouble?"

Adam looked him up and down before answering. "No trouble," he said. "No trouble at all. Here." He gave me one of his cards. "Call me if you can't make it, okay?"

"Okay," I said. "But what if *you* can't make it?"

He considered this a moment, then dismissed the question. "I'll make it," he said.

Raitlin's presence was like a small friendly thorn in my side. I wrote my name and our phone number down on the upper left-hand corner of his card, tore the card in half, and handed the relevant portion back to him. "I don't have a card," I said. "I hope you don't mind."

Adam laughed. "I don't mind at all. Makes me look at the darn thing in a whole new light. See you, Eve."

He was in his car before I got the joke.

It made me unaccountably happy to think Adam had paired me with him, even as a nickname. I was so unaccountably happy, I wasn't the slightest bit annoyed with Raitlin, who offered me my coat as his excuse for having intruded.

I accepted it gladly, even for the small walk back into the restaurant. It was unseasonably cold.

"Are you seeing him?" Raitlin asked, just before we got to the door.

"Yes, I am," I said, almost proudly.

"Behind our backs? Tsk. Tsk."

"What?" I said. "Oh. I'm not *seeing him* seeing him. I'm just seeing him once, next month, to ask his advice."

"Well, you know what they say. Having one date with a policeman is like eating one potato chip."

"I don't believe anyone says that, Raitlin. You just made it up."

He smiled. "Guilty as charged."

At the end of our Riverbrook dinner, I tried to rise to one of the many occasions no one was talking about—Carolina's return, David and Raitlin's possible marriage, my baby.

Carolina said something about the early bird getting the worm, and I responded (out of where, I have no idea), "Yes, but the second mouse gets the cheese." That led to a general discussion of "Animal Metaphors." and I found myself talking about a science piece I had read. Someone's pet cat had been successfully cloned, but its coloration was nothing like the original. The scientists said the cloned kitten was exactly like the DNA donor cat, but in a new suit of clothes.

"Well," said David, sounding peeved. "I guess I know who I am in that story."

I didn't. I was both surprised and glad when Raitlin said in a loud but somehow mild voice, "Leave her alone, Davey."

"Hush, children," Carolina said. "If you raise your voices any more, you'll scare the wait staff."

I suppressed the impulse to laugh. Since my excursion outdoors, dinner had felt very awkward. Incredibly so. It had also felt very *family*. "This is the way it should be," I said to the three of them, at large.

They turned as one to look at me. Before, I might have been threatened. Now, the common insistence of the gesture amused me. I was invincible. I was woman. I was pregnant.

"We don't follow you," Carolina said. The two men shook their heads in agreement. They laughed. I laughed. "I don't know. This conversation feels exactly *right* to me. Of course, I could do without the tensions, but they're *there*, and since they're *there*, it's good that we can talk about them, or *around* them. All our tensions are rising to the surface. Like bubbles or balloons."

"Never mind our schoolgirl," Raitlin said. "She has a crush on a guy in uniform."

I was about to snap at him when a line from a long ago poem came to my rescue. "Think what you like," I said. "You're entitled." I saw myself as an ocean liner that had somewhere to get to and sailed calmly on.

"My name is Barb!" came over to the table. She asked if there were anything more we wanted and I said there wasn't. "Well," said Barb hesitantly. "Are you folks here celebrating any special occasion?"

"An amicable divorce," Carolina said. Barb's smile collapsed like a soufflé. She looked at me as if for help.

"Don't listen to her," I said. "What we're *really* celebrating is the *marriage* that comes after the amicable divorce."

I thought it possible that Barb might literally throw in the towel—drop her little dishrag on our table and quit. Years later, she would tell her grandchildren about the strange people she met as a waitress.

I had trouble getting to sleep that night. I would start to fall and then jerk awake, the way you do in nightmares when you're falling, and about to hit bottom. Eventually I got up and opened the closet door. There were my clothes, hanging on their color-coded plastic hangers—white for dresses, blue for slacks, green for shirts and blouses—and all my shoes were in a shoe bag, hanging on the wall. There was no jumble on the floor. No umbrella standing stiff in the corner like a dead, black bird.

I went back to bed and was finally able to slide into sleep, the way the ambulance had slid into traffic, light spinning, but no siren on.

Chapter 11

A Metallic Frog

I began my online research the next day. I started with "rapist," and then checked the "Where can I learn about acquaintance (date) rape?" This gave me a list of women's crisis centers, and then a "Where can I find an online sex offender registry?" I tried that, but Michigan wasn't one of the states. I skipped over writing and poetry by rape survivors, and the literature about the best ways to survive sexual abuse. There were some weird coincidences. The name of the search engine, for example, was "homeboys interactive," which reminded me of Tat, who had called himself a "Georgia home boy." That led me to wonder if the "G" stood for Georgia, and I was right in the middle of wondering this, when I saw a spate of articles about the G-spot. But articles on the G-spot quickly trailed off into "How Females Ejaculate" discussions.

I decided to refine my search to "drug assisted" date rapes, and learned that they were on the rise, and hard to prosecute, since victims often don't recall the details of their "non-consensual sex."

I didn't know exactly what I was looking for, until I read this passage in "The Vaults of Erowon": "If you know what you're doing, experts say, you know that anyone can accidentally overdose on GHB. Avoid mixing with alcohol." The same article listed the nicknames for GHB: Scoop, Grievous Bodily Harm, Liquid Ecstasy, Liquid X, or (because of its taste) Salty Water. I had complained about the salty champagne. And Tat had said it was because of the cheese goldfish. "GHB's most popular nicknames, however, are 'Goop' or simply 'G'.

I'm not sure what I felt by the time I turned off Raitlin's computer. I looked around inside of me expecting to feel that old sense of "competence"—I had tracked down some useful information, hadn't I? I now knew, or could reasonably assume—that I had been drugged with GHB. Tat had almost certainly put it in my champagne, whence the salty taste.

But a feeling of competence was nowhere to be seen. I was shocked, I was furious, I was agitated. Partly, I couldn't wait to tell Officer Ferrier what I had learned. Partly, I didn't even want to go to meet him anymore. Maybe he was just posing as a police officer. Maybe he was even in league with Tat: it was awfully convenient that he just happened to show up right after I left the hotel. No. That was being paranoid. Still, he was a man. Not just an ordinary man, either: he was a man who carried a gun, and was presumably not averse to using it.

But that was exactly the kind of man I needed, wasn't it? He would help me track down that bastard. He must have been laughing up his ass the whole time, warning me about the thorns on the roses—probably stolen roses, given the way they'd been thrust together. And the bartender and the elevator guy, if there was one, maybe they'd been in on it, too. No, that was far-fetched. What about that pizza guy?

What had he said? He had been on his way up with a delivery and somebody said a woman needed a doctor.

There had been Tat and Joe asleep in the kitchen and a bartender and a boy in a white coat who wanted to be a doctor and an unknown man who had told the boy in a white coat that a woman needed a doctor.

And Officer Ferrier.

How many men did that make? Too many.

I had to trust someone, if I was going to follow through on this. Maybe I shouldn't. But he had *known*, that bastard. It wasn't some accidental thing.

And he had left me lying there unconscious. The tales on the net were full of people who choked on their own vomit and died.

I had to track him down, and I couldn't do it alone. The police at large wouldn't help.

All traces of GHB had been out of my system within twelve hours.

If I were going to track this guy down, I needed help.

I could walk away from it all, of course. I could walk away from Tat and the other man and the Carrigan and my whole past; I could even walk away from my future, in the form of Officer Ferrier.

The baby began to kick in no uncertain terms. I patted my stomach, what Raitlin called my swelling belly. "Okay, okay, little girl" I told her—I was sure the baby was a *her*— "You're the one thing I can't walk away from."

I decided to go ahead and meet with Adam at Riverbrook. He seemed knowledgeable. He seemed confident. He seemed *safe*.

I would meet with him, but I would interview him. I would interrogate him. I knew how to ask good questions. I wouldn't confide in him at all, not unless he confided in *me*.

I had to trust someone.

I wanted to track this monstrosity down, and I felt incompetent to do so. Confident, but incompetent. A contradiction in terms.

The next day Carolina apologized for not being a very good listener. I was sitting at the kitchen table, tracing its deeper scars with one finger, thinking idly of carving my initials in a tree. "Do you want to talk about what happened?" she asked.

"No," I said. "That's okay. I'll talk to my doctor when I see her next week."

If not by the words themselves, it was obvious by my tone that this was a slap in the face. Carolina's cheeks reddened as if the blow had been physical. "I guess I'm Semmelweiss," she said.

If it had been Raitlin, I wouldn't have asked, but I felt sorry for Carolina. It must be hard to have fallen into a household where she didn't really belong. I asked who Semmelweiss was.

Carolina laughed. "One of my schizophrenic leaps," she said. "I just meant that when I see a pregnant woman not eating right, I want to stick a diet under her nose."

"I'm doing pretty good in that department, aren't I?" .

"Oh, absolutely," Carolina said. "But—Well, do you mind if I ask you a couple of questions?"

"No," I said. "Not if they're about diet. Just don't start spouting 'protein' at me, and trying to talk me out of being vegetarian."

Carolina laughed. "I wouldn't dream of it," she said. "Well, I would *dream* of it. It's exactly the sort of thing I would and do dream of. But I wouldn't actually *do* it. All I would say, as one vegetarian woman to another is, 'Expect cravings.'"

"You mean 'pica'", I said—"Sudden cravings to eat wood or baking soda?"

Carolina laughed again. I was beginning to feel unpleasantly like a stand-up comic. "No," she said. "I mean meat cravings. Every pregnant woman I've ever worked with who was vegetarian had some degree of meat cravings."

I wanted to make a joke about the baby's being from Texas, given her cravings for steak, but I didn't quite have the heart or nerve for it. I thought of again trying to confide in Carolina about the rape, but didn't have the heart or nerve for that, either. She was so focused on doing what was right for the body, for the baby. She was all about nature and nutrition. I doubted that revenge was really in her line, and, no doubt about it, revenge was what I was after.

"Here," said Carolina, shoving the cutting board at me. On it lay a knife and five tomatoes. "Make yourself useful, will you?"

"I'm not a good cutter," I said. "I'll make a mess of it."

Carolina just gave me a dismissive wave, so I started. But these were not the tomatoes I was used to, pale and dry and antiseptic-looking, untouched by the sun. These were dark red misshapen globes, with bruises and discolorations. "These tomatoes look human," I told Carolina. "They're organic, that's why."

But, now, with the word "organic," they looked like the bloody uncooked innards with which my father had made gravy for Thanksgiving.

I touched one tentatively with the point of the knife, and it sprang a leak—first spouting and then oozing little seeds in a kind of gelatinous blood. I cut a slice from the side and it fell over, exposing the moist wet red insides.

"They're really fleshy," Carolina said from behind me, as if this were a good thing.

"I'm sorry, Carolina," I said. "I can't."

"Too squeamish?"

"Absolutely."

"Okay," she said. "You go sit down and vegetate. I'll find a way to put you to work later."

Dinner that night was close to being peaceful and normal. Raitlin hardly said anything, and what he did say was of the "Pass the salad, please" variety. David was full of stories of the product design lab. He had invented a vacuum vise, and was happy with the concept, and the design. Did we want to see it? We all said we did, and he brought it out. He asked me to be his "beautiful assistant" in demonstrating how well the vise worked. I stood and everybody clapped. It was ridiculous, but I felt like some refulgent Aphrodite rising out of the sea, glorious and pregnant.

He showed me how to raise the lever-arm at the vise's side and instructed me to pretend I was working a miniature pump. I was surprised when he told me to stop. "My lovely assistant has pumped all the air from under the vise, thus creating a vacuum," David told us. "You might say a vacuum is an absence, a nothing. But how wrong you would be. Not even God himself could move this vise as long as its foundational vacuum exists."

He turned to Raitlin, who was sitting forward, head on his hands, elbows on the table, still clutching his white dinner napkin, eyes closed as if he were praying. "Raitlin?" he said.

Raitlin opened his eyes and smiled. "What is it, my love?" He spoke gently, as if to a child. I felt a flash of envy. No one in my life had ever addressed me in that tone of voice, had they? I had never addressed anyone in that tone, either. I would, though. I *would*. My baby would grow up hearing that tone of voice every day of her long and happy life.

"What was the name of that Greek who said, 'Give me a fixed point and I can move the universe'?"

"Archimedes, I think," Raitlin said slowly. "But I'm not sure. I have no certain knowledge of anything at this moment. I'm not exactly stupified, but I'm quite *astonished* to be this happy. Let's all of us skoal, shall we, to this moment of grace, to this world that once contained Archimedes and now holds us and our heroic little vises—no pun intended— a world soon to be graced by a new and beautiful life."

"Here, here," said David, clinking glasses with Raitlin.

"Here, here," said Carolina, clinking glasses with me.

"God bless us all," I said, "each and every one."

Then for some reason we all stood and clinked our long-stemmed glasses together. I downed my sparkling grape juice while the others polished off their wine and the baby did a somersault. "Come on gang," Raitlin said. "There's something I've always wanted to try." He led us over to the dining room fireplace. "This has never been used," he said. "It's never even had wood in it.... When I say 'Now' I want everyone to throw his or her glass—if you will pardon the intrusion of correct grammar"— he smiled– "into the fireplace.... Ready? One. Two. Three. Three and a half. Now."

We tossed our glasses into the empty fireplace, and they shattered with one chaotic accord.

"Well," said Raitlin after a moment. "So much for that. I suppose one has to actually be Russian and tragic to really feel the merit of a gesture like that."

I got the broom and the dustpan and swept the fragments up. It was only the bowls of the glasses that had shattered: the stems and bases were intact. I was grateful to have a useful task.

At the moment I tossed my glass into the fire, I'd seen another fireplace. It was empty, like Raitlin's fireplace, but there were books burning on the floor in *front* of it. A girl was kneeling by the burning books. She looked like me. She was mostly not there. Water was pouring in; a ship was headed right for the doorway.

The image didn't make sense, and I knew why. It didn't make sense because it was *true*.

The truth went deeper than sense.

My second appointment with Dr. O. was on May 14.

Both Carolina and David had offered to drive me to the doctor's. Raitlin had a "conflictual engagement," but offered me the use of his "chariot" for the occasion.

I was afraid that if Carolina went to the doctor's with me, she would somehow end up more involved with the pregnancy than I wanted her to be. I was tempted by David's offer. David tried his best to be supportive but he was clearly too focused on his vise and his relationship with Raitlin to devote much time or energy to me and my baby.

He and I had taken a walk the day before. Sappho had apparently escaped. David was "of two minds" about it. He said he thought Sappho might actually do pretty well on her own, at least during the warm months, and that she'd probably have the good sense to come back home if it got too cold for her.

I said I thought Sappho was Raitlin's rabbit.

David said he had gotten to be the rabbit's foster parent.

I said I thought that it was interesting one could have parental feelings toward a rabbit, and someone else's rabbit, at that.

David said Raitlin had encouraged him to have parental feelings by involving him from the beginning in the rabbit's care, and decisions regarding her.

He said Raitlin, for all his cynicism, was a lot more open and inclusive in his plans and preparations than I was.

I said if David was talking about the baby, I hadn't been aware he wanted to be included. I said maybe it was easier for some people to feel parental about a rabbit than it was for them to be involved with a real baby.

He said he had tried many times to involve himself. He said I seemed more willing to use his help, moment to moment, than I was for him to become involved on any sustained basis.

I told him he had seemed so happy with Raitlin, I hadn't wanted to upset the dyadic apple cart.

He said it was I, on the contrary, who had been "happily withdrawn," and "amply abetted" by Carolina.

I said that wasn't fair, that I had been as open as I could be.

"You haven't," David said. He was flushed in that way people are, when they speak unkind truths. "You haven't told me the first thing about the baby."

I said I had. I pointed out all the books we'd read together, the times we'd spent joking about plans and procedures.

"How do you feel about the baby, Susan? Are you sorry it was too late for an abortion, or is the baby some kind of weird blessing in your life?"

"I don't know," I said finally. "And I don't mean that as a cop out, either. I honestly don't know. Sometimes I'm able to think about her—the baby, I mean—like some kind of immaculate conception. That's obscene, isn't it?"

"No. It's too understandable to be obscene."

"Well, I do. I don't remember the rape except as a kind of painful—I don't really remember the rape. I guess the closest I can get to it is imagining I went to a sperm bank and had myself inseminated. I never thought of getting an abortion.

When I first found out, I fantasized about finding the bastard and then I just kind of let that drop."

"What were you going to do when you found him?"

"I don't know. Find a way to get revenge or justice or something. But I start out on revenge, my mind always slides off into thinking about the baby, and then I go soft in the head. I start out thinking about shooting somebody in a dark alley, and I end up wondering what kind of stroller to buy."

"Well, I've got the answer to that one. Don't buy any kind of stroller. I've already put in an order on one."

I said I wanted him to be involved, but it didn't seem fair, and he did seem too wrapped up in work and Raitlin to have much left over for us, me and the baby.

David said he hadn't been feeling that great and, besides, he was afraid of muscling in on my act. He said he was aware, for example, of the possibility I might want to go to the doctor's alone this time. "I would be really glad to take you again," he said. "But if you decide this is something you need to do on your own, you don't have to worry about hurting my feelings. I promise you that I'll respect your need for independence, that I'll understand, and do my best to support you in your decision."

"Okay," I said, half-kidding, and half-not. "Then I think I'll take Raitlin up on *his* offer of a chariot and go by myself."

"Well, fuck duddle you," David said.

We both laughed, and I felt oddly close to him again, closer than I had felt any time since our one night whatever. I guess I expected him to press the point, to say something like, "Seriously, would you like me to drive you?"

But then he said he had to get back to the design lab, and started to walk away, leaving me alone with, and semi-regretful of, my decision.

"Wait," I said, meaning to call him back and ask if I could change my mind. But when he turned, I suddenly felt embarrassed by whatever had sparked the impulse—dependency, maybe, or childishness— and asked, instead, whether he thought if he were a stranger, he could tell I was pregnant.

"Definitely," he said.

He walked away, laughing and coughing at the same time.

Just as Carolina had predicted, my waistline had disappeared. The next afternoon I was walking down the produce aisle of the supermarket, and a young man with a full grocery cart had made a point of stepping aside to let me pass. "Congratulations," he said.

A gray-haired lady with a cane waved me ahead of her in the checkout line.

As I drove to Doctor O's, I steeled myself for a full revelation of the baby's conception, but I changed my mind in the office. Dr. O. was clearly rushed; she was also clearly pleased with what she called my "admirable preg stats." When I told her the gist of what had happened, that I had been drugged and raped on New Year's Eve by a virtual stranger, she just nodded. I asked if there was something I should do differently, given the circumstances of my baby's conception.

Dr. O. was nonplussed. "We've done a complete battery of tests already. That's part of our regular practice. You're healthy, as far as we know, and so is your baby. I'd be glad to monitor you more frequently, given the circumstances, but other than that, and saying I'm really sorry you had such an awful ordeal, I don't know what else to say."

I asked about genetic testing.

"You mean DNA testing, to determine paternity?" she said. "Well, that's very expensive, for one thing. About $2,000 at the going rate. And having the baby's DNA tested won't tell you anything unless you have paternal DNA to match it against." She shrugged.

"So there's nothing really—No special, I don't know, test, or advice you have for me?"

I was glad no one was with me to hear the way I was groveling. Why? What did I want?

"Look, Susan." Dr. O. leaned forward and patted my hand. "My heart goes out to you. If you decide you want to do DNA testing, I think the police would be your best bet. The whole situation is really kind of out of my league."

I was looking forward to meeting Adam so much, I almost expected something to go wrong.

It rained in the morning, but they moved on long before it was time to leave for Riverbrook.

It took me forever to get ready to go out. Raitlin and David and Carolina asked me at about four o'clock if I wanted to play Scrabble. I said I was just starting to get ready. "Right," Raitlin said. "Because you want to look nice and you've only got two hours."

"Hush, Rait," Carolina said, making Raitlin into a nickname that almost sounded normal. I wanted to hug her, so I did. David laughed.

I took a long, lukewarm soak, hoping the length of the bath would somehow make up for its tepidness, that over time, I would soak up as much warmth from this bath as from a short bath in satisfyingly hot water. But I just ended up feeling wiped out and bedraggled instead of really clean.

At first, I put on lingerie, (defined by me as silk underwear) but that made me feel sleazy, so I switched back to cotton. The cotton panties were big enough—they were from my sit-in-front-of-the-television-and-eat days—but my bra was too small. I didn't think I had time to go out and buy another one—though I was kind of looking forward to the maternity department—so I made do by attaching a little piece of string on the front clasp to expand the closure. That did the trick. True, the bra now gently pushed my breasts apart so they pointed in slightly different directions, but I didn't care. Cock-eyed was okay. Cock-eyed was exactly how I felt.

I brushed my teeth and tried to floss, but the string kept getting caught in my teeth, so I made a mental note to buy waxed next time and contented myself with an electric tooth-brush brushing. I used a blow dryer on my hair, gave myself a different part, and used the house scissors I found in the kitchen to snip away at my bangs and trim a little off the sides.

The effect was not bad. I put on lipstick and powder—both slightly darker than I usually wore— and gave myself an underarm spritzing with some Chanel #5 deodorant cologne.

I looked at myself in the mirror and noticed that my mouth was in a funny kind of "o," like the choir boy candles my mother had loved to light on Christmas Eve.

It was only when I saw the little "o" moue of my mouth that I realized I'd been whistling "Deck the Halls." And it was only when I realized I had been whistling "Deck the Halls" that I realized I was happy. Well, maybe not happy *yet*, but definitely on my way there.

The baby was being very cooperative. No somersaults, no handstands. She was resting, for once, cradled in the bottom of my belly.

I went back and forth about taking the car, but in the end, decided against it. If I walked, I thought, I could slip out the side door, and avoid all notice. Not so. Raitlin and David and Carolina came crowding into the corridor and saw me off, with much complimentary fanfare and teasing about "my fella." Their send-off was to be expected, but it surprised and delighted me.

"How long has it been?" Raitlin asked, as he opened the door to let me "loose on the world."

"Since what?" I asked innocently.

"Since you had a date," David said.

"This is not a date," I said. "It's a business meeting."

Chapter 12

Birds Without Crumbs

I walked down the driveway, turned left, and made my way down Newhall. It was a warm summer evening, balmy and nun-like. The street was what novels always called "bathed" in a light that seemed nostalgic and tender.

I was glad I'd chosen to walk. It gave me time to enjoy the feeling of a moment coming slowly into focus. One way or another, I thought, this was bound to be an important evening.

Despite everything, including the feeling I really shouldn't be, I had given way to full-fledged happiness. I felt beautiful and productive. A real Madonna.

A small knot of children was playing one of their mysterious games on one of the front lawns I passed. They laughed and scattered as I walked by. One little girl of about nine looked at me and let out a kind of whoop.

"I love you," she called.

I expected the children around her to make noises and catcalls, but none of them seemed to find her statement in the least remarkable.

"Why?" I called back, as if we were having a perfectly normal conversation.

"Because you're nice."

"I love you, too."

Inside me, the baby was awake after her long nap: every child I saw provoked a round of calisthenics. "You'll be out playing with them soon enough," I said aloud.

When I walked in the foyer, I was surprised to see the guy from last month, the guy who'd been wearing a greasy apron and telling everyone the show was over. He was apronless this time— down on his hands and knees, scrubbing the floor. Maybe he was being punished for ordering customers around.

Adam was already seated in a corner booth when I came in, but I didn't see him because he was behind a revolving glass case full of pie. He slid out of the booth and stood as I walked toward him. His salt and pepper hair was meticulously combed; he was wearing dark blue pants and a gray sport coat. He looked nicer than I remembered— not handsome, but spruced up somehow— more presentable. The baby gave me a little punch as if to say, "See how respectful and endearingly old-fashioned he is?

"I didn't see you at first," I said. "You were behind the Leaning Tower of Pastry."

Adam actually blushed. "Sorry," he said. "It's just habit by now. I always try to position myself so I see someone before they see me. Even if it's not—you know—like that."

I might have asked him what he meant by that, although I was pretty sure I knew, but the waitress came up. She, too, had a "Hi! My name is Barb" name badge on. I said, "Wow, that's kind of weird. When I was in here about a month ago, our waitress was Barb, but she looked a lot different."

The waitress flushed. "It's her name tag," she said. I'm Cynthia. I'm new, and they don't have my ready yet, so—Well, they didn't think anyone would notice."

"Observant," Adam said. I felt pleased with myself. The baby made a jerky little movement. Then there was a pause. Then another little "jerk."

"What's going on in there?" Adam asked, with a kind of rueful grin.

"Observant yourself," I said. "I think the baby's hiccupping or something."

"You're having a baby. Wow." Adam paused and looked intently at his menu. "It doesn't seem fair," he said after a moment. "Life's greatest experience, and it's reserved only for women."

"You had to have known," I said. "That I was pregnant, I mean."

"Yeah, but some pregnant women don't like you to talk about it, you know? It's sort of like a facial scar or something in that way." Adam turned a not bright but certainly *significant* shade of red. "That was stupid," he said. "I just meant, sometimes people don't want to talk about the obvious right up front."

We ordered dinner. Adam ordered steak, after asking my permission— "I've heard some pregnant women are sensitive to the smell of meat"—and I got a salad.

I had thought I might feel odd or awkward sitting across from him, but it wasn't. I found myself wondering whether people looking at us thought we were a father and daughter, a husband and wife—or just two people out on a date.

I asked Adam where he'd gone to school, and he grinned. "Interview time, eh?" he said.

I bridled a little at this. "I just think I should try to—"

Adam looked so distressed I broke off. "I think it's good, what you're doing," he said. "I mean, what you *want* to do. You sort of *have* to interview me– because otherwise you won't know– if I'm the right person to help you. If you want to use a– legal pad or a tape recorder or something, that's– fine, too. I'm used to that." He had a funny, even endearing way of talking. He grouped words together and then paused between them. I had an image of, who was it, *Topsy?* crossing a river in winter by jumping from chunk to chunk of ice.

"I don't need anything like that," I said. "Can you just tell me about the FBI symposium you went to?"

"A good memory," Adam said. "It was a Mass Disasters Symposium for law enforcement officers. They talked about plane crashes and fires and all kinds of stuff like that." Adam looked down at his plate as though he were suddenly not hungry. "Symposia are hard on the system, you know? I mean, the stuff they tell you. One of the cases we studied was that walkway collapse down at the Atlanta Hyatt. Do you remember about that? It was last New Year's. There was a party there and people crowded the walkway and it collapsed."

"That's awful," I said.

"What made it worse is that all the law enforcement people showed up really quickly to help."

"What's worse about that?"

"Wait. They listened to their instinct, see, and their instinct was to help the victims, so they rushed to the scene. They should have hung back and kept lanes of traffic open, so the medical people could get in. When law enforcement people let their instinct to help take over, that's no good for anyone."

I wondered if he were trying to tell me something personally. "Is that your specialty?" I said. "Mass disasters?"

Adam laughed. "No. Mass disasters don't have a unit. I am—or, until recently, *was*— Chief Command Officer of the Identification Unit."

I wasn't sure what an "identification unit" was and said so.

Adam seemed delighted by my comment. "The Identification Division responds to every major crime," he said. "We check for fingerprints, that kind of thing."

"I wonder what law enforcement did in the days before fingerprints." I hadn't meant the comment to sound adversarial but somehow, it did.

Adam didn't seem to notice. "Actually, fingerprints were known about and used in ancient China," he said.

"But ditto identification must be crucial in a lot of cases."

Adam shook his head. "Not so as you'd notice. Most people don't leave fingerprints at the scene of a crime."

"They remember to wipe them off?"

"No, they just don't leave any. What you really need are fingerprints on the crime weapon, and most firearms are oily. The oils of the firearm counteract the oily fingerprint residue, and you don't get anything useful. You're more apt to get usable info from foot prints or tire track molds, that kind of thing. And handwriting analysis. I started out in fingerprints, but I was promoted to handwriting after a year."

"Which do you like better?"

"Handwriting, I guess. There's a big gray area in handwriting." He paused and shrugged. "But being a cop on the beat is better than either one. It's the most down to earth, know what I mean?"

I felt like a schoolgirl, but I couldn't help asking. "Can you analyze my handwriting?"

Adam frowned, but produced a small piece of folded unlined paper from his pocket and pushed it across the table, along with a finely-tipped ball point pen.

"What do you want me to write?" I asked.

"I can't tell you what to write. Just write whatever comes into your head. About a page. And then sign it three times. Once with your regular signature, once with your signature done lightly, and once with your signature done darkly or heavily."

I wrote a page and signed it three times, as Adam had asked me to do, but no sooner had I handed the page over to him than I felt embarrassed.

"I'm sorry," I said. "I've turned this into a parlor game, haven't I? I didn't mean to."

"Do you want to keep going or take this back and think about it for a while?" he said.

"Well, I believe in the proverb that where there are two alternatives, I should take the third," I said. "But I can't figure out what that is, at the moment. I am curious. It's just— Well, never mind."

Adam smiled broadly. "There are other, better ways, of learning about a person," he said.

He looked at me as though considering whether to tell me something. "Fingerprinting is pretty dangerous work."

"You mean because people shoot at you to shut you up?"

Adam laughed. "Not exactly. I meant because all the paper dust can cause emphysema. Unless you wear a mask...."

Adam pushed his plate over toward the condiments. His steak was virtually untouched, as was his potato, though he had eaten most of his corn, a side salad, and a roll. "I'll take it home," Adam said, as though I had asked him a question. "It won't go to waste, believe me."

"Now...." He looked up. "Are you ready?"

I said I was.

"Pretty trusting," he replied, clearly teasing me. "You're supposed to say, 'Ready for what?' before you say 'Yes.'"

"Adam?" I said. My voice quivered oddly in my ears. Why was I so nervous? "Forget the handwriting analysis, okay? I'm curious, of course, but I don't want to waste the time now. I trust you, I think, and I can't say that about many men. I can't say that about many *people*, period. Fate seems to have thrust you upon me, twice, at points when I needed assistance, so—I want to tell you what happened and see what your reaction is and whether you're willing to help me or not."

Adam nodded, as though he'd been expecting this from the beginning. He folded the piece of paper again, and put it back in his pocket, then patted his pocket with his right hand, the way the father of an infant might pat its back to help it burp. I thought it was tremendously endearing.

Silence fell like snow. For a moment, I had a glimpse of Adam and me (and baby makes three) in one of those heavy glass snow globes that you shake to make the snow swirls. I realized we were both waiting for the other one to speak. "I may never want you to analyze it," I said.

"Fine by me."

"You still want to keep it, though—the paper?"

Adam flushed. "I like what you wrote," he said.

I stifled the impulse to ask for the paper back again. I hadn't written anything compromising, had I? Just stuff about being pregnant. Asking for it back again would be suspicious. Suspicious and stalling.

"How should we do this?" I asked.

"Well, A), I'm here to help," Adam said. "I'm not here to make judgments in any way whatsoever, and B), there's what I call 'the CRs of I—the 'Cardinal Rules' of Investigation." He grinned, daring me to ask.

"Okay, fine," I said. "I'll bite. What *are* 'the CRs of I'–"

Adam's grin widened. "I thought you'd never ask. The CRs of I are, 'Look before you leap' and 'Listen before you act'. If a person feels free to tell me something, I make it a point to listen. Unless it's an emergency. Every investigation is like a chicken crossing the road. You've got to look both ways, and you've got to listen."

"You're making me nervous by trying so hard to make me feel *less* nervous," I said. "But go ahead, by all means. Why *did* the chicken cross the road?"

"What makes you think she did?" Adam paused. "You're not even smiling," he said.

"I'm too busy identifying with the chicken," I told him. It was ridiculous, but true. Seeing that *I* was the chicken who might not cross the road—ask Adam for help, tell him what had happened—made me determined to go ahead. And now that I had decided to go ahead, I didn't know *how*. "Don't you have some techniques of interrogation or something?" I asked. "I seem to be finding it difficult to begin."

"I'm not a big fan of the word—techniques," Adam said. "It sounds cold. Freezing, actually. What we're doing here is developing a bond, a friendship, not necessarily to bring up any past situation too fast or too soon. As far as technique— Well, 24 hours a day, 7 days a week, you need my help, you need to cry on my shoulder— Anything— I'm here to help. Any way I can. You can rely on me."

I knew if I didn't say something quickly, I would embarrass us both. "You could ask me questions," I suggested, knowing somehow he would reject that idea.

"I don't like to ask very many questions," he said. "Questions don't leave the lanes of traffic open, if you know what I mean. I know you'll tell me what you need to tell me on your own timetable. But you're welcome to ask me anything— I'm more than open to that."

"Are you married?" I said.

He flushed. "I was. I have three sons. We've all been in the military. It's a bond between us. There's nothing I wouldn't do for those guys."

I knew I was stalling, but I couldn't help it. I *needed* to stall. For just a fraction of a fraction of a moment, when Adam had said 'I love you' I heard it as though he'd said it to me. "What was your wife like?" I asked. And punished myself with a *You idiot*.

Adam flushed again. This time, he looked shame-faced. "She was abusive," he said.

"You mean name-calling abusive, or something else?"

"I mean alcoholic, taking slugs at me, burning me with her cigarettes abusive."

"To the boys, too?"

Adam looked shocked. "No. Never to the boys. She knew I would have killed her."

The starkness of that statement, coming from him, gave me pause. But there was something about the admission that he, too, had been a victim of abuse that made me feel freer to talk to him. I felt bad at having pushed him into such personal territory and said so. He looked at me for the first time as though he thought I was odd. "You had to do that," he said. "If I can't talk about personal stuff, I can't listen to it, either. You know what I mean?"

For an answer, I began to tell him everything I remembered of New Year's Eve. He asked my permission to jot down the events as I said them, and I must have raised my eyebrows at this, because he said— "Requests are not questions. Requests are respect. Questions can be invasions."

When Adam was done jotting, he reached across the table for my hand. "May I?"

I nodded. He took my hand and squeezed it briefly, then carefully replaced it on the table and withdrew. I began to cry, but when I saw his look, I felt guilty. "Don't worry about me," I said. "I don't know why I'm crying. Not because of *that*. It's stupid or pathological or both."

Adam shook his head. He looked *stricter* than I'd thought possible. "I don't think there are stupid reasons for crying," he said. "I remember showing my ex this slogan I thought was really cool: 'Each moment we live teaches us why.' I wrote it out on this little sign I had on my desk at work. When she left, she wrote this before it with a marker— 'We cry from the moment we're born.' Since then, when I look at it, it says, 'We cry from the moment we're born: Each moment we live teaches us why.'"

"That's terrible," I said.

"Maybe," Adam said. "But if it's terrible, isn't it terrible because it's so true? Anyway, I've been known to cry for no particular reason at all. Just out of a kind of weltschmerz."

He must have seen my look. "World pain," he said.

"Does what I've said tell you anything, Adam? I mean do you notice anything particular? Or is that a stupid question?"

"Don't," Adam said. "That's part of the recovery, you know. Not calling yourself stupid any more.

"As for what I noticed—Well, 'Georgia Home Boy', for one. That's another nickname for GHB."

I hadn't seen it. I started to criticize myself for that, but pulled back, remembering what Adam had said about not calling myself stupid anymore.

"Well," I said, "I thought of going to the police. I mean, this guy may be a real rapist—I mean, he is a real rapist, obviously, but—"

I couldn't finish the sentence for some reason. After a moment, Adam nodded. "He might have done to other women what he did to you." It was not a question.

"Yes. So I think I owe it to *them*—as well as to *myself*—to try to track this guy down. I have no proof, of course. It would just be my word against his. But I need some kind of closure on this." Adam just nodded. I wanted to ask what his nod *meant*. "Do you think he was telling the truth about being a translator, or was that all just made up?"

"In my experience, lying is kind of addictive," Adam said. "Bad guys don't just lie about the important stuff. They lie about everything. I guess part of the appeal of being a criminal is you force yourself to be awake all the time, in a way that most of us just aren't."

"'Appeal'?"

"Well, 'seduction'," then." Adam shrugged. "Words by themselves—terms—don't interest me very much. I'm not what you'd call a wordsmith."

"Anybody who uses words like 'weltschmerz' is a wordsmith in my book," I said.

"You haven't been to the sensitive crime people, I take it?" he asked, as though the question followed logically.

He sounded almost smug. I thought of offering him my knuckles to rap. "I don't even know who 'the sensitive crime people' are," I said.

Adam's face and voice had been wiped clean of any expression that I could interpret. "Sorry, that's just lingo. You haven't been to the police, is what I was asking."

"Aren't you the police?"

Adam hesitated. "No," he said. "Not anymore. I quit."

"When?"

"About a month ago. Right after that Riverbrook fender-bender."

"Why?"

Adam smiled, and shook his head. "I can't really tell you."

"Security reasons?"

Adam shook his head vigorously, like a dog shaking off water. Then he laughed. "You seem to like making me out to be glamorous," he said. "I like that." He picked up his water glass, and Cynthia appeared out of nowhere to fill it. "I can't tell you because I don't really know. I just quit. Too many years on the force, I guess."

"So are you, you know–?"

"Penniless and wandering the streets?" He laughed. "That was one of my default options. No. I do contract investigation work. I don't know. It suits me. Plus, now I can help you in a more *untrammeled* kind of way."

It was Adam's idea to take his coffee outside. "Are you sure you don't want anything? Tea?" I said I was in the mood for a vanilla steamer. Adam went back inside. He reappeared almost instantly. Cynthia appeared a moment later and put a piece of apple pie in front of him, and a drink in front of me. "This is on the house," she said to him. "The pie and—" She actually managed to glance in my direction— "your steamer."

There was a cool breeze blowing through the vines twined in and around the wrought iron "walls" of the empty take out patio. In the daylight, anyone could tell that the vines were dusty, the walls needed fresh paint, and the candles on the tables were a disturbingly greenish shade of yellow. But at the moment, the illusion worked.

The "steamer" was delicious.

We sat in silence for a moment. The baby began to do cartwheels. I thought of pointing this out to Adam. I imagined his laying his hand on my belly. I imagined his laying his hand on my heart.

"What do you want?" Adam said.

Lyn Coffin

The question came so close to fitting in with what I was "seeing," it unnerved me a moment. Then I came back to what we were doing, what we were supposedly *about* here.

"I want to find him. I want to find him without his ever knowing he—" I was about to say 'knocked me up', but I pictured Adam, wincing— "got me pregnant."

"And then what?"

"I want to try to find out if he's done this before, or—since—" The awfulness of that thought threw me off-track a moment.

"Do you want a taste?" Adam said, indicating the pie. He had cut the point of the wedge off and pushed it across his plate at me—a little pie-triangle, complete with cheese.

"Thanks." I picked it up with my fingers and ate it gratefully. "I like cheese a lot better than whipped cream," I said. "Anyway—I want to find out who he is. I want you to help me track him down." My voice sounded a little more vehement than I would have liked, but Adam only nodded.

"Then what?" he asked again.

My mind blanked. An image flashed into my mind of Adam grabbing Tat by the collar—grabbing him and punching him and beating him up, of Tat falling to the ground and Adam kicking him, of Tat groaning and Adam kicking him again. I saw blood and teeth on the pavement and Adam, turning back to me, and laying his hand on my belly again, and this time it was bloody and the blood of my father soaked through my belly and filled the placenta and the baby began to choke.

Adam reached across the table. "Hey," he said. "It's okay. That was a stupid question. That was me rushing in, not allowing space for the traffic.... You don't need to know what you want to come next. One step at a time, okay?"

186

"But are you okay with this? Are you really going to help me?"

"I told you," Adam said. "I'm in. I'm not a very religious person, but I'm a believer, Susan. I believe I came into your life for a reason.... I only— Well, sometimes I curse myself that I didn't press you right then, right on New Year's day six months ago. I knew something was wrong. If you'd been someone else, I would have pressed you, but I— Well, it was one of the few times when I didn't believe what my training was telling me. I thought I was— I thought I was just making up trouble in order to give myself an excuse to—try to get closer to you.... I don't know. It doesn't make sense.... Never mind. This isn't about *me*. Not now. Sorry-" Adam's voice faded into silence.

"I think you say 'sorry' more than I do," I said. Adam smiled. He pushed up the shirt sleeves in a "going to work" gesture and began to eat his pie. He had tattoos on both arms.

"I want to know what we do, how we track him down."

"I think we need to start at the Carrigan, and go from there," Adam said. "It's like Hansel's trail of breadcrumbs, you know, except it was made by the witch. Most of the crumbs have probably been eaten by the birds, but there are always some you can find, if you look hard enough."

"Hasn't the trail grown cold by now?" I asked.

Adam smiled. "Yeah, but cold isn't so bad. Cold can actually make things better. It's 'wet' you have to worry about." He looked at me. "Do you want to come with me? It might be difficult."

"You mean I'd muddy up your investigation, somehow?"

Adam shook his head. "There you go again. I'm just going to call in a marker or two and ask some questions, that's all.... I meant it might be difficult for *you*—for you to go back there, for you to have them see you pregnant, and hear what they have to say...."

I considered the unpleasant truth of this a moment. "Well," I said. "I always went there at night. I don't think I know any of the day staff. If we went there in the morning or early afternoon, I doubt if anyone would connect me with—whatever."

"What about Joe?"

"Joe always works the graveyard shift."

"Okay, then," Adam said, almost happily. "I'll set it up."

"What did you mean by about 'calling in a marker'?"

Adam shrugged. "People owe me favors," he said. "It's called networking. The thing is I don't want to necessarily bring up situations too fast for you—too soon. But it would be good if we—moved quickly on this, given it's been a while."

"I'm ready," I told him. "More than ready."

He smiled and shot me one of his 'I wonder whether I should say this' looks. "If you like—and I say this in the most respectful, tentative way—you could be my wife. I mean, I could introduce you to people as my wife. That way, they wouldn't—you know—think anything about your– about the pregnancy."

"That sounds good to me," I said.

For some reason, we both laughed nervously, and shook hands on it.

Adam walked me home. We stood awkwardly on the cement front stoop. There was hardly room for two people, especially when one of them was pregnant. Adam leaned closer. I thought at first he was going to kiss me. "I'll call you as soon as I get us in," he said.

"'Get us in'?" I really needed to go to the bathroom, and I kept thinking one of the gang might be eavesdropping on our little tableau.

"Into the hotel," Adam said, pulling away. He started backing toward the steps. "I'll call you as soon as I know something," he said. "Take care of yourself and the baby, okay? I hope-"

Adam's voice stopped abruptly. Most of his body was already angled away from me; he had his left hand on the wrought-iron railing. But as he stared up into my face, an odd thing happened. His right hand came slowly forward—came forward inch by inch, as if drifting, as if *floating* toward me. At the furthest extent of his reach, the tips of his fingers touched my belly. There was a micro-second of touch. I felt heat. I felt warmth. I felt *connection*.

Adam's expression didn't change. I don't think he *had* an expression, in fact. He seemed to be in another world. I don't think he knew that he had touched me. Maybe, in a sense, he hadn't.

Somehow about the touch reminded me of something I had seen, high up. Something holy. Something sacred. And then I knew: it was the Sistine ceiling.

The hand reaching out. The fingertips just touching.

God, awakening Adam.

Chapter 13

Talons Without Birds

It felt wrong to go back. Not because it was dangerous in any realistic, they-might-be- watching-me way. But because it felt like I was tempting fates I didn't believe in.

It helped that the trip fell on July 4th. I told Adam that we had chosen an auspicious day for our outing. He said I was putting it mildly, that the Fourth of July was the only day he could be sure the manager would be out of town.

The desk clerk on duty seemed to be expecting us, but clearly didn't register me any more than I registered *him*. His whole attention was focused on Adam, who was looking especially spiffy wearing a sport coat and tie, and carrying a black pilot's case, like a briefcase but wider.

"How's it going, Deedge," Adam said.

The clerk flushed. He took off his glasses and wiped them on his sleeve before replacing that. "It's D.J. now," he said. "D.J. or Dwight."

Adam nodded. "Things going along okay here, D.J.? I know it was kind of a surprise, hearing from me."

D.J. looked at Adam's face as if trying to gauge his seriousness. He shrugged. "Yeah. It's okay, though. Like I said, I'm happy to help out." He looked over at me and squinted as if he thought I might be a figment of his imagination. "I've got a good memory," he said, as though that followed logically from his former statement. "I never forget anything."

Adam smiled, as though D.J. were making all the sense in the world. "I've always appreciated that about you, D.J.– I was wondering if the wife and I could have a look-over the books for a minute or two."

D.J. blanched visibly. "We're not exactly ready for anything like that, uh–"

"—Just Adam," Adam said.

D.J. nodded. "I'd like to help you out– Adam." He seemed to have trouble saying the name. "If you could give me a couple of days, I could see what I—"

Adam looked at him quizzically, then broke into a rueful grin. "No, I don't mean *those* books, Deedge," he said. "I just meant—you know—the register."

D.J. laughed and made a mock gesture of wiping his sweaty brow.

"Now, *that* I can do," he said.

He waved us behind the counter, and with a touch or two on his computer screen produced the guest register for that day.

"Great," Adam said. "Now, let's go back in time, okay? Back to the night of December 31ˢᵗ, 1999."

"No problem," the clerk said. Again, a touch or two, and there on the screen was a list of hotel patrons— "Guests"— with their addresses, their license plate numbers, a listing of credit card numbers, phone numbers, number of guests, and entry notations—"6 a.m. wakeup call;" "Early maid service," etc.

"Would you excuse us for a moment?" Adam asked, peering intently at the register. I thought for a moment he meant *me*, but D.J. grew red in the face. Mumbling something about making us a fresh pot of coffee, he backed away and disappeared through a curtained doorway.

Adam gestured toward the register. "Scan the names, okay? See if anything—you'll forgive the pun— registers, for Tat."

I scanned the list of names obediently, looking for anything that might be connected with the man we were looking for. I found a Thomas A. Tuttle, of Athens, Georgia—initials "TAT"— and a Tate Jefferson, of Long Beach, California— Maybe his name was really Tate?

I pointed these out to Adam, and he nodded. He took a tiny camera out of his case, snapped a picture of the register sheet, and put the camera back. "Just like in the movies," he said. "But I think we may have already found our guy." He wrote down the names and the information that went with them on the top sheet of a small note pad he pulled out of his shirt pocket.

"Tuttle is a 'Georgia Home Boy'", I pointed out. 'So that fits."

"But you said yourself he didn't sound like someone from the South. And the Georgia Home Boy was almost certainly one of his sick private jokes and stood for GHB.... No, the thing is not to get too complicated in investigations. He had the drug, he was planning the rape. For him to use his real name is possible, but unlikely. 'Never investigate the possible till the likely has been exhausted.'"

"Look at the sheet," Adam said. "Tell me which entry stands out. Don't think presence, think absence."

And then I saw it. There was one entry that had no last name, no first name, no address, no credit card information.

The word "M A N A G E R" was written across the line, two letters to each heading except the last.

"What does that mean?" I asked.

"Maybe pay dirt," Adam said.

D.J. came back with fresh coffee, and we stayed for a while, making conversation. Adam seemed content to sit and shoot the breeze with D.J. I was impatient to get out of there. The baby had begun a series of gymnastic exercises, and the smell of old smoke in the office, which seemed to come curling down at me out of the thick yellow wallpaper, made me feel queasy.

In a short space of time, Adam managed to throw quite a few questions at the bespectacled D.J., whose glasses glinted and flashed ominously in my general direction, so I couldn't read his eyes.

Unfortunately for our researches, D. J. didn't seem to remember much about what had been going on in the hotel over Christmas break, though he'd heard from room service there'd been some wild happenings. "Was Emma on then?" Adam asked.

D.J. looked askance at him. "Emma's not with us anymore," he said.

He paused. Adam nodded and shrugged. If I had been D.J., I would have asked him what a nod and a shrug were supposed to mean, but the gestures apparently reassured the desk clerk, and he continued.

"Mary did everything," he said. "You know Mary?"

"From way back," Adam said. "Back when we were green around the ears.... So Emma wasn't even working here over the holidays?" Adam asked.

D.J. shot a look in my general direction. "Don't I know you?" he said.

I froze. My whole body froze. My hand had been traveling from the counter to my belly, to check on the baby: it stopped midway. I could feel the smile on my face solidify like water turning ice. My mouth set in the open position, but not a sound came out.

Adam stepped a little closer to the counter. "I don't think that's very likely, do you?" he asked the clerk. A look passed between them. All of a sudden D.J. was looking not at me, but through me. I was invisible. He became suddenly voluble. "Mary and Marty did room service or tried to. Not my idea of a dynamic duo, if you know what I mean. Not that it mattered.... You know them?"

"I know Marty a little," Adam said.

D.J. didn't seem to have heard his answer, or care that he hadn't heard it. "This place was dead. The place was dead, the manager was gone. Mary and Marty were doing their thing. When the cat is gone, the rats eat ice cream, know what I mean? Say no more, D.J. Say no more." He seemed to have frightened himself with his own advice.

"Some kind of trouble?" Adam asked. No answer. "If you're curious about something, I could call in a marker or two with my buddies on the force, find out what happened."

"Nothing happened," D.J. said. He took out a Kleenex from under the counter, moistened it with spit, and began to wipe off his computer screen. "Like I say, the place was real kaput."

"Well, my very significant other and I—" Adam leaned in a little closer to D.J. "The two of us (he winked at D.J., ominously, it seemed to me) are thinking of having another couple or two join us for a live-it-up weekend before the baby comes. Do you have any suites we could test drive?"

D.J. frowned. "What do you mean, 'test drive'?" he asked.

"You got any suites we could take a look at?"

"I guess so," D.J. said. "But I need to stick it out here at the desk."

"That's okay. Just tell us where the suites are and let us borrow the keys. That would be great."

After a moment, D.J. capitulated, giving us a map with "x's" and several keys. I was tired of being a jungle gym for my unborn infant. My books said it was my twenty-seventh week of pregnancy.

All I wanted to do was lie down, or at least sit down. Adam winked at me.

We turned away from D.J., who seemed curiouser and curiouser, but Adam turned back. "So, you don't remember much about Christmas break?" he asked.

"Unfortunately, no," D.J. said.

Adam looked at the books again. He pointed at the single word, "Manager" defiantly straddling several columns.

"Not much," D.J. said, finally.

Adam nodded. "Yeah, I know. I get that problem myself, sometimes. Kind of like early Alzheimers or something."

D.J. looked at me nervously, and then looked back. "It's nothing like that. I just don't always feel interested in speaking out, in saying what I saw. You know what I mean?" Adam shook his head no.

"I remember the suites were vacant except one. I remember thinking the suite guy must be calling in a big favor. Otherwise, I couldn't understand the manager's giving him a lair. That's what we call the suites." He looked at me as though he were saying something in code and expected me to get it. I didn't. D.J. looked back to Adam.

Adam nodded. "I see what you mean. Do you remember anything about that guy?" His tone was infinitely respectful—flattering, almost. Somehow, the tilt of Adam's voice managed to imply that D.J. knew more about the human psyche than most. He was addressing D.J., I realized, as though he were an expert witness of some obscure sort.

D.J. considered this possibility not at all. "Nah," he said. "Just that he was a weasel if I ever saw one." The cliché, "It takes one to know one" popped unbidden into my mind.

"Okay, well, I appreciate your help, D.J. I've got a good memory myself, you know what I mean?" D.J. nodded and allowed as how it would be best if we could keep our inspections short.

I was fairly sure he had been warning us, so I was surprised when Adam invited me to stretch out on top of the bed in the first suite we came to. "Make yourself comfortable," he said.

"You were pretty tough on old D.J.," I murmured.

"Me? I was a pussy cat."

"You kept bugging him about stuff."

"Another of the CRs of I, Susan." A pause. I would not give him the satisfaction. The pause bulged like a tiny dam from the weight of too much water.

I couldn't stand it. "Okay. I'll bite."

Adam's voice was still mild, but his eyebrows had a suspiciously high arch to them. "Rule Number One: Never cut anyone off. Rule Number Two: Take your time. Rule Number Three: let evidence dictate theory."

"Those are different than the rules you told me before."

Adam smiled broadly. "Yes, they are."

"Never mind that. What point was there asking D.J. what he did between Christmas and New Year's? Did you really think he remembered? I mean, do you remember what *you* were doing?"

"Well now— That's a really interesting question, he said. "Yes, I do. But let's focus here, okay? I need your help checking out the suites," he said. "I could do it myself, but then you wouldn't get the chance to trigger your memory."

A half an hour later, we had seen every suite but one—a suite tucked in a back corner of the fifth floor, next to the fire escape. Nothing.... We went back to the main desk and returned all our keys. "Do you think we could look at this suite, too?" Adam said.

"That's the manager's own suite," D.J. said., suddenly reluctant.

"You could call him if you're worried about it," Adam said. "I saw it was empty, though, and he and I go way back. I'm sure it'll be all right."

D.J. fumbled in a drawer and produced a set of keys on an eagle key-ring. "There's no copy of these," he said, clearly nervous.

Adam smiled. "I'll bring them right back."

I stepped into the room, and something more basic than memory hit me like a battering ram. I could hardly breathe. There was a musty smell that made me sick. The bilious green of the rug was hard to take.

And then I saw the picture. The fire in the fireplace was not burning, but the books on the floor in front of it *were*. An ocean liner faced the viewer: it was apparently coming right for the house. A picture of the leaning tower of Pisa had been hung crookedly on the wall—the world had been knocked cockeyed so the tower could be straight. There was a mirror over the fireplace, a snapshot stuck in the mirror frame. The snapshot was of a man with green snakes for hair—no, it was leaves. A bust of the same man, with the same hair, stood in an alcove, looking blindly on. There were two girls. One was looking out the window at a kind of ice field. The other girl (they were twins) knelt by the burning books. She might have been praying. She might have been reading. In a moment, she would get the answer she was looking for and the book she was holding would burst into flames. The girls had well-defined heads and limbs, but their bodies had been reduced to suggestions. The bodies you *thought* they had were really the walls and floor of the room. There was a tree in the room: its roots stretched out along the floor.

I recognized the picture. I felt dizzy. Someone had turned on the ceiling sprinklers, and water was cascading down my cheeks. Then I realized that there were no sprinklers. I was sweating.

I sat down on the carpet, and staggered up again, a deep sea diver, frozen from too much water, burning from too much air. I sat down on the bed and it scorched me.

"I'm sorry," Adam said. "I needed to be sure." He pulled a chair out from the desk and offered it to me, but I was afraid I'd fall off a chair. I allowed myself to slide back down to a sitting position on the floor, but this time I sat on my hands. The rough shag carpet was grass green—like a meadow. The feet of the antique desk had been carved into balls gripped by talons, talons without birds. I recognized those talons. I heard a plane overhead.

This was where it happened.

It was as though nothing more could happen here ever again. No one could ever breathe here, certainly not me. Not even Susan, whoever *she* was.

Poor Susan.

Adam was waiting. He had an odd expression on his face. He wasn't smiling. He wasn't frowning. He wasn't friendly. He wasn't hostile. What was he? He was neutral—benevolently neutral.

I trusted that neutrality. It was smooth as rock. No foothold for any emotion. I struggled to speak.

"I remember the picture, the carpet, the animal feet on the bed, even that plane," I said. "It's all tangled. But it was here. *I* was here."

I saw a map. I saw a skull and crossbones.

"Could you try the other half of the suite?" he said.

I nodded. After this, I could try anything.

He unlocked a door and went ahead of me, into a room about half the size of the first one. I stepped into it, feeling like Alice entering the world behind the mirror, and looked around. There was no series of shocks here. Everything looked plain and generic. I felt nothing except a blessed absence of associations.

I had never been here.

"Can you wait in this room a minute?" Adam asked. "I need to run some tests. I'm sorry to push this along, but I'm afraid D.J. out there is going to get nervous and come looking for us."

I turned on the reading lamp and sat down in the desk chair. "You go ahead," I said. "I'll be fine."

The baby wasn't moving.

I got up and knocked on the inner door. I felt a little like the hysterical heroines of old movies, the ones who aren't good for anything but to do exactly what the hero says not to. That, and scream their heads off when the bad guy shows up.

"Adam? Can I come in?"

"Of course. It's not locked."

I went back in the room. Adam had opened his pilot's case on the bed. Stuff was spilled across the bedspread.

"What's all this?"

"I'm thought I'd go into investigative high gear for a moment."

"Is there anything I can do?" I asked.

"Not really. I need to do everything myself to keep the chain of evidence clear."

He got down on his hands and knees in the corner between the wall of windows and the door to the adjoining room. He stopped and looked up at me. "Is it hard just standing there like that?"

I said it was, a little.

He got up, stood in front of me, and considered. "Maybe you'd be more comfortable sitting on the windowsill behind you? May I...?"

"Of course," I said, not knowing what he was asking.

Adam put his hands under each of my arms and lifted me up and back. I felt light again. Not feather light, as I had once been—still big, but light now, light like a balloon.

In a moment, I was sitting on the window ledge.

"How's that?"

"Great," I said. "It's like a nest. A hard sort of nest, but still—"

It was true. There in the room where I had been attacked, where D.J. and the authorities might break down the door at any moment and arrest us for whatever it was Adam was about to do, sitting like a kid on a windowsill, my legs dangling down, I felt more comfortable than I had in a long time.

The baby stirred a sleepy kind of "what's happening" kind of stir.

I sighed.

"What's the matter?"

"Nothing. Baby woke up from a long nap. Proceed with whatever you're doing."

Adam crossed the room and got back down on his hands and knees in the corner farthest from me. There was a small click, and a strange kind of quivering blue light came on, like the light used in nightclubs trying to be cool.

"What are you looking for?"

"Seminal fluid or blood, basically."

Whatever comfort I'd been feeling drained away. For long moments, there was just me sitting on the ledge in the flickering blue light, watching as Adam crawled back and forth across the carpet with his magic box, clicking the switch.

Adam "swept" the rest of the room without stopping at anything.

While he finished with the carpet sampling, Adam took a picture of the bathroom, two pictures from the doorway looking into the other room, and eight pictures of the room we were in, four from different heights and angles, one of the bed, one of the desk and chair, two of the picture on the wall. Then he locked the door to the adjoining room again and asked me to examine the bathroom for a moment and see if I remembered anything.

"I know this is hard," he said. "You don't have to lie down or anything, but if you could kind of look around and try to remember anything you might have seen or grabbed onto or anything."

"I told you about the picture," I said. "I was looking at that some of the time, I think. I stared up at the ceiling. I don't suppose this matters but I remember that piece of yellow wallpaper peeling up in the corner up there."

"Good," Adam said. "That's just the kind of thing I mean." He stood on the desk chair, and took a picture of the peel I had mentioned. "Anything else?"

With a sudden wrench, I remembered my hand closing on something hard and round. I went and put my hand on the doorknob.

No, that was too smooth and too cold. The fable of Goldilocks came to my mind. The porridge had been too hot, then too cold, then just right. "I remember things in my hands," I said. "There were these little globes. I couldn't hang on and I couldn't let go. I was on the ground in a meadow and there was something—I don't know. My face was in the grass. I couldn't breathe."

"It's possible," Adam said, to no one in particular.

All of this seemed to be taking a very long time. I was relieved when Adam finally repacked everything in his case except for the Polaroid, a pad, and a pen. I was even more relieved when he ushered me out into the hall and told me to stand guard.

That one whispered instruction was enough for me to feel excited and involved again.

Adam must have seen my look, because he flushed. "Sorry," he said. "I was just kidding. I am almost done, though."

He stood in the doorway and took two more pictures of the room; then he took one of the door. He labeled and dated the three photos on the back and initialed them like the others before putting the zip-lock bag with the photos away in his case.

I didn't want to face D.J. at the check-in desk. I was afraid he would look at me, and I would blurt out something incriminating.

I didn't think I could face anyone for a while, except Adam.

Chapter 14

A Dolphin out of His Element

Adam and I stopped at Riverbrook on the way home. We ate grilled cheese sandwiches and pickles, and Adam had chocolate chip ice cream for dessert, joking that he was more pregnant than I was.

"What happens now?" I asked.

"Well, with your permission, I become a regular drop-in visitor at the hotel. I eat lunch there, hang out with the manager, maybe buy him a few drinks. I'll talk to room service, the kitchen staff, maybe the guy who parks cars. It's probably better if I do this stuff on my own, because, you know, like you saw today, most people don't want to talk to a couple."

"Anything else?" My voice sounded a lot more hard-edged than I had meant it to be; for a moment, I was afraid I'd offended him. But Adam laughed.

"Yeah. You and your case are going to be like a moonlight job for me for a while," he said. "I'm also going to run a couple of private credit checks through this organization I belong to, talk to a few bank officers and a few police officers, do some lab work, and call in a few markers on the law enforcement front, stuff like that."

"Anything I can do?"

"Absolutely." Adam grinned. "You can try to cultivate patience, which will stand you in good stead with the baby anyway, you can not give up on me, *and—*" He stopped abruptly and flushed as though he'd said a dirty word or made some unexpected faux pas.

But I was on to him. "—And what?" I insisted. "What else can I do?"

"Well—" When Adam was on uncertain ground, I had noticed, his voice slowed and slurred into a kind of blurry drawl. It did that now. I wanted to hug him.

"Well, you might want to consider—you know—childbirth classes. Like Lamaze?"

I considered him a moment. His face was really flushed. I hoped it wasn't sadistic of me to enjoy a moment where I was the cool one. "Actually," I said, "Those husband-coached classes are more what I've been thinking about. David was going to do them with me, but then he got kind of busy, and now he can't."

"I know," Adam said. "You told me."

Suddenly, I thought I knew what was going on. "Are you saying you want to be my partner?" I asked.

Adam began to laugh. Not his normal, deep, full-throated laugh, but a bubble-up-in-you-can't-stop-if-you-want-to kind of chuckle.

I tried unsuccessfully not to feel hurt. "I'm sorry," I said. "I thought you wanted to be my— you know, partner. I guess that was just wishful thinking or fantasy on my part. I certainly don't want to—you know—"

Adam's merriment stopped as abruptly as it had started. "No, no," he said. "Of course, I want to be your partner. I couldn't think of anything more— It's just that—I—uh—Don't laugh now— I used to help out at a childbirth course."

"What?"

He shrugged and shot me a guilty look. "I'm sorry. I probably should have told you. It's just some pregnant women seem to feel—I don't know— intimidated when they learn I actually—*know* something about what they're going through."

"You taught a course to pregnant women at the high school?"

"No." It was as close as I had ever heard Adam come to sounding irritated. "I helped out, is all. And it wasn't to women, it was to couples."

"Ah, yes. Can't leave the devoted husbands out of the picture now, can we?" In my mind's eye, I saw a wall of vines. A big, green snake was crawling through the vines. The snake of bitterness.

"Why are you talking like this?" Adam said. He paused, and sipped at his coffee, as if deciding whether to say more. He liked his coffee really hot. "The couples aren't always married, of course. And some of them are—lesbian couples."

"Right. And I suppose the next thing you're going to tell me is that some of your best friends are lesbians."

"Wow." Adam stared at me in what looked like astonishment.

"Now you're going to tell me the cat's got your tongue."

"No." He was clearly angry. "Now I'm going to tell you your tongue's turned *into* a cat. I don't know where all this homophobia's coming from, but I don't like it."

"I don't either," I said, and started to cry.

Adam nodded, and his look softened, but he did not reach across the table or make any move toward me at all. "Aren't you going to try to comfort me?" I asked after a series of minutes had trudged by like a parade without music or floats.

"No, I'm not."

"Why? Is that another cardinal rule of investigation?"

Adam flushed. "If you want to know why I'm not trying to comfort you, ask decently. I don't respond well to mean questions."

I didn't feel like crying any more. I felt really exposed, and angry. It occurred to me that we were having a fight. Our first fight. I wasn't sure about what. "Fine," I said. "You like patsies. I'll be a patsy. Why didn't you make any move to comfort me, when I was clearly in distress?"

Adam leaned forward. "First of all, just because I'm a man doesn't mean I'm uncomfortable with feelings, or someone who tries to head women off from having them. Secondly, it's been my experience with some women—With you, as a matter of fact—that they cry when they're angry."

"Well, I'm angry now, and I'm not crying," I said.

"Yes, you are," he said.

He was right. "Do you want to tell me what's going on with you, Susan?"

"I don't know," I said. "I'm supposed to feel all happy because of this baby and sometimes I am, you know. I mean, I'm glad I'm pregnant, even though—you know. And I keep thinking of people with awful fathers who turned out great. I've got some money that my mother left me because it came from my father and she hated him and didn't want to be dependent on him. But I feel like everything is out of sequence. I still haven't caught up to the fact I was raped, and I feel guilty about being raped, and I feel really angry about feeling guilty, and sometimes I have dreams that a stork flies out of a garden where a woman lies dying and hands me a baby wrapped in cabbage leaves and when I open it, it's a stone. And when I wake up from the dream, I'm always afraid the baby's died inside me, and I'm carrying around a stone. And sometimes I wonder why you're even bothering with me at all because I'm so *flawed* and I don't have any friends except Raitlin and David and they're gay and that shouldn't matter but it does. It bothers me that they're together. I sometimes I think it's *wrong* even if I know it isn't. Maybe that's because my father, you know, when I was a kid. I don't know why that should color my ideas about Raitlin and David, but I think it does. I hate myself sometimes. Except when I start to hate myself, then I start to hate my baby, and not because of who her father is, but because of who her mother is. And then I start wondering again why you're bothering with me, which is a bad thought because I think you might be in league with Tat, like he's paying you paying you to follow me, and when the baby is born, you'll take her away, or something. And mostly I know that's garbage and I think you might be in love with me or at least in lust with me, but I don't see how, when I'm so big and awful. David has this gurgle in his chest and Raitlin made a crack about it at the table the other day and David said he could kill Raitlin and later, I had to track David down and ask if that was true, could he really kill Raitlin because of whatever, and he said No, of course it wasn't. And when you talked about your abusive ex-wife you said she hadn't abused the boys because if she had, you would've killed her. It's like I've got all these thoughts and feelings and *imaginings* laid out on a table in front of me like a tangle of underwear in some bargain basement and I know I'm supposed to be able to sort them all out, but somehow I can't, so I might look down and find I've got on one sock and half a slip— And I know that you don't believe in cutting anyone off, but I wish you would, because I feel like I'm Little Red Riding Hood and I've wandered into the woods and the wolf is after me and I don't mean you, only my picnic basket doesn't make a very good compass and I'm lost and it's getting dark and I have no idea where my grandmother's cottage is and I'm afraid that even if I figure it out and actually get there, by the time I'll get there, she'll be dead, and the wolf will be ready for a midnight snack, meaning *me*."

I stopped. I didn't really want to stop, but I had hit the wall mentally, even *imagistically-* I lay by it now, not bleeding, but breathless.

Adam nodded—not very sagely, I was happy to notice. He held up one finger as if in warning. He wasn't actually smiling, but his mouth had a kind of softness to it, as if a smile could bud there any moment. I had expected, or dreaded, his visceral disapproval. I would not have been surprised if he had gotten up somewhere in the ranting and left without a word.

But he had survived the *anschluss*, and so had I. He was marshalling his resources now for a response: even if it was a rebuttal, that would be something. I had not succeeded in making him abandon or reject me, and for this failure, I was truly grateful.

"Could I hold your hand a moment?" Adam said.

I stretched out both hands, palm up, meaning for him to choose, and he put a matching hand over each of them. His hands were like blankets on mine, and this somehow prompted me to notice that the baby had been quiet for my whole harangue. Usually, when I was agitated, she was agitated. I had apparently fallen into a private whirlpool this time.

Adam smiled a slow, broad, *sun dawning* kind of smile. "It will take me years to properly respond," he said. "Lest you think of that as a cop out, no pun intended, I am going to say a few things back to you, not so much in answer as in *acknowl-edgment* of your verbal—"

He paused, and I finished for him— "diatribe?"

Adam laughed. "I was going to say 'fountain', but if you need to insult yourself, I won't try to stop you this time."

I laughed. The waitress started to come over again, but when we started to slide our hands apart, she turned abruptly, and marched off, whistling.

"The way I see it," Adam said, "you and I are a lot alike. That speech you made just now was jumbled, but in a really *telling* sort of way.

"I kind of believe that people are divided up into tribes or something, that there are *types* that cut across national and color and gender barriers, and most people stay a member of one tribe all their life, but some people don't. I used to be a member of the *doer* tribe. I could think and speak and feel with the best of them, but I was most *me* when it came to doing something, and I was least me when I felt stymied or paralyzed, and that was the gift my wife gave me, because I didn't know how to respond to her verbal and emotional abuse. It was like she tied me in knots inside for years, like she *imprisoned* me, and the funny thing is that gradually, in my imprisonment, I had a chance to meet myself, to discover who I was, and that man was someone who didn't really like, didn't really trust, *doing* at all. I didn't want to be the one breaking down doors or waiting in a squad car, hoping for a burst of action that would settle the bad guy's hash. I became a *seer*, I. The joy for me now, the interest, the beauty—is in seeing what *is*."

Adam smiled, and pointed to the table closest to us. "Take that lemon meringue pie," he said. "That guy is eating his pie, and his eating is an action, an activity, but lemon meringue is a seer's delight. Doers like hunks of meat, chunks of things that are tough or chewy or resistant, that put up a fight. Pie, on the other hand, melts in your mouth. It rewards a kind of slow receptivity. Lemon pie is always a blend of lemon and sugar. Sometimes the mix is too sweet, sometimes too sour. Sometimes "lemon" includes the zest and the fiber. Other times, it just means "juice." Lemon is always easily identifiable as lemon, of course, but under that, lemon can be green and unripe, or full and soft, bitter, or sour, or tangy, or even sweet. And you don't just have the lemon gel to consider. Like Gaul, lemon meringue pie is divided into three parts: the yellow gel, the crust, and the meringue." He sighed and stared down at his plate. "This pie is really good," he said. "I rarely get swept away by thoughts or feelings," he admitted, "but I sure am a sucker for tastes."

"See? You *are* a wordsmith," I said. "So much so, I didn't even care that you didn't say anything about why we're alike."

"Ah. *That.*" Adam just smiled and got up to pay the check.

He walked me to the front door and said, "I'm going to see what I can find out at the hotel. If you're sure you want me to, you know, partner you at a class, I'd really like to do that.... Just because I got off on lemon meringue pie doesn't mean I'm not thinking about what you couldn't keep from saying back there." He rubbed his hand over his hair ruefully. "Boy, that's a lot of negatives all in a bunch," he concluded.

I asked him if he had gotten a haircut and he admitted he had. But he was not to be pushed off course. He touched his fingertips to my belly, a little longer this time. Inside me, I could feel the baby give a leisurely stretch. "I think I'm falling in love with you, Susan. Or have. You're the realest person I know. The only person I know who's like you is *you*." He put his whole hand flat on my belly and spread his fingers. I felt a sudden surge of warmth, and tenderness, and joy.

"I'll keep in touch, okay?" He seemed awkward to the point of distress.

"Adam?" I asked. "Are you sorry you said what you just said? You seem all, I don't know, out of water all of a sudden."

He smiled. "See? That's what I mean. You're fearlessly yourself. 'Out of water' is exactly what I feel now. I feel like some big dolphin who leapt out of the ocean in a paroxysm of love or enthusiasm and all of a sudden he realizes he's not a mammal at all. He's nothing but a big fish, out of his element, unable to breathe the ordinary air."

I reached out and pulled him as close as I comfortably could. "You're wonderful," I said, and kissed him.

I gave everything I had to the kiss, and got it all back again in spades, endearing little cartoon spades like the one tattooed on Adam's left hand, innocent and brave.

The next two weeks were agonizingly quiet. Adam called me every day to say he was on the trail but had nothing definitive to report yet. These calls were the high point of my day.

Both David and Raitlin seemed to be going out of their way to avoid me. David had developed some kind of chest cold or bronchial condition. He rarely laughed or even smiled any more, there was a kind of "coony" look to his eyes, as though he hadn't slept, and sometimes when he was in the middle of talking, you could hear a kind of gargle in his voice. My pregnancy books, in the words of one, told me to "avoid sick people like the plague." The same author who had started out saying, "Whether this is your first pregnancy or not, it's an exciting time for you. Having a growing baby developing inside you is an incredible experience," and promised to help me "see clearly" how my baby and I were changing and growing, now warned me that I should limit contact with "sick people" like David as much as possible.

Nobody actually seemed to be eating meals anymore. I ate odd things standing up in the kitchen. Cooking and eating had come to feel like extremely dangerous activities, things best done on one's own in the dead of night.

Sometimes I started off on a cleaning rampage, only to break off after five or ten minutes. My books said tension and stress were bad for me and my unborn, and I needed to learn to relax.

The end of July broke everyone's heat records. Comedians were making "How hot is it?" jokes on the television. The sun lay exposed on the eastern horizon like a half-cooked egg on a piece of damp toast.

I was rummaging around under the sink, looking for fresh sponges, when I came across a zip-lock bag three quarters full of cleaning rags. I reached in, and was about to select something, when I remembered. In the weeks after New Year's, David had groomed Sappho with flannel squares. The flannel squares had blue jean backing. There had been a lot of them. Now, they were all gone.

I grabbed the bag and went looking for David.

I finally found him in shirt sleeves in the basement. He was sweating but looked miserable and cold. I thought of warning him about mold and mildew and its possible effect on his asthma or whatever it was but thought better of it. Something about the look on his face warned me not to jump into an interrogatory mode too quickly.

I found myself asking about what he was making, as though that were the sole reason for my descent into the nether regions.

David coughed, and I saw him glance quickly at the contents of the tissue before throwing it away. I turned away, feeling a wave of fear and helplessness.

"Did you ever find out what you're allergic to?" I asked.

David shrugged. "Probably mold. The doctor doesn't think it is allergies now, anyway. It's some kind of bronchitis. I'm surprised you asked. For the last month or so anyway, you haven't seem terribly interested in anything except the baby or Adam."

He sounded jealous. I didn't take even a small pleasure in that fact.

"I'm sorry, David," I said. "I know I've been kind of distracted. I don't know what's the matter with me."

"Well, that makes two of us." David spoke gruffly, but I could tell by his expression he'd been at least partially mollified. "You're going to have to come somewhere in my general vicinity if you want to see what I'm working on," he said. I got a little closer.

He was holding a thin disk of pale wood, about the size of a dinner plate—a series of narrowing rings or grooves had been cut into this.

"What is it?" I asked.

"What does it look like?"

"A wooden maze."

David seemed pleased. "No."

"A wooden Frisbee?"

"No. It's a fruit bowl."

I picked up one of the discs and whacked him with it. "A fruit *plate*, maybe. A wooden disk can't be a bowl—it's missing a dimension or something."

David was like a little kid at Christmas, suddenly. He picked up three wooden pegs, about pencil thickness, though much shorter, and plugged them into three equidistant holes on the edge of the disk and placed it back on the counter. "Now it looks like a toy—a three-legged moon lander, or something," I said.

He chuckled. "Observe and be educated," he said. He produced a banana, two pears, and three apples from his backpack. He placed the fruit on the center of the raised "plate," and it began to sink. "Voila!" David said. "You see? This is a bowl that fruit makes of its own weight."

"Maybe you should call it 'The Pregnant Fruit Bowl'," I said, patting my belly. I picked up the "Rosetta Stone" dishtowel David used to dust his workspace and began to swat him with it.

"You're such a brat," David said, laughing. He grabbed a paper bag and began to swat back.

"I know," I said.

David picked up a wooden spoon for a sword, using his bag now as a shield. I grabbed a ruler.

We went on like this for a moment or two. Dust swirled, and David subsided into a chair, laughing. He didn't cough, but his breathing had gone from mock huffing to labored, and I was concerned.

He held his right hand to his right side as though it hurt.

"I don't really know what's wrong with me," he said.

I sat down next to him, and mentally willed him to look me in the eyes. "You always think that," I said, after a long moment.

"Look, though." David got up and went to the workbench; he got a crumpled Kleenex and a magnifying glass and brought them back to where I was sitting. "Look," he said. He opened the Kleenex to reveal a gelatinous smear of yellow-green snot.

"Truly disgusting," I said.

"The stuff is greener than it's supposed to be. And it has flecks in it."

"You're being a hypochondriac." I got up and tossed the kleenex at the wastebasket. I missed. The Kleenex fell on the floor. David considered a moment, then picked it up with a pair of fireplace tongs and put it in the basket.

David frowned. "Lately, I've had to fight off all these paranoid ideas."

"Like someone's poisoned the water? That kind of paranoid idea?"

"Why do you think I drink bottled water, Suse? No. Like the glue on my envelopes has been poisoned. It tastes funny these days."

"No one would want to kill you, David."

"Because I'm so nice?"

"That, too. But you're not important enough for someone to want to kill you."

"Thanks, I guess," David said. "I have trouble breathing sometimes. And low energy."

He looked suddenly very lost and vulnerable. He shivered.

"If you have trouble breathing, you shouldn't hang out here in the damp lower depths, David. You should go to a doctor and get something."

"I did," David said. "It didn't help."

"Then go to a doctor and get something *else*," I told him.

"Yeah," he said. "I guess I should."

"Definitely."

"What about you? I don't see you going off to the doctor, either."

"I'm not sick, David. I'm pregnant.... Carolina's looking out for me."

"Does she have you drinking Echinacea tea?"

"She tried. Mostly, she measures me and says the baby and I are fine."

"Consider yourself lucky."

"I do. And speaking of lucky, when are you and Raitlin going to get married?"

"We did it already," David said.

I must have shown my hurt, because he said, "It was a really private ceremony, Suse."

"Fine. But—"

"I mean *really* private. Just the two of us, and a witness."

"So he and Carolina are divorced?"

"No." David made a face. "They decided not to do anything official. Our marriage was just– you know– symbolic." He shrugged. "I guess Carolina's here for the duration."

"The duration of what?"

"Your pregnancy, I guess. Maybe even after that." He sighed. "I kind of miss the old days— just the three of us, rattling around."

I got up and started to leave. The expression on David's face was kind of blurry, as though an emotion were coming into focus. I stopped and waited.

He hesitated, clearly searching for words. "You know that I'm in therapy," he said.

"I do."

"Well—the other day my therapist made a very interesting comment." He paused, but I had ceased being willing to play the straight man, even for David. I said nothing.

"He said that a good therapist, and sometimes even a good friend, often needs to be just one half-step ahead of his client, or his comrade. He said that speaking the truth can be a powerful gift, but so can waiting." He glanced down meaningfully.

"Go on."

"I gather that you've been working with your Officer Ferrier—"

"Adam."

"I gather that Adam has been kind of—helping you— uh—*sort out*—what happened to you on New Year's, right?"

"As a matter of fact, he is. Which reminds me— Remember those jeans I didn't want to bring from the apartment, the ones I said were too big for me?"

"Yes?"

"Right. Well, it suddenly occurred to me that those jeans must have been the source of the jean squares you used to use to groom Sappho."

"And?"

"You said something about not washing them because the oils in unwashed clothing made her fur look good. Do you know where those squares might be? They're not under the sink and there's a possibility Adam could get—*evidence*—off some of those squares."

"Wow," David said. "Well—" He stared off into the corner of the basement.

I waited, trying not to let myself feel how much might be hanging in the balance.

"Well—" David said slowly. "If they're not under the sink, they might be in the window seat in the living room."

"What?"

"Raitlin said something about using them to wipe off his corn plants."

We went to the living room and opened the window seat. Sure enough, underneath a pile of newspapers and magazines, there was another ziplock bag two-thirds full of flannel squares.

"What mischief are you two up to?" Raitlin said, coming stealthily up behind us.

We both jumped guiltily. "Raitlin," I said. "Did you get these flannel squares from under the sink?"

"Yes. Have I behaved in a culpable manner?"

"Did you wash any of the squares?"

"No. I thought David had already done that."

"So they're just the way you found them?"

"Yes."

"You did good, Raitlin. I'm going to turn over this bag of squares to my friend Adam. I think he might be able to get some evidence from them. You know—fingerprints or something."

Raitlin and David exchanged one of those intra-couple, 'you know what I'm thinking' looks. I knew what they were thinking, "Semen." "Semen" was what all of us were thinking.

Raitlin frowned. "It's been over six months, I. Don't fingerprints and—*stains*—or whatever kind of dry up, and disappear?"

"Apparently not. Adam says he's taken fingerprints and semen samples off of materials that are ten years old."

"Wow." Raitlin frowned. "Makes you want to mind your p's and q's, doesn't it?"

"I've *always* wanted to mind my p's and q's," David said. "The only trouble is, you insist on minding them for me."

I thought he was kidding, but he left the room right away, and I thought I could tell by the jut of his back, that he'd been obscurely serious. "What's David upset about?" I asked Raitlin.

"Damned if I know," Raitlin said. "I want him to get a chest x-ray, and he thinks I'm being over-protective or something, but that hardly justifies his little display. It's married life, I guess. Pique goes with the marital territory, it would seem. It's part of the matrimonial equipage."

"Speaking of that, when did you guys make it official?" I asked.

Raitlin blanched. "I'm sorry, Susie," he said. "It was three weeks ago."

"What exactly did you do?"

"We had a minister friend over and said a few things, made a few promises. That was it...." He considered me closely a moment. "Not everyone thinks about marriage the way you do, Susie. You're a kind of throwback, you know."

"What do you mean?"

"You're so Victorian about it. Marriage. It doesn't mean any more than the paper it's written on. Which in our case, is none."

I was trying hard not to cry. Luckily, the baby was being really nice. It was moving around inside me, but gently, in a very reassuring and even consoling kind of way.

"What about Carolina? I though you wanted to, you know, get divorced from her so you and David could really—"

"The whole divorce-remarriage thing was just too expensive and wearing on everyone concerned. Carolina and I decided to keep our pro forma liaison, and David and I decided it was more exciting, and therefore more appropriate, to maintain our "Can't we just be significant others?" status." Raitlin shrugged.

"So Carolina was in on it, too?"

"She was our witness, kiddo." Raitlin moved to chuck me under the chin, but I jerked my head away. "Sorry, Susie-Q," he said. "But you know you're–" The sentence slid into a sigh.

"I 'know' that I'm– what?" I asked.

"Oh, Susie-Q," he said in an entirely different tone. "How to put this? – Much as we love you, as much as we know you love us, I think we–?" He paused. "I think the idea of our being married, being a couple– It seems to make you uncomfortable.... You might be a touch– homophobic."

"Homophobic?" I said.

"Homophobic. But you can't help it, probably. Probably a consequence of your twisted childhood."

"Wait. What's happening. First I find out that you and David– slight me– don't have me at your *wedding*. Then you say the reason is I'm homophobic.... I don't think I'm homophobic at all. I make every effort to– I think it's *good* you and David are together. I wouldn't dream of trying to–"

Raitlin cocked his head at me with a sad little smile. "It's okay, Susie. I know you're trying. You probably suffer more from your wretched little attitude than we do. Anyway, let's just pretend this little frog didn't jump all slimy out of my mouth, okay? Besides, we probably would have invited you anyway if you hadn't seemed so preoccupied these days, what with Adam and the baby and all. Or if we'd thought for just a millisecond about how it would affect you. I'm really sorry we hurt your feelings. Don't let it bother you, okay?"

"You're not just making stuff up, are you, Raitlin? I mean— is this really the way you see things? You said yourself, you have this problematic relationship with truth and all."

Raitlin grimaced. "See, people think that falsehood is an attempt to kill, or at least *muffle* the truth. Even in the bad old days, I never saw it like that. The lies I told others—even the ones I told *myself*—they were attempts, perhaps misguided, but still attempts, to *improve* the truth, to jazz it up, make it more interesting. What I've told you just now—this small admission of mine, which apparently caused you some pain, for which I'm sorry—this *confession*, if you will, can safely be stowed under the rubric of truth, for the simple reason it wasn't *interesting* enough to be falsehood. As the cleanly stand next to the godly in attainment, so the truthful is adjacent to the boring." With that, and what I can only describe as a tiny flounce, Raitlin left the room.

I called Adam right after that and told him about the jeans. He sounded, as always, glad to hear my voice; he also sounded oddly miffed, or disappointed.

I told myself not to be paranoid. "What's the matter, Adam?" I asked. "Am I calling at a bad time?"

"No, of course not," he said. "It's just I assumed those jeans had been discarded or given away a long time ago. I should have asked you about them at the get go.... Never mind my male vanity. It's good you found them."

"Do you want me to bring over the squares?" I asked. Adam said it would be great to see me, but he was "right in the middle of something."

Something small but kind of nasty snapped in me like an icy twig when he said that. All of a sudden, I realized I was suspicious. Maybe even jealous. I wondered if what he was right in the middle of involved a beautiful, non-pregnant woman. I told him that now would be a really good time for me to come over, if he didn't mind. He said, "of course" he didn't mind, that he was in the middle of putting together a chain of evidence, and the jeans would certainly be part of that. I asked if I could help him put together the chain and he said no, that was something he needed to do by himself.

"You're afraid I'll muck it up, aren't you?" I asked, wondering who was talking.

"I've got better things to be afraid of," Adam said darkly. He asked if I could bring one or two pieces of fabric from a pair of my own jeans, "just for comparison." He hesitated a moment, then suggested that "things might work better" if he came to where I was. The more he seemed to be putting me off, the more suspicious I became. I asked him if there was something he was ashamed of in his house.

There was a pause. Adam took a deep breath and sighed. "Look, Susan—" he began. There was a note in his voice I had never heard there before. He sounded unhappy, disapproving –almost grim. "I've been wanting to have you visit me since the morning we met," Adam said. "It's just—I've figured some things out, and I thought— Well, never mind. Come on over. I'll explain when you get here."

He gave me directions, and we hung up.

I found an old pair of jeans, and cut off the bottoms, which were too long for me, anyway, to take to Adam.

No sooner had I started out that I began to have deep misgivings. I had never visited anyone—any man, that is—in his own home alone before. *"What ifs"* started to stampede through my brain, none of them good. I told myself (and the baby) that I was being silly. Adam was helping me; he had put himself and his expertise at my disposal. I had been alone with him in a hotel room. Not just any hotel room, either. I had been pushing him to help me all along, and he had done so, behaving all the while like a rough-hewn gentleman. I had trusted him from the beginning. I was behaving like a perfect ninny.

Chapter 15

Banners and Snakes

I might have driven the car right off the road had it not been for the weather, or the absence of it. It was a cloudless, windless, August day. It was a day so unremarkable as to be unusual. All the world was room temperature: the weather seemed to have disappeared.

Then, as I turned off I-94, a new thought hit me. I reflected on the instability of threesomes. Before I got pregnant, my relationship with Raitlin and David had seemed very fluid, sometimes volatile. We were different now, the three of us. We were more solid, and more separate. I decided the baby had a lot to do with that.

I recognized in my musings the latest form of the "I'm only the carriage, not Cinderella" syndrome. Only now I wasn't even full-bodied enough to be a carriage. Even as I swelled with my baby, I was thinning out: I had become a balloon—a fragile membrane between the "inner" and the "outer" worlds, the dark world of water, where air came in a hose, and the light world of air, where hoses were for water.

I found myself remembering a line from some famous poem, "I have it in me so much nearer home/ To scare myself with my own desert places." I had always resonated with that line; I had understood it, I had lived it. Now, with the baby, it was as though a desert, an empty space, had sprouted rocks: behind and under these rocks, animals that didn't bite could scurry to safety; between the rocks were fields of cactus, and every cactus had sprouted a flower.

I had quieted down quite a bit by the time I reached Adam's house. Sherman Court was a cul de sac that angled off a narrow, one-way street. Adam's house was a little yellow Cape Cod almost at the end. There was nothing remarkable about the house, unless I counted the three large flags in the window. I rang the bell, and waited a moment, but nothing appeared to be happening inside, so I leaned forward and peered through the little observation window.

There was a tall man, not Adam, just inside the door. He was dressed in camouflage, and he looked angry. I stepped backward off the stoop, lost my balance, and started to fall. Someone caught me from behind, too quickly for me to really panic. It was Adam.

"Sorry," he said. "That stoop is pretty small for a pregnant lady."

"Where were you?" I asked.

Adam smiled. "Believe it or not, I was across the street, borrowing a cup of sugar so I could entertain you," he said. He showed me a fistful of sugar packets, then he unlocked the door. "You lock your door even when you're just going across the street?" I asked.

He rubbed his head ruefully with his free hand. "I guess I belong to the 'You can never be too careful' school," he said.

He stepped through the door ahead of me and waved me inside.

"Was it your roommate I saw?" I asked.

"Probably not, since I don't have a roommate," Adam said. "Oh, you mean *him*." He closed the door behind us, and there was the guy in all his 6 foot plus camouflaged glory.

A mannequin.

"He's kind of scary," I said.

"If you think he's bad," Adam said, "wait till you see all the heads." He laughed, probably at my expression, and led me into the living room. The walls of the living room were plastered with framed photographs, showing Adam in uniform, shaking hands with unsmiling men in uniform, or smiling men in pin-striped suits. Several of the photographs were signed and dated; some of them had been taken on ships or in front of planes. There was an enormous television.

Flags were on every wall. A Navy flag, a Marine flag, and a U.S. flag were standing on a tripartite stand in the bay window.

When I shot Adam a questioning look, he shrugged. "One of my sons was a Marine," he said. "The other had to settle for the Navy."

"You're serious, aren't you?" I asked.

Adam nodded. "About the Marine Corps, I'm very serious."

I hardly had time to take in the heads in military paraphernalia and the flags, when I noticed the stairs. There were gun belts looped all the way up the banister. They looked like long strings of gigantic firecrackers.

Adam laughed out loud. "You haven't seen anything yet," he told me. He led the way downstairs to his basement. "Welcome to Firebase Manderley," he said. I still didn't get it. "As in Scarlet's house?" I asked.

Adam smiled. "You mean Rebecca's house?" he asked. "Scarlet's house was Tara."

It took a moment to realize he was right. I had been using the "Scarlet's house" phrase so long, "Rebecca's house" just didn't seem right.

"It doesn't matter, anyway," Adam went on. "In this case. Firebase Manderley was named after you."

The basement had been draped in camouflage. There were maps up on the walls. Lanterns hung from peg boards. Artificial vines had been wrapped around the support poles. "Welcome home," said Adam.

The baby kicked hard as though in response. "Are you serious?" I said. "You named a firebase in your basement after me?"

Adam laughed.

I gave him the two zip-lock bags of jean squares.

"Which squares are from the jeans you were wearing New Year's Day?" he wanted to know.

I hesitated. Adam shook his head in what I took to be mock disapproval. "Always label and date," he said. "Remember. Thoroughness is the Cardinal Rule of Investigation…."

I looked at the two zip-lock bags. "No, wait. I know. The red flannel squares are from that night. Here." I handed back the two bags and waited as he labeled and dated them.

"So what did you find out?" I wanted to know.

"About your case?"

"Adam Ferrier, you're stalling," I told him. "Yes, of course, about my case."

"Well," he said. "First, I'll need to run these jeans under the light, and fingerprint you."

After he had run the UV light over all the samples, and bagged and labeled the stained ones, he cut down the side seams of the pocket from the suspect jeans and ran the light over what had been the bottom of it.

It seemed to me a strange thing to do. "Do you really expect to find—you know, semen—at the bottom of a pocket?"

Adam shot me a strange look. "You'd be surprised," he said. He asked where the other pocket was.

"I think that was the first piece David used to groom Sappho—the rabbit," I said. "It's nowhere to be found."

Adam nodded. There was no stain in the main pocket, as it turned out, but Adam discovered a crumpled piece of napkin in the fob pocket.

"I don't know how that got there," I said. "I went through the fob pocket this morning,"

"Napkins are hard," Adam said. "They feel like fabric a lot of times. You have to be really looking."

Holding the napkin fragment by the edges, he smoothed it out. The piece was the top right corner, roughly rectangular, about two inches in length and width. On the left edge was part of a letter, maybe, and then 'MA'. Under that, someone had written in tiny print 'out early to work the cold' and then, under that, 'Sunday, 1-5'.

"What do you think it means?" I said. "I was thinking 'MMA' could be the last part of 'Emma', who went out early to work the cold on Sunday. I remember at the Carrigan, you asked D.J. if Mary or Emma worked Christmas. He said Mary, but he could have been lying, or misremembering."

Adam smiled a little sadly. "I admire, as always, the fertility of your imagination, Susan. But I'm an Investigator, not a psychic. I haven't any idea yet what the note means. My only advice would be not to add things except as a last resort. You're adding an 'E' to 'MMA' before you've taken 'MMA' out for a spin. Not only that, but 'out early' doesn't seem to go with 1-5, unless we interpret that as 1 to 5 in the a.m."

"You think they're initials?"

Adam shrugged. "Given the capitals, I'd say that's a possibility. If it's okay with you, I need to take your fingerprints," he said.

"I've got nothing to hide," I said, and stepped back into the room. A very sweet but acrid smell lingered in the air. The baby gave a little shudder, and I felt sort of dizzy.

"Let's finish this in the upstairs lab," Adam said. "It's warmer up there."

I thought he was serious. I pictured rows of test tubes and electronic equipment.

As it turned out, by "the upstairs lab," he meant the kitchen.

He put a small white filing card down on the kitchen table.

Once again, Adam seemed to know what I was thinking. "There are three kinds of fingerprint cards," he said. "Application cards—like when someone applies for a law enforcement job– has blue type. Immigration fingerprint cards are green. Criminal are red. Criminal cards are all I've got, but it doesn't mean anything. Really. Look." He produced a felt tip marker and drew a bold green line right through "CRIMINAL."

"Make you feel any better?" he asked.

The baby lurched inside me, as if personally affronted by the card. "Not much," I said.

"You have a funny expression on your face," Adam said. "What are you thinking?"

"I'm thinking my baby is a comedian," I said. "It's pretty active these days, and so am I. Whenever she—or he—tumbles around in there, or does pretty much anything, it always seems like a kind of commentary on whatever's happening.... Which reminds me, I checked about the childbirth classes–"

"What did you find? There's a six-week series at the high school on Thursday nights at 7:00, starting August 15th. It's a little late, though, so if you found something sooner–"

"No. The class I found starts two weeks later. Yours is better."

Adam nodded. "We should be finished on September 12, nine days before your E.D.D.– your Estimated Delivery Date."

"Adam. I know what E.D.D. stands for."

"Of course. Well, I meant to tell you about the class but other things kind of crowded it out of my mind."

"What other things, Adam?"

"Let me take a set of prints. Then we'll talk about the other things."

He rolled my fingers on the black ink pad and took a series of prints. Then he gave me some "Plumber's Friend," and a couple of handi-wipes.

Adam prepared us a pot of chamomile tea. He poured it out, and offered me sugar, which I accepted.

"When I was at boarding school, we had high tea every Saturday afternoon," I told him. "Once, it was served by the headmistress herself, one Miss Madeline I—for "Imperious"— Witherspoon, who probably didn't like me any more than I liked her. When I got up to her serving station, she had already poured me a cup of tea, and her sugar tongs were already poised over a bowl of those quarter-teaspoon "dots." She glared at me over her bifocals. "One lump or two?" she said. And I told her, "Sixteen, please." It was a real satisfaction to watch her put dot after dot in my cup, until the tea was overflowing."

I sighed and patted my belly for reassurance. The baby was quiet.

"Why are you telling me this now?" Adam asked.

I had to consider a moment before I knew. "I'm nervous," I told him. I knew the question that was coming next.

"Why are you nervous?"

He sat down at the table with me, and, really, he didn't look the type to make anyone nervous. He looked like the kind of guy who poses for granola ads—big, and strong, and wouldn't hurt a fly— unless, of course, it were a very *bad* fly.

"I don't know," I told him honestly. "You seem different today. Guarded, somehow. Or wound up. Maybe it's just the house…. All this ammunition and paraphernalia makes me a little nervous. Not to mention firebases named after me."

Adam nodded. "I'm sorry," he said after a minute. "I've got something to say, and I don't know how to say it. I don't *want* to say it at all, though it's good news, of a sort. I keep telling myself I have to say it, but…."

He paused and took a taste of his tea. Adam had rinsed the pot with boiling water, before making the tea. The tea was very hot. "Anyway," he said, after we had sipped for a few moments, "I guess I should just say what I have to say. It's good news, actually."

"That's the second time in a minute you've told me that," I pointed out.

"Yeah. Well—the thing is, I'm pretty sure I know who did it to you." Adam's voice didn't sink; it just stopped. I waited a minute.

"Who raped me, you mean?"

"Yes."

"Wow. That didn't take you very long. Are you sure?"

"Okay. I'm going to try to tell you where we are. This is difficult stuff to say, and difficult to hear." He shrugged. "I'm going to try to say this all in one breath, so to speak, because otherwise I—" He got up and got a green metal box which he put down in front of me.

"What's this?" I asked. "Evidence?"

Adam laughed a strangled kind of laugh. "No. It's gingersnaps. For fortification…. Okay. So, when you and I left the hotel, here's what I had. You recognized Room 125, and Room 125 was listed in the suite on the "Manager's" tab for New Year's Eve. Now, basically, there are three types of people that get put up by a hotel manager. His friends, his business associates, and law enforcement."

"If the manager has personal guests in, he pays either everything, or nothing. Usually everything. If he has business associates in, he pays everything. That's the way it goes. If he has law men in there—excuse me, law *people*—he generally pays the food, and the law people pay their own bar tab. They're not supposed to drink, and—Well, it just works out better if he—the manager—doesn't have anything to do with their drinking on the job."

I didn't understand and said so. "Are you saying hotel managers put policemen up at their hotel as a way of buying them off, so they'll turn a blind eye to violations or something?"

"That's a good question," Adam said. "I haven't really explained the thing very well. If a manager wants to buy off police personnel, he doesn't put them up. People would find out about that. It would be sure to backfire. No. If a hotel manager wants to buy someone off, he does it in the time-honored way—Gets him or her on the take, gives him or her money."

"So, why—" I began.

Adam held up his hand. "There are really only two times when law enforcement people would be the official guests of a hotel. One is if a group like the Federal Law Enforcers has a convention or something."

"I didn't think police people could have a union." I said.

"They can't. But the FLE is close. It's a big lobby group, and it's everywhere."

"Never mind. There was only the one suite listed under 'Manager'," I said. "If there were a convention—"

"Well, first of all, if there were a convention, not all the law enforcement people would be given complimentary rooms, no matter how vacant the hotel was. Secondly, the organization would be listed on the books.

"There's really only one time when a law enforcement person stays at a hotel and is both complimentary and under-cover."

"Wait." Shock was making me feel stupid, and disoriented. It wasn't possible that I was sitting in Adam's kitchen, eating gingersnaps while the baby moved around lazily inside me. It wasn't possible that he had gun belts draped over his banister, and that we were talking casually, on a bright August afternoon, about the horror that had happened almost thirty-one weeks ago. I looked at Adam. He had that earnest expression on his face that people get when they want you to know something they haven't actually said.

"Are you saying the man who raped me was a *policeman*? Do you know him? Oh, my god. Is he a *friend* of yours?"

A wave of disgust passed over Adam's face. His lip curled. "You're in shock, Susan, so I'll let that pass. The answer is no, he's not a policeman— and, no, I don't know him."

He paused, as if considering whether to say more. "At this point," he said slowly, stirring a dot of sugar into his tea cup, "I have all you need to go ahead. Name, rank, and–"

"You know his name?"

"I believe so, yes."

I looked Adam square in the face. "What is it?"

"Let me tell this my way, Susan, okay? I've already—"

"Adam," I said. "Go ahead and tell this any way you want. But I want his name *first*." I was about to say something about his "owing me" this much, but I stifled it. That was a line from late night television: Adam didn't owe me anything. It was all the other way around.

Adam considered a moment, then nodded. "Okay. Randall Lee Smith."

"Wait. So Tat was—I mean, Randall was Tat?

"Yes."

"'Lee' was his middle name."

Adam nodded.

"You know this?"

He nodded again. "I couldn't say so in a court of law, but, yes, I know this. I even know where the 'Tat' came from— It's a nickname Randall got stuck with back in grade school, after he tattled on some of his buddies. And 'Lee' was his parents' idea of a tribute to General Robert E."

I felt sick. The name Randall Lee Smith had turned into a name banner and then a snake. It wrapped itself around a stone and sank into my consciousness. I felt as though I had swallowed it.

The baby kicked. It was almost as though she felt I had swallowed a stone, too.

"'Randy'," I said. "That's like a bad joke."

Adam nodded. "Maybe I should get you something stronger to drink. I don't think just this once will hurt you."

"I'd like that," I said.

I was a little nonplussed when Adam poured us both shots of whiskey. "Did I misunderstand you?" he asked.

"I thought you meant coffee," I said. "Never mind. This is much better for an occasion like this. Time-honored, and all"

But when I went to actually take a sip from the little glass, the baby freaked. I felt as though I might throw up. "Oops," I said. "I guess the baby's a teetotaler or something."

I started to laugh.

Adam looked concerned.

"I'm sorry," I said. "I know I'm not supposed to be funny or anything now. But after I said, 'teetotaler', it occurred to me tea was the only thing the baby really seems to like."

Adam's face furrowed. It occurred to me that he looked like a completely confused cartoon character. The phrase "bulldog of befuddlement" came to mind.

I began to laugh in earnest, and the laughter, as it had in childhood, carried me straight into tears.

Adam sat back down next to me. I leaned forward a little, hoping, I think, that he'd put his arm around me. But he turned my chair to face his more directly, leaned forward, and put both his arms around me. We sat like that for what seemed an awkward length of time.

I pulled away, finally. I didn't want to, but I needed a Kleenex. Before I had the wit to ask, Adam pulled a box of Kleenex out from a little shelf under the kitchen table. "Miracle man," I said, and began to cry again.

He didn't put his arms around me again, and I think that helped me to come back to what I normally think of as my senses. "I got some stuff on your shirt," I pointed out. "You should probably run the UV light over it."

Chapter 16

"I" Said the Lamb

It took me a while to calm down. By the time I would have been able to hear more, Adam had to leave.

He got up and stood uncertainly in the doorway. After a second, I went and joined him there.

"This is part of why I thought a later visit might be better," he said. "Would you mind waiting here until I get back?"

I said I would wait for him if he could promise he wouldn't be gone too long.

Adam shot me a funny look that kind of quelled me inside. I hoped he hadn't heard what *I'd* heard in my response: I'd sounded silly, simpering, and coy, like some kind of bedroom farce stereotype.

"I'll be gone about two hours," he said. "I'd make it shorter if I could, but I'm a witness in a check kiting case in Kenosha."

"Nothing worse than kiting in Kenosha," I told him.

"Well, I can drive you home if we leave right now," he said.

"But then you'd have my car to deal with, wouldn't you?"

"I don't think you should be driving right now," Adam said gravely.

I wanted to protest but didn't. The room wasn't exactly spinning, but it was certainly tilting. I felt dizzy and confused. My tongue felt thick in my mouth.

I looked back at the kitchen table. There were still two full shot glasses of whiskey on the table. "I knew a teetotaler once," I said. "He'd never had anything to drink until one time he was at an initiation where everybody was drinking saki, which is clear, and they said he had to drink one glass. So he did and got really drunk. Only they hadn't really put saki in his glass. They'd only put water but he got drunk anyway, because he *thought* it was saki. He was really drunk, even after they told him it was water. He had a hangover and everything."

"Look," said Adam. "I've got my cell phone on. Here's my new card. It has the number on it." He handed me a gray business card with a magnifying glass in the top left corner. Across the top it said, "Questioned Document Examinations/ Latent Fingerprint Examinations."

"This is cuter than your other card," I said.

Adam shook off the remark. "Feel free to go upstairs and lie down," he said. "Call me if– Well, if anything. I'll be back in a couple of hours. Take good care of yourself."

He went out the back door and was gone.

All of a sudden, I really wanted that whiskey.

I went to the kitchen table with every intention of downing both Adam's whiskey and mine, but the baby had other ideas. I held the glass to my nose, and I got a whiff of something that smelled like turpentine. Not just turpentine, either. Turpentine that had been left out in the sun. Turpentine with paint flecks in it, rainbow-swimming, oily, iridescent turpentine.

I ran to the little bathroom off Adam's kitchen, and made it just in time.

To say I vomited into the toilet bowl would be a radical understatement. My mother had said the worst thing about "baby me" was my tendency toward projectile vomiting. She claimed she stopped taking me to restaurants after one episode resulted in spatters on the faces of people sitting across the table from me.

This was like *that.*

After a series of dwindling, but still explosive, discharges, I made my way back to the table and sat down. I felt too exhausted for anything but a certain kind of fear, almost as familiar to me from my childhood as the vomiting.

My mind circled rapidly around a number of distinctly distressing possibilities: there were nerve gas canisters in the basement, and they were leaking; the baby had died; I was falling into the chasm of insanity. Etc. Etc.

My mind kept going like this, even after my body had asserted a kind of sleepwalker's autonomy. I went to the sink in a kind of daze and drank a long glass of warm water from the tap. Then I exited the kitchen and begun to trudge up the stairs—taking care not to touch the ammunition belts wound around the banister.

The second floor was very small. I felt at first like Alice, an Alice who had stumbled into a kind of wedding cake house. I imagined that there was a tiny attic above the small second floor, and a miniscule turret above that, and a hollow spike above that.

I took off my shoes and lay down on the bed in the far bedroom, because it had a white chenille spread folded across the foot of the bed.

I pulled the spread up to my chin, and lay on my back, staring at the ceiling. It was a nice, sloped ceiling. I could hear something (squirrels?) running over it, occasionally dropping nuts (?) that rolled like marbles—bump, bump—down the roof. Every time the roll began, I waited for the sound that would mean it had stopped. And every time, the roll ended in silence.

As I lay there on the bed, I turned from Alice into Goldilocks, and then somehow into a bowl of porridge.

I wasn't too hot: I could feel the sun outside beating down on the roof, the roof lifted in protection against it, the house like a man with a brown raincoat, shielding me from the elements.

I wasn't too hot, and I wasn't too cold. The chenille spread was like a cloudy lamb—giving me its coat for warmth. "'I', said the lamb, all wooly and warm. 'I kept her safe from the summer storm....'"

I was like a bowl of porridge—no, that was too messy. Nutritious, but gloppy.

I was a cradle—clean wood, warm and rocking in the sunshine.

And there was a baby in the cradle. A sleeping infant.

It was hot in the room.

I pushed off the chenille spread, put my hands down on my mounded belly, and I began to croon. The song I crooned was half notes, half words, and half silence. I told my child that I loved her, that I would take better care of her than I ever had of myself, that she was a gift, a pearl of great price. I told her she was the reason I had been born, and in no way a burden. I spoke to her of the lotus that springs from mud– that springs from mud, and travels through water, and is ready, finally, to greet the summer air, fresh and fragrant, intact and pure.

I asked her to forget the mannequin with a rifle downstairs, the gun belts on the stairs, the mistakes I had made, and would make, all the ways I would let her down, and had let her down already. I begged her to forget the ugly name she had heard down below, in the kitchen— the name that had made me vomit half-curdled bile—

And for a moment I saw her sitting on God's lap and God looked like a tall, bearded black man dressed in white, and they were worlds that should never have been apart that had come together and they both were smiling the same smile and smiling it at me, at me. And I asked Them for a sign, for another name to put in the place of Randall Lee Smith— a beautiful name, to be a covenant.

And a bird, a real bird outside a real window— sang its short but liquid song in answer, over and over outside Adam's bedroom window. And it sang the name "Lucy."

"Your daughter is Lucy," the song said.

I saw the words, "I Love Lucy," written across a cartoon heart on an ancient, grayed over television screen. It was a joke, which made it more precious.

I saw us going sledding. I got on the sled behind her, and down we went, and the slope that had seemed too precipitous leveled out, and soon we were flying inches above the ground and even though I couldn't see her face, and I so much wanted to, I could feel my daughter leaning back against me and laughing and we were flying over a world that was dazzling and white and would provide a safe and happy landing.

My hand, moving around under the pillow, touched a piece of paper.

I pulled it out, struggled to a sitting position, and began to read:

Dearest of All,

I send you this message from a world
more yours than mine. We're two halves
of one event, and the love I give you is
the truest part of me, offering deep, reliable
connection.

For a moment, it was the baby, sending me a letter from a world more mine than hers.

Then, with a shock I recognized the message as the one *I* had written to *her*, to Lucy, in response to Adam's asking me for a handwriting sample.

I was touched that Adam had saved my letter to my baby. And kept it under his pillow. The letter itself, the words I had forgotten writing, touched me, too.

I began to cry for all the ways in which I was not adequate to what I had written.

I lay on Adam's bed, which was narrow, and cried for myself, for my baby, for the good intentions I had, and the courage I didn't. And for the first time in my life, the progression reversed. The crying led to laughing, and happiness swept over me. I was pregnant, I was happy. I was having a daughter. I *had* a daughter.

"Lucy," I told her. "I'm not much, but everything I have and am, is yours. I want you to be born more than I've ever wanted anything in my life. I promise to do the best I can to keep you alive and help you be happy."

And I saw my father, reaching in for me, reaching in past the shoes and the coats, and the umbrella in the corner. He reached for me and held me. He put me in his lap and loved me. But he didn't do anything more or other. This time, he didn't do anything wrong.

And I saw my mother, reaching to hold me, to comfort me. But unable to protect me. Maybe unable even to *try*. She had failed at the first duty of a mother. I might fail Lucy in many ways, I probably would, but I would not fail her in *that*. Maybe my mother had not died because she made the terrible mistake of loving me. How did that even make sense? Maybe her terrible mistake had been not loving me *enough*....

When I woke up, Adam was standing over me, and the bed was wet. There was a sweet smell in the air.

I found myself remembering boarding school, and all the extra sheets I'd had to launder.

Adam looked kind, but grave. "If you should stand up, stand up slowly" he began, which terrified me. "It's August 5th," he said, as though that explained everything.

"Meaning what?"

"Meaning, I think we'd better go straight to the hospital with you. You've had an early spontaneous rupture of the membrane. Don't worry, though. The folks at St. Luke's have seen plenty of that."

The Titanic was far out on a dark sea. Its watertight compartment sprang a leak. The ship was going down. Nearly everything that mattered would be lost.

Adam sat down slowly on the side of the bed and started to put on my shoes for me. He got one on, then said, "What are you doing, Adam?" and thrust the other shoe into my hand.

I heard a voice in my head, "Diddle diddle dumpling my son John. One shoe off and one shoe on." The voice couldn't sing worth a damn.

"Will you allow me, please?" Adam asked.

I nodded, not sure what he meant.

Adam turned away his head, like a kid who covers his eyes when he doesn't want to be seen, he reached under my shirt and probed me gently for a few long moments.

Adam withdrew his hand, and wiped my belly dry with the bedspread. He tucked the chenille throw around me, as though I were a frankfurter in a bun.

I felt scared. A stranger in a strange home.

"Okay," he said. "I'm going to lift you. Don't struggle, okay. I promise not to drop you.

He bent over and hoisted me into his arms. It wasn't at all like the movies. The noises coming from Adam made it sound as though his chest wall were collapsing. Adam rose uncertainly to his feet, turned slowly and walked toward the door. I felt as though I was sleepwalking through someone else's dream.

When he reached the door, he turned sideways, and we edged out into the hall, inch by inch. We moved down a hallway that seemed to lengthen as we moved.

Rounds of ammunition uncoiled from the banister like metal snakes and clattered to the floor below as we staggered down the stairs. "Don't worry, they're not live," Adam said.

The words, "not live" made me shiver.

Adam carried me slowly through the kitchen. I remembered a story where the women of a city overwhelmingly besieged were allowed to carry out one thing—each carried out a child, or a man. I opened the door, and we stumbled into the sunlight. Adam kicked the door shut behind him with one blow of his foot.

Adam's car was still in the driveway. I opened the passenger door, and he slowly lowered me in. Then he knelt beside me on the pavement and helped me put the seat back to its "full recline" position.

He got in the car and backed carefully out of the driveway. "The weather is really strange today," he said, to no one in particular.

I wanted to say that I was nothing but a membrane between inner and out weather, and the membrane had ruptured. I wanted to tell him I had been sealed off, once, from everything that wasn't me. I wanted to say I was once a riddle. I wanted to say that the answer to that riddle was "an egg," and "an egg" was a riddle inside a riddle, and the answer to all riddles was a baby.

I said nothing. Lying nearly supine, I looked up and out. I saw the whole blurry world through a glass, brightly, and the tops of trees were most of what I saw. The leaves were a bold, even flagrant green, vying in brilliance with an infinite sky. There must have been a gentle breeze blowing: the trees seemed sometimes to be wringing their hands.

Adam took his car cell phone out of its holster, and dialed with one hand, steering with the other. "St. Luke's hospital," he said first. Then, "Emergency Room, please." Then, "This is Adam Ferrier, recently of the Ann Arbor Police Department. I'm on my way to the hospital with a 31 weeks Primigravida, with premature rupture of the membranes. We should be there in about five minutes. Can someone meet us with a gurney?"

Then Adam made another call. "Hi, Carolina. It's Adam. Susan and I are on our way to the hospital," he said. A pause. "No. The membrane spontaneously ruptured."

I wanted to ask him not to say "spontaneously." "Spontaneously" was a good word, I thought; it should be reserved for good things, not wedged between "membrane" and "ruptured."

"Hold on, I'll ask her," he said into the phone. And then, to me, "Do you want Carolina to meet us there."

"Yes, please," I said. "That would be nice."

In a matter of seconds, we were pulling into the circular drive in front of the hospital. I sat up with difficulty. I wanted to tell Adam about the funny thing I'd seen on television, but even before we'd come to a stop, Adam was beeping his horn.

Two men came out from behind sliding glass doors, on either side of a gurney.

"We've got her," they told Adam. Adam opened the passenger door, and fell back, out of sight.

The two men lifted me onto the gurney, and they pushed me toward the hospital entrance. Just when I thought my shoed foot was going to hit the doors, they parted before us like a glass sea. I wanted to sink into the gurney, but before I could do that, people appeared.

There were four people now, one at each corner of me. I was like a white cloth, and they were going to set the table.

Someone said, "One, two, three, transfer," and I found myself in a bed. Someone had taken off my one shoe. Both shoes disappeared. When I was in my sixth grade, there was a girl who died during a school party at the roller skating rink. I had taken off her skates.

The bed was soft. Someone unwound me from the chenille throw, like a mummy in reverse. My own pun delighted me. From mummy to mummy.

They put me in a clean white cotton shift, no underwear, put my head on the clean, white pillow, put a clean white cover across my legs and chest, leaving my belly and arms exposed.

Someone put a needle in my arm. I looked up and saw clear liquid dripping into me. When I was little, mother had washed my hair with "White Rain." I looked out the window and saw August skies, clear and dry. But I could smell the rain.

A female nurse tore off a piece of what looked like big, yellow scotch tape, and slid it with coy rudeness right between my legs. When she brought it out again, the tape was a deep, deep blue. "PROM," she said.

I wanted to tell Adam, who had somehow managed not to disappear at all, that it was like the baby and I were playing with the world, like that movie where Charlie Chaplin was tossing the world like a ball back and forth between his hands, except in reverse: the world was tossing *us*, and tossing us gently. I was Winkin and she was Blinkin and the big round world was Nod.

I felt curiously calm. I was in the eye of the hurricane. Nurses and doctors were coming and going, so baby and I didn't have to. From time to time, I asked myself what would happen next, and gave myself my mother's answer, "Time will tell."

The two nurses wheeled the three of us—my bed, my baby, and me— out of the room, and into an elevator marked "Freight." Adam stayed by my side the whole time, holding me by my unconnected arm. He told me we were headed for Labor and Delivery—where Carolina would meet us.

It was sort of like being at a three-ring circus, and I was the center ring.

They put us in an ante partum room, because, one nurse said, they didn't want to "tie up a birthing room for you, when you're liable to be here a long time."

I asked if she meant "like overnight."

"Like days or weeks even, maybe," she said cheerfully, and left.

Carolina showed up, holding a sheaf of papers. Then Dr. Oberdorster showed up. Dr. O. was the "on call" obstetrician that night and, thus, our consultant by default. She looked and sounded like a completely different person. Maybe it was because the pink and green were gone: she was a vision in dazzling white.

Carolina seemed enormously relieved to see Dr. O. "I have some pressing business elsewhere in the hospital," she told me. "But you're obviously in capable hands...." She indicated Adam with her left hand, and Dr. O. with her right. "I'll be back as soon as I can," she said. "Then we'll work out a birthing plan," she said. She gave Dr. O. a "thumbs up" gesture and left as quickly as she'd come.

Dr. O. stood by the bed, across from Adam, looking down at me as if she were waiting for me to say something.

I asked if she didn't want to examine me. She said, "No, not really," that all the information was on the chart, and examining me at this point would put the baby "at risk."

She asked if I had any questions, and I asked her what was going to happen and she said, "That depends on you whoever."

Adam flushed at this. Dr. O. stood up a little straighter. "You probably know by now that you're here because of PROM, premature rupture of the membranes."

Adam started to ask a question. Dr. O. held up a finger. She turned back to me. Now *he* seemed to be the odd man out.

"What about Carolina?" I asked her. "Can Carolina be here with me as my doula?"

"Of course."

Adam cleared his throat. "I—uh—am not sure how much time Carolina will be able to spend with us," he said, looking at me with a "tell you later" look. "There's been a last minute change in plans."

"Well, never mind," Dr. O. told him. "The nurses here are extremely capable." She turned back to me. "You may not feel like you need bed rest," she said, "but right now, it's essential.

I recommend, above all, a positive attitude about staying in bed. A positive attitude may make the difference in how long bed rest helps you avoid having to deliver your baby before it's is ready to be born."

Adam turned toward the doctor. "What about her position?"

"You're right," Dr. O. said, as if he had made an astute observation, instead of asking a question. She turned to me, pursing her lips.

"Lying on your side increases blood flow returning to your heart, thus increasing blood and oxygen supply to still growing Baby," she said.

I rolled obediently over onto my side.

Adam and Dr. O. exchanged a look. "The left side would probably be better," Dr. O. informed me.

I changed sides.

Dr. O. bent over and pushed a button. The middle of the bed rose a bit, and the foot of the bed was not far behind. "It's probably better if you rest in a position where your hips are higher than your shoulders," Dr. O. announced, stuffing pillows under me where they didn't belong. When she was satisfied that my position roughly approximated that of a beached whale, Dr. O. stopped.

"I have a feeling that when you go home, it will be with a baby," Dr. O. said brightly. "Seriously… we may have to give you something if you start having contractions, and Baby will do better if we keep an eye on it here."

"But I don't know what I'm supposed to do," I complained.

Dr. O. pulled the last bit of coat out of my fingers. "Think of yourself as a star in the play where nothing happens," she said. "We want Baby to stay inside you for as long as possible."

Without warning she turned back to me and probed my belly for a moment. She nodded. "Baby's head is not yet engaged, but it appears to be thinking about it. Unless and until the football is in the center's hands, I don't want you getting up for any reason. When nature calls, use a bed pan."

She turned to Adam. "I recommend reading her books and giving her backrubs. There's probably nothing on the mammoth television up there—" she gestured— "but the slop is at least presented in living color."

Back to me: "They'll be checking your vital signs every three hours—blood pressure, pulse, temp, respiration. Make sure to get a menu. When you're in the hospital for a while, the choice between jello and rice pudding begins to seem pretty important."

Dr. O. held out her hand to me, palm out. I would have given her a "low five" slap in acknowledgment, but I was busy at the moment being a whale, looking around at the dunes.

"Nice to meet you—Adam," Dr. O. said, already half out the doorway. She turned back. "And, mom–?" she said.

"What?" She was scaring me.

"Take it easy."

She was gone.

It was getting late, I realized. It was always getting late. Things were only early when you didn't know it. After that was late, then later.

Adam pulled a chair closer to the bedside and sat down. "Feel like holding hands?" he asked.

"Yes," I said, producing a hand for him to hold. "'Cold as paddocks though they be/ Yet I hold them out to thee'."

Adam smiled, and began to rub my small, cold hand between his warm and ruddy one. "Who said that?"

"My father, for one. But it wasn't original with him. I don't think anything was original with my father, except for bad behavior."

I looked at him. He was strong. He was comfortable. He was *here*.

"When's Carolina coming back?" I asked. "Where are David and Raitlin?"

"You're asking the wrong guy."

Adam mumbled something about the possibility of my calling home. But before anything along those lines could happen, there they were, the three of them. Carolina came in first and led the way around Adam to the far end of the foot of the bed. Next came David. He looked as though he'd seen a ghost, or was one. Last came Raitlin, who stood uncertainly between David and Adam; Adam pushed back his chair and stood to greet the trio.

They all stood, and I lay blinking, under a light that might have been stolen from the interrogation room in a Russian prison.

Finally, after what was probably only a handful of seconds, we all began talking—we talked quickly, zipping in and out of the weave of each other's formulations like cars on an expressway in a hurry to get home.

All of us were careful to say nothing very real. I think we all realized that this place, this hospital, was all too full of the real as it was.

I introduced Adam to David and Raitlin, and was surprised to hear Raitlin say almost proudly, "The Officer and I have already met." Then I remembered Riverbrook, and how, lifetimes ago, I had stood behind a window in a warm room and watched as Adam took command of a difficult situation.

But the difficulty embedded in this situation (other than myself) was clearly something foreign to Adam. If anything, he was more ill at ease than I was. He started sentences and then abandoned them when it became clear they were headed where he didn't want to go. And he apologized constantly.

Raitlin was quiet, for the most part. He answered whenever called upon, but, after his initial offering, volunteered
nothing. David had, for him, a lot to say, but his voice was
weak, and shaky, and whenever he began speaking, at least
one of the rest of us jumped in to finish the thought, or the
sentence; it was as though he were a drowning swimmer, and
needed us to save him.

Carolina asked me what I needed from home. Raitlin produced a pad, David produced a pen, Carolina asked questions
like "What do you want to sleep in?" and I listed items, and
Adam wrote my responses down, because, as I pointed out, he
was the only one of us who had truly legible handwriting.

After this "group" project. Carolina said she would drop the
suitcase off at reception within the hour. A nurse came in and
announced the end of group visiting hours. We all brightened
considerably at this, and the three of them left, each bending
and kissing me awkwardly on the cheek before they left.

Carolina turned in the doorway—What was it about hospital rooms that seemed to encourage people to speak from
the doorway?— and said, "You're in good hands, Susan." She
seemed to me to mean Adam, more than herself. "My status
here at the hospital is unclear, but I'll be in first thing tomorrow morning to check up on you."

After Carolina's departure, Adam and I looked at each
other, bobbing gently up and down in the wake of her departure.

A nurse came in to take my vital signs and asked Adam
to step outside for a few moments, so I could use the bed pan,
"etcetera."

After all the checks— the baby's heart rate continued to
oscillate right around 140— Adam re-entered, with a hospital
tray and several pages of multi-choice menus for the following
days.

He went down to the cafeteria to eat. I stared at the hospital tray. Raitlin liked to say that expectations were premeditated resentments, and I had always taken that to mean "high" expectations. In this case, though, my expectations stood me in wonderful stead: I had expected the food to be lousy, and it was actually not bad. I had expected "cold," and it was "lukewarm."

I thought I wasn't hungry, but either Baby had her own ideas on the subject, or I was wrong: I ate a lettuce salad, a roll with butter and something called "eggplant surprise."

When Adam came back, I was drinking the last of the tea.

He brought in the suitcase Carolina had left for me, and said he thought he might call it a night. He still had some research to do on the check kiting case, and there were some other things that needed his attention.

He kissed me on the cheek. "Adam," I said, "Would you be adverse to *really* kissing me?"

"Silly," he said, as if to a child he couldn't resist. He kissed me on the mouth, so gently it was almost a tease. I clutched at his shirt, not wanting him to go, wanting to bring him back down to me. "Wait," I said. "Don't go. There's something I want to ask you."

"'Ask. Demand. I'll answer'," Adam said.

"Does it bother you to think of Raitlin and David, you know, in bed together and having sex?"

Adam looked puzzled. "I've never thought of them in bed together and having sex."

"Okay, but if you did— It's just that Raitlin said I was homophobic and I'm wondering if that's maybe true."

Adam shook his head. "What in the world makes you think of this now?"

"I don't know, but— If you did think of them in bed together and having sex, would it *disquiet* you? Because it does me."

Adam laughed. "If you think of them bowling, does that make it easier?" he said.

"No. Thinking of people bowling never makes anything easier."

He laughed even louder.

"So I guess Raitlin is right and I'm homophobic, huh?"

He kissed my hand. "If you say so," he said. There are worse things to be. But I think it's usually disquieting to think of other people having sex, particularly family members." He was still kind of laughing. "As long as you don't find yourself making queer jokes, or mock anyone with limp-wristed hand gestures, I think you'll be okay."

We said good night, and Adam left.

I listened to the sound of his boots going down the corridor, getting fainter and fainter.

I fell immediately into a troubled sleep.

Chapter 17

The Beehive

I started out every day thinking I was ready. Every day, Adam would drop by for a long visit. Every day, we would do breathing exercises, and talk about the baby, and what might happen when labor began. Every day, I would somehow push what had happened eight months ago to the back of my mind.

Once, a male nurse came to take my vital signs while Adam was there. The nurse's name was Randall. I looked at Adam, and Adam looked at me.

I lay in the hospital, day after day, in a kind of white fog. Sometimes, it felt to me as if I were the one waiting to be born. Lying on my left side in the Trendelenburg position, wrapped in white sheets and blankets, with a fetal monitor belt and a contraction belt wrapped around me, I seemed to myself like the beehive of the vagina picture in Dr. O's textbook, only white not red. I kept hearing my mother talking about battening down the hatches.

My mind seemed to have jumped ship, or derailed, or whatever the metaphor was. My consciousness no longer progressed the way it once had, tunneling forward with all deliberate speed. Instead, it crawled sideways, or gazed up at the sky or dug a hole in sand, or, in general, seemed comfortable with the idea of not moving ever again. I found myself remembering things I had forgotten and forgetting things I had once remembered.

All that was left of the rape was a name that stood out in hideous clarity.

I was in the same place, day after day—a place that worked hard to stay as it was. "Different menu, same bed," was how Adam put it.

I was in the same place, in the same position (as far as I could stand it: sometimes I cheated, and rolled a little toward my front, or a little toward my back). There was nothing I could do differently. Baby, on the other hand, apparently felt freer than ever before. She had never been more active. Hardly an hour went by without inner activity of some sort. I pictured her doing calisthenics, trying to get ready for her big entrance.

I was, in a way, in thrall to the baby I held captive within me. Sometimes I would talk to her and try to persuade her that the hospital world was a safe place— unlike the outside world, which was real and dangerous.

The next time Adam came to visit, I asked him where Randall was. "Why do you want to know?" Adam asked.

"I don't know why," I said. "But the closer the birth gets, the more real it gets, the more I have this insane fear that, at the last minute, that scumbag is going to show up. He's going to show up and claim that I wanted what happened to happen. He's going to say I told him I wanted to be pregnant—by him. That he wants to have fatherly rights. I keep thinking that he's around the corner somewhere. That he works at the hospital. That the next guy coming through that door will turn out to be *him*, and he'll grin at me, and say he hopes it's a girl, so he can rock her in his arms, and cradle her and stroke her little limbs with his big red hands.

"I know you've been pretty much alone in this, Adam. I said I wanted to know, and I set out to know, but now I'm afraid to know. I'm afraid you're going to tell me that Randall is a doctor, that he works here. I'm afraid that, somehow, by my sending you out to find *him*, he's going to find me, to find *us*. I'm afraid I'll have to deal with him again. I'm afraid if he does show up, I'll go crazy and shoot him through the heart and have to go to prison for the rest of my life and hear how he's raising our daughter to despise me because of course he's too horrible to die. And then when I get out of prison, after years of horror, Lucy will come to me and say she always knew I was good, she just wondered why I didn't come to save her from all the awful things her father did to her when she was young and innocent and couldn't protect herself.

"I worried at first we weren't going to be able to find him, Adam. And now I'm scared he'll find us—any day, any moment. He'll thrust himself into our lives, into *her* life. And he'll demand his *rights*."

"He's almost certainly won't show up here, Susan," Adam said slowly. "Randall lives near Traverse City. He was here on assignment but got transferred. He's unlikely to come back."

I rolled over on my back. My whole left side was numb—and it hurt. My waters had broken, so technically the birth process had started, but baby showed no inclination to emerge. I was in a hospital, but I wasn't sick: I was trying to keep gravity's paws off my baby. I was a mass of concerns and contradictions.

"Tell me."

Adam nodded. "Okay…. Well, let's back up a little. Remember, I told you that three types of people stay *gratis* in a Manager's Suite?"

Adam was sitting in a chair over by the window, against a backdrop of trees and skyscrapers. The trees were very tall, and the skyscrapers relatively low, so that foliage and buildings ended at about the same height. The effect was more than a little comical, as if some cosmic barber had drunkenly tried to even everything off.

"Well, I found out that the manager is kind of a penny-pincher: whenever he brings family members in for a 'free stay,' he makes them buy their own meals, meaning he actually clears a profit, even on so-called 'family freebies.' That leaves the other two kinds of Manager guests I told you about—business people and law enforcement people. In both cases, the manager foots the whole tariff, so there's no difference there. But business people are notorious drinkers—work hard, party hard—that kind of thing. And everything goes on the tab. The room service bills are horrendous, etc., etc.

"That's where a law enforcement person is different. The manager would probably be willing, would *definitely* be willing, to foot the bill for everything. But law enforcement people aren't allowed to drink on the job. If a law enforcement person has a free room, he's on a job, an assignment. He's not supposed to be drinking. He goes down to the bar, brings his drinks up, pays cash. That way, the record they leave behind only shows room service charges for food and non-alcoholic beverages. That's the main difference between business folk and law personnel– the paper trail they leave behind."

Adam paused, and lofted the orange skin into the empty waste basket. It made a tiny thwack.

"But what was a law enforcement person doing at the Carrigan?"

Adam smiled. "You gave me the answer to that yourself.... Remember how you asked me if I knew what I'd done between Christmas and New Year's?"

"Yes." I rolled over on my back for a blissful second or two. My left side was beginning to feel raw.

"Well, I remembered exactly what I'd done: I was busy being an expert witness.... Did you ever read about the Outlaw trial?"

"Even if I had, I wouldn't remember it now," I confessed. "My brain has turned to mush, along with the rest of my body."

Adam laughed. "Well, it was a trial they had to hold over—That's what Randall was doing at the Carrigan. He's a US Marshall, and he was guarding a witness."

"Are you sure?"

"Yes. He was responsible for the Outlaws' accountant. They brought him in from Chicago for the trial. That's the guy Randall was seen with. Randall was in the Manager's suite with the accountant in the adjoining room."

"The whole time?"

"The whole time."

"Was he involved, too?"

"No. He was probably sleeping...." Adam sighed and leaned forward clapping his knees with his hands. "He was probably drugged, too. With some kind of sedative."

"Have you ever killed someone?" I asked. The baby began punching me with a series of surprisingly forceful little jabs.

Adam shot me a look as if wondering who I was, or what to say. "I was on the force for twenty-seven years. I've killed when I had to."

"Would you– I mean, if I asked you to, could you– ?" The question hung in the air.

"What would you do if you were in my place?" I said finally.

Adam shook his head. "I hate that question, Susan. It doesn't make any sense. If I were in your place, I'd be pregnant. The room would be full of reporters."

As if on cue, David came in. David looked ashen. He reminded me of the self-portrait of Matisse's I had once seen, where the white of the face overlapped the dark of his hair.

I asked what was wrong. No one answered me for a minute. "I'm not sure," David said finally. "They're doing some tests today, and maybe I'll find out."

"What kind of tests?"

David smiled wanly. "You don't want to know," he said.

"I do, though."

David looked at me. "I want to talk to you," he said. "Alone." Adam got up but then Carolina and Raitlin came in, and a bevy of nurses. The nurses clustered around the fetal monitor while a doctor I had never seen before– pale and pimply, looking all of fifteen years old– gave them a little lecture on preterm procedures. Then everybody but Adam left as quickly as they had come in.

"Adam? I've been thinking about Randall. I just– I want him gone," I said.

"He is gone."

"I mean gone gone. Out of the way. Unable to do this to anyone else. Other women won't be as– lucky as I am, I don't think. I mean you. They won't have you."

"Have you thought about this?" Adam asked.

"Of course I've thought about this. I've thought about it and it's what I want." It was only when I said it that I knew it was true.

Adam blanched. "Susan," he said. "First and foremost, I'm a person of the law. I'd do anything for you, you know that–"

"Then do it," I heard myself say. "You know where he is. Find him and do it. Don't tell me about it, just do it."

"You don't know what you're saying."

"I do know what I'm saying."

"You're in the hospital about to have a baby and you're–"

I put my hands on my belly. I think I actually had an impulse to cover up the baby's ears during this discussion. "I suppose you think we should just– No, *I* should just... Let bygones be bygones."

Adam frowned. "I don't know what you're saying at the moment," he said

"Well, I don't know who you are, so I guess that makes us equal. I guess neither of us knows anything about the other. I guess we're strangers."

I tried to speak slowly and casually. I don't think most observers would have detected anything funny in my voice. But the baby's heart rate went up about fifteen beats per minute; she wasn't fooled.

Adam didn't move or say anything. He seemed to have turned to stone. "Adam? Say something."

"Look." Adam sounded as distressed as I had ever heard him. "I want to ask you a question, but I know you're in a bad way here—Well, not a bad way. I don't mean that. What I mean is, you had a terrible thing happen to you, and now you're in the hospital and all nervous—Well, I don't know that—but you might be nervous or in an un-normal state right now."

"Just ask your question, Adam, okay?"

"Okay. Why did you come to me at the beginning, I mean?"

"I wanted to know the truth."

"Why?" Adam seemed to get taller. From where I lay, beached on the bed, he was the tallest person I'd ever seen.

He was standing with his back toward the window. The sun was blazing right behind him: he was the dark center-piece of God's flaming eye. "I don't really know," I said. "I've always believed in it, in the truth. Setting things straight."

Adam sighed. He came over and sat down again in the chair by the bed. "Most of the time, in my experience, truths have to be pieced together like stained glass windows—sometimes, if you're not careful, your hands get cut."

"No cut hands in this hospital, please," a nurse said, coming in to take my vitals, and duly note the baby's heartbeat.

"It's really weird even to be talking about this in a hospital," Adam said when the nurse had left. "I feel like I'm releasing toxins or something."

"Would you tell me what happened, Adam? I think I'm ready."

"Okay, I'm going to skip over who told me what, and the exact times and dates involved. I'm going to tell you the story I pieced together. Randall Lee Smith is a U.S. Marshall. He came to Ann Arbor right after Christmas, guarding a witness for the Outlaws trial.

"My source told me that shortly before that our guy was sent to Chicago, and arrested someone who turned out to have less contraband than expected."

"So, you're saying that Randall might have gotten the drug he used—the GHB—from that con in Chicago and come to Ann Arbor, hoping for the chance to use it?"

Adam held out his hands to me, palms up, as though he had no more to say on the topic.

"Okay. Go on."

"Okay. He came to Ann Arbor, guarding this little accountant guy. Randy spied you—"

"Is there some way to keep 'me' out of it? I know that sounds ridiculous, but—"

Adam considered a moment. "Randy spied this waitress. He probably slipped some sleeping pills to the witness, locked him in his room, persuaded the waitress to have a drink with him in the bar, put the GHB in her champagne. He and the waitress ride up in the elevator...."

"Does he have a record? Has he done other things?"

"Not officially, no. There are some notes in his file– rumors, suspicions, unsubstantiated reports. Randall seems to have been skirting along the edges of trouble for most of his time as a marshall.... Back to the issue.... I lifted prints that match yours and Randall's from the back legs of the desk.

"Your fingers are wrapped around the back of the ball. Your thumbs are on the inside, pointing back, toward the wall. Your fingertips are splayed, indicating tension or pressure. Your left hand is on the rear left leg of the desk, and your right hand is on the right. Randall's prints are on the outside of yours."

"What do you think happened, Adam?" I said.

He nodded; his expression said he'd been waiting for the question. "I think Randall put you on the floor and climbed on top of you and held your hands down on the desk legs hard enough so your fingers splayed. And then he raped you from behind. And I think while this was going on, the back of your head rubbed against the underside of the desk. And when he was through, he stood up, and some of his semen splattered on the rug. And some of it spilled out of you. And then I think he put you in jeans that were probably his, judging by their length. I'm not sure about the man in white— maybe he really was mis-delivering a pizza or maybe there was a pizza box in the witness's room, and they sent a bell boy to your door with it, just to see if you were rousable, and would leave without making trouble."

"Randall threw your skirt and panties in the laundry chute, and someone from the hotel threw them out. I have a witness who said there was blood on the skirt, but not the panties. Another witness said the reverse was true."

Adam sank into his normal chair by the bed. He was looking at me as if he expected something. I wasn't sure what it was.

"The thing of it is, evidence can only take you so far. The semen samples might turn out to be from someone else. Everything I've told you is consonant with consensual sex. There was no scalp material on the underside of the desk—just the hair. It might not be yours and even if it is…. Everything I've found can be made to look another way. We still have the fact you didn't report anything. It's just your word against his—a U.S. marshall. You can bet, if anybody even mentions trial, Randy will sit down with some expensive counsel and make sure he gets his story straight and he'll almost certainly fight you every step of the way.

"And you don't clearly remember what happened. This could all be made to look like you wanted to get laid. I know you're telling the truth, but somebody else—Well, it's just my theory about where the drugs came from. And the hotel people are motivated to protect marshalls. They get a lot of law enforcement business. Randall is important to them, and you're not. You're dispensible.

"They'll come after you with everything they've got. And not just *you*—They'll come after me and Raitlin and David. They'll drag in ancient history about my ex and me—how she called the cops and showed them her bruises—bruises I gave her trying to defend myself. They'll question our *alliance*. They'll investigate Raitlin and David and bring up the whole gay issue. We've got no proof of anything at this point. DNA testing would connect your baby to Randall. He might even take the line that you were 'remiss' not to tell him about the pregnancy. It's his child. He'd almost certainly ask for visitation rights, to look good. Hell, he might even ask for custody, given what they'll describe as your unsavory life style and habits, consorting with wife abusers, living with sexual deviants. This is not New York, after all. This is Ann Arbor."

"Couldn't Joe testify on my behalf?"

Adam shook his head. "They've got Joe for drinking on the job. He's afraid of losing the little he has. And he's no friend of yours, anyway. My hunch is he had a thing for you, and you turned a cold shoulder. He'd be a hostile witness at best."

"If I ever thought of a trial, you've convinced me otherwise. The idea of that creature asking for some kind of rights is horrifying," I said finally. "I'm not even sure if I could recognize—"

Adam grimaced, and reached into his back blue jeans pocket. He pulled out a picture of a picture. It was Tat.

I don't think I made a sound. I was glad I was lying in bed. I was glad the baby kept doing little bumper car maneuvers inside me.

"I remember him," I said.

Adam looked gray, and implacable. "I called in another marker from a guy in Chicago. He taped the guy in what I supposed you'd call–" Adam's mouth twisted– "casual conversation."

Adam picked up a bottle of "Mountain Spring," and took a long draw from it. Then he sat down by the bed.

"Look, Susan," he said. "I'm going to say something, and I'm probably going to botch it. I'm probably saying this too early, or too late, but.... I know you were abused. I saw it right at the beginning. I wish to Christ I'd said something, done something, right then—but I didn't. Of course, you're a beautiful woman—a beautiful woman about to give birth to someone else's baby. I expected to hate Randall, and I did. On this tape, my friend led the conversation to, you know, women. Women and—*escapades*— He started talking about broads and babes with legs and racks and– And Randall—*bit*. He bragged about it. About you. Not explicitly, of course. But they said Ann Arbor women were hot to trot, and he made a joke about 'a waitress who couldn't wait for it' and a special that wasn't on the menu. He said there was 'no case like a rape case.'"

The words that had been pressing to get out, got out finally: "Am I a 'rape case' to you, Adam?"

I had wondered what Adam, angry, would look like. Now I knew: the planes of his face turned gently, like shades. And where there had been opening, and light, there was closure now. Other people got red in the face and looked volatile, Adam had tears in his eyes.

"I'm really sorry to be telling you this, especially now, when you're in the hospital, waiting, but I realized when I was listening to the tape that I'm screwed up, Susan. Not like he is, God knows. But for years and years now, there's been this, I don't know—hunger in me. And I wanted a woman to love and be loved by, and I wanted that to be physical and something else—mental, spiritual—I don't know. And it was like I could have either one, but not both. Because the women who drew me in, with their laughs, their caring for people, seemed all bottled up when it came to sex. And the other women, the ones who were easy in bed, were all messed up otherwise.

"This isn't what I wanted to say, though. What I wanted to say was that listening to Randy in that bar made me sick. It made me want to kill him. But I've been your willing agent in all of this. And I've fallen in love with you, of course. Which is not the romantic thing it is in the movies. It's a horrible pain in the neck, to be honest. I've got feelings for you I don't

THE AFTERMATH

know what to do with. Scary feelings. I'm forty-nine years old, and I've been married, and raised three boys, and I've never felt like this.

"And when you say something like you wonder if you're just a rape case to me, I feel angrier than I've ever felt in my life, and the worst part is that always before when I've been angry, I've wanted to hit someone. And even though I have never and would never hit a woman, even when that woman was hitting *me*, I've wanted to. And now—when I get angry at you, I want to hit *myself*. I want to beat myself up for being who I am, for being a rough-necked, hairy, primitive man who's not worthy to love you or be loved by you.

"And this doesn't mean that I think you're perfect. There are spaces in you that scare me, deserts where there ought to be gardens. But the opposite is true, too. And I don't know if any of that can be changed or will change. And it doesn't matter.

"I want you to live with me, you and the baby. I want to marry you, if you'll have me. I was going to buy you a ring, but something in me said you wouldn't want that. My sense is that a ring would scare you, at best, and weigh on you, at worst. If I'm wrong, I have no doubt you'll tell me.

"So what I did was get you this. At first, I thought a diamond, to go with my spade tattoo. But it didn't seem right. Anyway, I hope this will do—" He let the sentence trail off and handed me a little white box. Inside, was a key chain with a medallion and two keys on it.

"That's the front and back door keys to my house," Adam said.

"What about your car?" I finally dared a look at him.

Adam laughed. "See, now? That's you to a 'T'. I talk about marriage and I give you my house keys, and what do you do? You ask for my car key. And the answer to your question is, nobody's ever driven my car but me. I might see things differently in the future, of course. Probably about the time *she's*—" he pointed to my belly— "ready to drive."

I pulled the key chain out of the box. The medallion was of Saint Francis. He was holding one hand out, palm up; he had birds at his feet. "St. Francis, Pray for Us," was written around the outside of the medallion.

Holding the key chain in my left hand, close to my heart, I reached out for Adam with my right hand.

"And–" Adam said. "Just in case, I bought a few things, and kind of spruced up the spare room. I don't know if you saw it, but it's big and sunny, and would make a great nursery. You could have my room, if you want, or bunk in with the baby."

For a moment, I saw myself entering the house, the baby on my hip. I saw myself in a rocker, rocking the baby to sleep in a big, sunny nursery. What I did not see was any gun belts, or mannequins in camouflage.

"Do you really think it would be good for a baby growing up with a bunch of military stuff?" I asked.

Adam shrugged. "I already took the gun belts off the stairs," he said. "That was stupid of me. I could put everything like that in the basement, put a Gone Fishing sign up on Firebase Manderley- another stupid thing. Maybe I'll sell everything and buy you a stroller with gun turrets." He laughed. "But, really, Susan. I just proposed to you, you know. You're supposed to say 'yes' or 'no' or something about that. I think. I don't know...."

"I don't either, Adam," I said. "I think I love you, but it's all too much. The rape, the baby, David. I'd like to say yes, but it would be so conditional, I think I should just– I don't know. Thank you for the keys. I really would like to try moving in with you. But even the question of marriage doesn't seem important next to the real question, the real thing I need to decide, which is about him. About 'Rat a tat tat....

"From what you were saying, a trial would be way too dangerous. Whether I won or lost, I might have "Tat" to deal with for the rest of my life, and so would the baby. I might even– lose custody."

Adam nodded. "In a rape case, the big thing the prosecution has going for it is the witness's testimony. And you don't remember. Or at least you didn't. You and I know why—or think we do: because of the GHB. But the law doesn't care what we know, it only cares about what we can *prove*."

I could feel my temperature sky-rocketing. I kicked off the blankets.

"Are you mad at me, Susan?"

"No, of course not. How could I be? But I think the world would be a lot better if women just had babies with other women. They could do it now, you know—the scientists? Birth could be all a matter of parthenogenesis. Think of it. Two women giving birth—only to girls. The world could go on. Only it would be a peaceful world. A virtually-crimeless world. Because the women of the world could live in harmony with each other and raise children in cooperation with each other. And there wouldn't be any wars or any rapes or parents abusing their children in closets, sticking their penises down their daughters' throats, making them gag, filling them with filth and terror. Some men will say anything to get their testosterone-soaked way with whatever female they happen to want to have *at,* never mind if she's under age or his daughter or a waitress who happens to be handy. If this baby is born a boy, I—I—I don't know what I'll do."

I could see my father in the closet, kneeling over me: I could feel myself starting to gag. And then I was under the desk, and

267

Tat was on top of me and I tried to pull away from him, but my head kept bumping the desk, and I remembered moaning because it hurt and because I thought it would be over sooner and then I remembered lying flat and father was still on me but inert and I thought he might be dead and then he started to dig into me from behind and it hurt a lot and I started to scream but Tat grabbed my hair and pulled my head back until I ran out of breath and passed out and just before I left myself and a mess of pain behind, I heard a voice in my ears that was mine and my father's all mixed up together, high and low in one twisted rope, and the voice said, "We're going to forget this happened. Forget it. Forget it."

The next thing I knew Adam was sitting beside me on the bed, and Adam's voice, the voice I had come to trust, said, "It's okay, Susan. I'd never do anything to force or hurt you." He began to sing a gruff sing-song lullaby.

"Hush a bye. Don't you cry. All the pretty little horses. Black and gray, white and bay. All the pretty little horses."

It worked, finally. The baby calmed down and, some time later, I followed suit.

I felt ashamed of myself, and it was hard to look at Adam.

Before he left, he sat back in his chair, took my hand, and, looking at the floor, said. "You didn't forget, Susan. You didn't forget what your father did. You didn't forget what Tat did. What that says to me is, you're a survivor. We'll see this through, each in our own way. I'll help you as best I can."

"What just happened, Adam? I mean, just now, when I kind of blanked out?"

"You had a flashback, I think. At least, that's the way it seemed. I know about them. After Desert Storm, I got them all the time."

"Do you hate me now, Adam?"

"Because of what you said? —Of course not." Adam sighed. "It's taken me years to stop hating myself, Susan. I won't go back there anymore, not even if I thought it would help you, which I don't."

Adam walked over to the window and stared out at the darkening world. "I should go. I'd like to kiss you good night, if that's okay."

"I think so."

Adam came to the bed slowly, as if someone were pulling him, bent down, and kissed me gently on the forehead. "What a world," he said.

He kissed me again, hard on the mouth, and I felt wild love rising in me. But even before it was over, I could feel Tat looming over us, grabbing me, having at me....

"Adam," I said. "I want you to kill him. To end his existence. I can't do it. But you can. I want you to do this for me, Adam. For me and the baby."

"Susan," Adam said. "God knows I..." He looked as though he were in agony. " It's an impulse, Susan. I understand the impulse. But an impulse is one thing and an act another."

"I know, Adam," I said, "but that's what I really want. I don't see any other way to be rid of him. He comes after me in nightmares."

"I know," Adam said. "I hope he stops."

And he was gone.

When I opened my eyes the next morning, the first thing I saw was Carolina standing in the doorway with Adam, who looked more than a little like an unsuccessful cross-dresser. He was wearing a vest that gave him the shape of a pregnant woman, complete with breasts and mounded belly.

I burst out laughing.

"Laugh if you like," Adam said, laughing.

Carolina was laughing, too. "Adam is modeling an educational device correctly referred to as an 'Empathy Belly'."

"I think it's a little late for that, don't you?"

Carolina smiled. "It's a left-over from a pregnancy class they give here. I thought we could set it up in a chair and provide your visitors with a little comic relief."

I measured out the rest of the day in hospital trays and vital statistics. I was lying in bed, alone, watching the shadows in the room lengthen as the sun sank behind the trees at the limits of my vision. I began to ask myself uncomfortable questions, and to arrive at even more uncomfortable answers.

I remembered the minister of my childhood saying, "Be careful what you set your heart on—You're liable to get it." I had wanted Adam to find out what happened, and, now that he *had*, I wanted more. I wanted him to act on his knowledge.

Maybe I could leave my knowledge of the rape and the thought of revenge behind me in the dust.

But Randall might have raped other women before me. Maybe if those women had done something, he would not have raped me. If I did nothing–if Adam did nothing to stop him, maybe he would keep going.

I was no vigilante and did not believe in a private citizen taking matters into her own hands. Not if that private citizen were me, anyway. But that was just what I had done, or made possible, wasn't it? First I asked Adam to find him. Then I asked Adam to kill him.

Now what?

All my reflections and fantasies and worries and agitation had a way of ending up, like tracks disappearing into snow, in the single proverb, "Where there are two alternatives, take the third." I was beginning to hate that proverb.

That afternoon, Adam and I played Scrabble. He won, but only because I generously allowed him "entwife" as his first word. Then we told jokes and non-controversial stories.

Adam even gave me a little childbirth-coaching class. After I had cleared it personally with Dr. O. and "the powers that seem to be," I persuaded a shoeless and hospital-gowned Adam to climb awkwardly up into bed behind me.

When he got into place behind me, his agitation was palpable. I tried to tease him about his obvious distress, but he was having none of it. "When people talk about going to bed together for the first time, Susan, this isn't generally what they picture."

We both laughed at this, and the childbirth practice went pretty well after that.

Chapter 18

The Boot and the Trout

I had bad dreams that night. I dreamt I was trying to put the baby into a shoe box, and she was too big. "She's too big for her britches," someone said, and it was true. The baby looked like a dwarf three year old and kept sticking out her tongue, which was long and forked, like a snake's. I finally managed to get the baby into a box, only to discover it was a brick.

I woke up abruptly.

When Raitlin came in and gave me a wan but non-sardonic smile, I felt a rush of appreciation for him. "How's David?"

"He's better today."

"What's the matter, Raitlin?"

"I can't say, Susan. You'll have to ask David that."

I started to protest, but Raitlin looked so distressed, I didn't have the heart to continue. "Look—I've brought you something to take our minds off cares and woes." He stepped back out the door and came back in carrying a hooded basket by its two handles; the basket was woven of what appeared to be pale green reeds. Raitlin handed it over to me with a kind of shy pride: it was soft and light and lined with a pink and blue striped flannel blanket that had been tucked down into the weave of the reeds. "This is really all you need," Raitlin said. "And it's not even tainted with bad karma."

"What are you talking about?"

"It was made in Bolivia, by workers who belong to a union. No sweat shop wages or unsavory conditions."

I was really touched. "Thank you so much, Rait. This is the first thing I've seen that I can actually imagine putting the baby into," I told him. "Other than myself, of course."

I gave the basket back to him, since it was bulky for the bed, and Raitlin sat with it in his lap for the rest of his visit. Our talk began rather superficially but evolved gradually into a discussion of what was meant by the word, "family."

"You were born into a family," Raitlin said after a while. "I've had to invent mine."

I thought of telling him what the family I'd been born into had been like but decided against it and said I'd never really understood why he'd agreed to my moving in along with David.

"I liked you," Raitlin said. "I still like you. You and I have a lot in common. Well, maybe not a lot– but our love for David. That gives me the idea that maybe I can help you."

"And that's why you let me move in? So you could help me?"

Raitlin favored me with one of his whiplash smiles. "Look, Susie-Q. I know I must seem like an old has-been or some twisted dirty old man to you. But I'm not even sixty. Sixty isn't old, you know, but I'm old. I'm prematurely old. I was probably *born* old. And you know why? The answer is, 'It doesn't matter.'" 'Why' only matters with things you can change."

The baby was exploring the inside of my skin, so gently it tickled and distracted me. "I don't know what you're saying, R, but please keep going. Sometimes, I catch up to you."

Raitlin grinned—a positively-Cheshire-cat-no-holds-barred-you're-my-kind-of-gal kind of grin. "Thanks for the nickname," he said. "Did you ever hear of patterning, Susie-Q? I don't know if it's been discredited or what—half the things I grew up with have been, you know—Hell, *I've* been discredited myself, as far as that goes—But there used to be this thing called patterning. A bunch of friends and neighbors would take this kid that had been brain injured so he couldn't move his legs or something, and they'd work with him, day in and day out, moving the leg up and down, up and down. The theory—and supposedly the results actually matched the theory in this one special case—was that even though the human mechanism was supposed to work by the brain's telling the leg what to do, if the leg repeated a motion over and over, it could work the other way, too, as a last resort.

"I'm like that, Susie. I was born without the aptitude for a family. But then I saw this stupid little maxim on a cocktail napkin of all dignified places, and it said, *"Friends are the family we make for ourselves."* And that's when I asked David to move in. And he, bless his soul, whatever obscure and idiosyncratic reasons he had, talked about wanting to bring you along into it, whatever it was, whatever it would become. Hell, he was probably afraid to move in alone with an old queer such as myself.

"And the thing is— I'm trying never to use "but" again, because everything is all connected with everything else by "ands," as far as I can see— my twisted little heart leapt for joy. It was a two-for-one special, don't you see? If I hadn't just met you, and been wowed by you, it would have been very different. But—I mean *And yet*— I *had* and *was*."

"You were wowed by me? You didn't just think I was the Susie-cream-cheese nebbish friend of David's, the downside you had to accept to get the upside?"

Raitlin giggled. It was the campiest he had ever sounded and it made me giggle, too.

"What did you find to like about me, anyway, Rait? My naiveté?"

"You're fishing, Susie. See, that's okay. The world is divided into fisher folk and non-fisher folk, and you and I are among the former. We just have to be prepared for what we hook, you know? We might come up with a boot instead of a trout—a big, black, shiny, fascist boot, not the pretty little trout we wanted to grill over our pretty little campfire."

"Raitlin, are you–?"

He waved at me. "I'm okay. I just haven't been getting enough sleep. I like that you're a survivor— I can almost see the high school yearbook, "Voted Most Likely to Survive." And I like the fact you always mean well. At whatever cost to yourself and those around you, you are still intent on operating with the best or most innocent of intentions."

Raitlin shrugged, then he leaned forward and took my hand. "Of course, you have beautiful eyes, darling, but this is not the place to catalogue them. I want to be one of the several men who love the pilgrim soul in you, Susie-Q."

I started to cry. Raitlin smiled, not unkindly, and produced a travel pack of Kleenex from his back pocket. I waved them away. "That's another thing I love about you— You're reliable in your reactions. Whenever you're overwhelmed and feel the need to punt, you cry."

I stopped crying.

Raitlin laughed.

Despite my best efforts, I laughed, too. "Maybe you're right, R. I'll think about what you said. Maybe not until after the baby is born, but I will think about it."

"Don't feel obliged, in any case," Raitlin said. "Look upon what I just said as a free trial-size sum up of your personality, offered by a fellow sufferer. No obligation."

Nurses came in and asked Raitlin to "vacate the premises" for a while. I thanked him for the basket. He smiled and said David had been working on a new and improved infant car bed. I started to ask him if David's flu was still the reason he gave for not coming to see me.

But Raitlin cut me off.

"You know," he said, standing sideways in the doorway; the nurse, clearly disapproving of and defeated by his continued presence, had to brush past him on her way out. "I never thought David would be my partner. I never dared to hope that high. When I heard you were pregnant, that just sort of cinched it. I saw myself as some kind of *pater familias*, I guess. As life goes for a man like me, that's rather a noble role, I think." Raitlin shrugged. "Then Carolina showed up and allowed me to add her to our little enclave. I know full well how abrasive and 'not what you want' she can be. But she's happy in good times, you know, and strong in bad times. And if you come to see her the way I do, as this kind of amazing *brick*—Well, she's a gift for all seasons.

"I don't know about Wilde, really; he's awfully wily, you know—wily in a way a straight pervert can never be. And yet, however it may have been for Wilde, *I* really wanted a family, Susie. That's the weird thing. Most of my life had gone by without my knowing what I wanted. I rattled around in that big old house, and it was a death trap for me. It was a death trap until you came—you and David and Carolina, bless her maiden-aunt-down-to-the-bedrock soul.

"Don't count on being able to figure your life out later, Suze. That's my advice. Life is like this multiple choice test and it's not that hard, but everything depends on your doing well, and they don't give you much time. Time pressure is part of the test."

Raitlin came back and stood by the bed. He took my hand slowly, and held it between the two of his, as though he had just discovered something valuable, but designed for an obscure purpose.

"No matter what you think of me, Susan, I want you to know one thing." Raitlin's voice and hands were shaking. I thought for a minute he was pretending to be emotional, but a glance at his face told me otherwise: it was grim and steeled. "I really love David," he said. "I mean, lay-down-my-life-for-him *love* David."

And Raitlin began to cry. He cried the way some little children cry, his sobs laced with great, big, ragged gasping for air. The nurse stuck her head in the door, and thought better of coming in.

And I knew without having to be told. I asked only for confirmation.

"He's sick, isn't he?"

Raitlin's nods turned into up and down keening.

"Cancer?"

"Yes."

"What kind?"

Raitlin stopped crying, blew his nose, pulled the chair up from behind him, and sat down on the edge, so little on the chair, I thought for a moment he was going to fall on the floor. He sighed once, then took a deep breath, as though he needed to get a running start on the words. "They took a half liter of fluid out of his right lung two days ago. Yesterday, they operated and took out another three. The diagnosis is 'Non-small cell Stage 2 metastatic adenocarcinoma, unknown primary, currently manifesting as a pleural effusion'."

"Oh, my god," I said. "Oh, my dear, sweet god."

Raitlin and I were hugging by then, hugging and crying together.

After a few moments, he pulled back and looked at me. "He has only a tiny chance of surviving this, Susie. One per cent, they said."

"Who said?"

"They did. The doctors. Three of them. They came into his room wearing their white coats and they sat down and said they could offer him only 'palliative care' and he had a one percent chance of long-term survival."

Raitlin clutched my hand really hard. It was surprising to me that it hurt. "You know what he told them, Susie? Do you? He looked at them in that sweet, I-could-be-contemptuous-and-I'm-not, way of his, and said, "Is there any chance you guys are in the wrong room?" Raitlin began to sob again. "I shouldn't have told you," he gasped. "This is the last thing you need—This is the last thing any of us need...."

"I'm glad you told me," I said. "I want to go see him."

"What, now? That's not even possible for you, is it?"

"What's not possible is that three doctors told David he has no more than a one per cent chance of staying alive. I want to see him, and, for once, I'm not just going to lie here and wait for someone to make that happen. I'm going to make it happen myself.... You're permitted to help, though."

Raitlin smiled through his tears. "Tell me what to do."

"Do you have time?"

"Absolutely."

"Well, first of all, go get that nurse that keeps poking her head in here. Tell her I'm about to leave here against medical advice."

"Wait, Susie. You don't have to leave anywhere. David's upstairs, on the eighth floor—in the cancer and gerontology wing."

"What—? Oh god. Well, I'm as sorry as hell to hear that, but it certainly makes it a lot easier. Just go tell the nurse I need to see her, then."

Raitlin did as instructed: in a few minutes, he was back in the room, said nurse in tow. "You want to take my vitals, right?"

She allowed as how that was right.

"Okay. So take my vitals, and then I'm going to use a bedpan—sorry, Raitlin—and then I'm going to lie absolutely still, like a perfect left-sided angel, while my friend here wheels me up to the eighth floor, to the cancer and gerontology clinic."

"Wait, Susie," Raitlin said. "I know you want to do this, and I want to help you, but—"

"Raitlin? Are you chickening out on me at this late date?"

I had meant it as a joke, but Raitlin turned pale; there was no doubt I had hurt him. I wanted to apologize immediately but was afraid the apology would only hurt him more. "I just think you need to check with David before going up there. I'm not entirely sure he wants to see you—or anybody."

"Of course. If he doesn't feel like seeing me now, that's okay. I'm not going anywhere."

Raitlin disappeared and Carolina came in. We talked about nothing, in between nursely probings and mutterings. She noticed my untouched dinner tray.

I mumbled something about not having much appetite. Carolina considered me shrewdly. "Raitlin told you, didn't he?" she asked.

"Yes," I said. "He did. Why didn't you or Raitlin tell me a long time ago?"

Carolina flushed. "We didn't *know* a long time ago," she said. "That's the short answer. The other short answer is, David asked us not to."

"Why?"

"I'm not good at speaking for other people, Susan. Especially not when they're David. You can ask him that question yourself, if you need to."

"My not eating wasn't all about David. I don't feel like eating, that's all."

"Are you having contractions?"

"I don't think so. Not really. Sometimes I have cramps or something, but there's no pattern to them. I'm not nauseated. I just don't feel like eating. That's probably just nerves, right? I mean, if I were having contractions, I'd know it, wouldn't I?"

Carolina stared at me. "Did you read that little book I gave you?" She didn't wait for my response, which would have been that I didn't remember her giving me a book, but that all the books I'd read indicated I'd have plenty of forewarning that labor was about to begin.

Carolina didn't seem to need a response. "Page 31," she said. "'Contractions in the latent phase of labor are mild to moderate, regular or irregular, ranging between 5 and 20 minutes apart, and become progressively closer together, not necessarily in a consistent pattern.'"

"Well, there hasn't been anything like that—" I began.

Carolina waved me into silence and submission with a single dismissive wave of her unoccupied left hand. "If I may finish quoting— 'Some women don't notice them at all.' Speaking of which, where are the books and games I sent over?"

"Still in the suitcase, probably. I haven't opened it."

"Why not?" The tone of Carolina's voice made it impossible to get angry with her. There was nothing accusatory about it at all. It was a neutral voice, a childlike voice. Curiosity had crowded out emotion.

"I don't know," I said, striving for the same honesty. "I guess I didn't want to be distracted."

"You're supposed to be distracted at this point."

"I know, but—Look, Carolina. This is a job, sort of. And I'm a one job at a time, do it right kind of person."

Carolina did the last thing I would have expected her to do in response to that statement: she grinned. "Me, too," she said.

We both laughed then—me, a little uncertainly, because I didn't know what was funny. When I'd recovered myself, I picked up the topic again. "The nurse last night said I shouldn't even ask myself if I were having contractions or not. She said the monitor would decide whether I was heading into labor or not."

"That's ridiculous.... Do you mind?" Carolina lifted up my hospital gown and probed my belly gently with her hands.

We both stared at the monitor screen, at the left of which was a green line crawling down along the edge like a snake.

"There's something funny here," Carolina said. She had me ring for a nurse—not the same one who had said the monitor would decide– and instructed her, not too politely, I thought, to check the monitor contacts. The nurse obligingly adjusted my green belt and fiddled with the back of the monitor.

"That ought to do the trick," she said, and turned to go.

"Wait a minute," I said. It had suddenly occurred to me that I didn't know anyone's name. "What's your name?"

"I'm Elizabeth," the nurse said. She gave me a big smile. "I just came on," she said, "but I'm here until late tonight, so we may have a chance to get acquainted. Holler if you need anything. I'll be back in a minute for vitals."

She waved and went out the door. *Elizabeth*, I thought. *Elizabeth is a nice name. And it goes with "Lucy."*

"That's better," Carolina said. I thought for a moment she had read my mind and agreed with "Elizabeth" as a good middle name.

But she was still probing, and still staring at the monitor. The baby's heartbeat had gone back to the wrong neighborhood—but that was okay: she was just relaxing.

As I stared at the green tracing on the screen, my belly began to fist itself. It tightened past tightening, and then it tightened some more. It went from odd to uncomfortable to very uncomfortable to painful. And stopped there. And stayed there—like a train behind schedule, waiting by a station marked: "Painful."

The monitor line rose gently in response, plateaued, then—as my belly relaxed—sank down again. The two seemed to be having a conversation, egging each other on. I was just the battleground for their competition.

The thought of contractions, which had been playful before, began to be a lot less funny. I asked the nurse to turn off the monitor. "I think the monitor is daring me to go into labor," I told her.

The nurse laughed, and said Dr. O. would be called.

Raitlin came back and said David wasn't "averse" to having me visit, but he wanted to wait until morning, when he hoped to be feeling "less himself."

"That cinches it," Carolina said. She didn't sound exactly smug but she was still a little annoying. She was staring at the monitor, as though it were a crucifix or something. The baby's heartbeat was plugging along in the "138" neighborhood again. Oh, well, she would be a tomboy, good at climbing trees. She would beat the boys at their own games and be queen of her own....

"What cinches what?" I asked. "What are you talking about?"

"You sound like someone going into active labor," Carolina said meditatively, almost as if to herself.

"How so?" I was waiting for her to say I was "dreamlike" or "focused" or even "intense." I could think of so many acceptable answers.

"You sound really irritable," she said. Now she had me. If I objected to her evaluation, I would only sound more irritable.

I wanted to say that I wasn't irritable but hurt. I was torn between feelings of grief for David, and shock and hurt feelings and anxiety for what seemed about to happen.

"Time for a little palpation," Carolina announced. "I want you to roll over and stay on your back for a minute."

After weeks of being told to stay on my side, I was thrilled by Carolina's command. I did as instructed.

She moved her right hand over my belly like a geiger counter. Her eyes were closed. For some reason, I thought of black and white movies, and men looking for treasure in old mines.

The baby's heartbeat went up a little. "139... 140... 144." It seemed to me she didn't like being prodded. I knew I didn't.

"Where's your watch?" Carolina asked.

"It's after 11:30." Raitlin loomed up behind Carolina, and put his big, silver pocket watch in her outstretched left hand. "Behold, I give you 'the mausoleum of all hope and desire'," he said. Carolina didn't crack a smile.

"Back into the background for you, kiddo," she told him. Then she handed the watch to me.

"Time this," she said, her eyes still closed.

I looked at the watch. 11:42 and ten seconds. 11:42 and twenty seconds. 11:42 and thirty seconds.

I looked over at Raitlin, but he turned away, clearly embarrassed, and walked over to the window.

"There's nothing happening," I told Carolina. "I'm not having a contraction."

"I know that," she said. "But from now on, there will never be 'nothing happening'. This—the trough you're in now—" (I saw pigs about to feed: the trough was full of apple peels and potato scraps) "is called an interval. You need to time those, too. An interval is not nothing, Susie. It's the time between contractions—regrouping time. We need to know the duration of the intervals, the duration of the contractions, and the intensity of the contractions—those three."

"I don't understand," I told her. She was still pressing too hard on my belly, and the baby still didn't like it: she was taking out her displeasure on me. I could feel something bony trying to poke up out of my skin, like a branch under ice. For the first time, I felt it might actually come through.

Raitlin, standing over by the window, looked unfathomably sad. Of course, he was thinking about David. I should be thinking about David, too. What kind of a friend was I? He hadn't even wanted me to know. Probably thought I couldn't handle it. He was right.

The baby jabbed me, hard.

And then, like a tidal wave, it hit. "Aaaah," I said, trusting Carolina to know that meant, "Contraction beginning." This time the contraction came with tidal, oceanic force. I was between a rock and a hard place, and the distance was narrowing. I was being twisted like a rope, squeezed like a dishtowel after all the water's been wrung out.

Just when I thought I couldn't take it anymore, it let go— the tidal wave that had been carrying me tossed me up on the dunes and retreated and I was left lying in the sand.

THE AFTERMATH

"It's over. Finally. I forgot TO TIME IT," i said fighting
to regain something more than composure—some faint sense
of myself—who I was and what I was doing, as though that
mattered in the face of what was happening, what I wanted
to happen.

"Almost a minute," Carolina said.

Adam came in, and I tried to cover my face with a towel.
I couldn't breathe, so I took it off again. Adam, Raitlin and
Carolina— they all began to laugh.

"Welcome to the funny farm," I told Adam. "I'm really
glad to see you." Then I turned to Carolina. "That's going to
come back again, isn't it?"

Carolina smiled. "You betchum, Red Rider," she said, a
little too gleefully, it seemed to me.

"So, what happens now?" I asked.

Carolina looked at Adam, who only nodded. That irritated me. Carolina was my midwife. Why did she need to be
checking with Adam before speaking? "I suppose I could give
you my second stage speech," she said.

"Let me just say 'hi' first," Adam said. He came over to
the bed but did not sit down. he took my fingertips in his and
gave me a funny little limp kind of shake. "Hi there, Susan,"
he said.

"It's nice to hear my name again," I told him. "Can you
stay?"

Adam looked at me, then at Carolina. Now, he was doing
it. "I'm here for the duration," he said.

Raitlin moved toward the door. "I think I'll sit this one
out," he told Carolina.

"As you wish," she said, and he left.

"Here it is," Carolina told me, moving in closer to the
bed, so Adam was forced to step back and to the side. "Labor

285

is a natural process that has pain as a normal component. The intervals between contractions are relatively free of discomfort. If you are prepared for the pain, you will not have as hard a time with it."

She stepped back and gestured to Adam. "Would you care to talk about the sources of pain?"

Adam looked at me. "Are you up for this?"

"I am."

Adam nodded. "Okay. Well, labor pain is basically two-fold. Contractions come when the uterine fibers squeeze together. The uterine muscle is composed of circular, longitudinal, and 'figure-eight' fibers, and these tighten the muscle in every possible direction, creating a painful sensation."

"Right," said Carolina. "But the uterus doesn't actually squeeze the baby out; rather, it slowly draws the cervix up over the baby's head—"

"It's sort of like when you pull a turtleneck sweater on," Adam said. "But the second, and more significant, source of pain occurs as the cervix and vagina are gradually stretched to allow the baby to pass through the birth canal...." He turned to Carolina.

"I couldn't have said it better myself."

They both looked very pleased with themselves. "Well, there didn't seem to be anything very gradual about that last contraction, I can tell you that," I said.

They smiled. They were doing everything in concert. It was driving me a little nuts.

Another contraction hit. Even as I was struggling up the steep sideways slope shown in the monitor, Carolina and Adam were orchestrating everything. "Would you mind being timekeeper?" Carolina asked Adam; it seemed to me she was talking too loud.

"Not at all." It seemed to me Adam was talking very loudly, too. Maybe because there was a roaring in my ears, like rushing water, only different.

The world got very dark. I felt as though I were going to pass out. I remembered a maxim from the first childbirth book: "Keep pain in perspective."

But the only perspective I could seem to keep it in was the perspective of someone who's staring it in the face, who's looking down its bloody gullet, hearing the gnash of its teeth, smelling the stink of its breath of its breath. *Don't forget*, I told myself. *This is what you want.*

Raitlin stuck his head back in the door. "Would you like a popsicle?" he asked. He didn't seem to be addressing me particularly: it made sense that my responding, 'NO! THANKS!' was general, too.

The pain was gone. I was alone again, under a darkening sky.

Despite my yelling, Raitlin stayed around after that.

Adam smiled beatifically at me, even as he asked Carolina about "the state of the pad."

She peered in under the gown and nodded. "Bloody tinge," she said. And they smiled beatifically at each other, as though "bloody tinge" was just the ticket.

Dr. O. put in an appearance a nerve-wracking while later. She did a brief palpation and examination. She and Carolina and Adam threw numbers and nods back and forth at each other, and stared at the monitor. I might have found this irritating, had my contractions not been tossing me back and forth at the same time.

Carolina informed Dr. O. that my cervix had been ripe since she'd first come in. I wanted to ask if that was why I smelled something like soft peaches in the room. But apparently I was not to do anything. Carolina and Adam and Dr. O. let me know that they had everything well under control. From time to time, I glanced at Raitlin, who would shrug and shoot me a quizzical, 'I don't know what's happening either' look. I wanted to hug him.

After weeks of lying on my side, I was encouraged by Meeny, Miney, and Mo, to get up and walk around the room. One of them said the baby was engaged—another referred to her as having successfully dropped. Somebody remarked that the importance of working well as a team in labor "could not be over-emphasized." But none of them seemed to think that I had much to do with the team, or what was happening. I was apparently some kind of a center, who would pass them the ball when they gave me the signal.

Dr. O. left to do her rounds, informing me for the seventh or eighth time that I was in the best of hands with Carolina and Adam "on board." She promised to return within the hour, and to be beeper-accessible until then.

I was too busy to pay much attention to her going. Carolina and Adam had me up and walking. The two of them gave me counsel in stereo, much of which only confused or at best, distracted me.

Adam suggested I "remain physically relaxed, even limp" during contractions. Carolina told me to focus my mind "on calming thoughts or visualizations."

Adam said I had "started off well in labor," and was likely to continue in that mode.

Raitlin took over the duties of timekeeper, while Adam and I performed what he called a "labor ballet," dragging the fetal monitor behind us as we tried eight different "postures," one by one. The first posture was called "slow dancing," but I thought it would better be labeled "marathon dancing:" I leaned against Adam as much as I dared and we shuffled slowly around the room.

"Where's the music?" I asked.

"Good idea," said Carolina. In a moment, Vivaldi's "Spring" filled the air. filled the air.

"Ah," said Raitlin. "Debeers diamond music. People always get it confused with Vivaldi." "It's that DeBeers diamond music. People always get them confused."

While Carolina rattled on about slow dancing's advantages—"It encourages rotation and descent, as well as adding comfort," I found myself developing a waking dream that Adam and I were marathon dancers about to win a great prize, if I could just keep going. But before I could really develop this fantasy, Adam said it was time to shift to walking.

Now he and I paraded around the room. In this fantasy, we were married. We were walking in the park, very much in love.

Immediately, Carolina was there to break off this posture, and instruct me in another. In this one, I stood at the foot of the bed. I leaned forward with my arms on the edge of the bed, and she produced a large blue beach ball, which she called "a birthing ball." I rested my chin on this. Now I was a little girl, resting my chin on mommy's tummy,

The next three postures were much less satisfactory from my point of view, since none of them involved Adam. Posture #5 was "the lunge"—I stood next to a chair and put first one foot and then the other up on the seat; then I "lunged" toward the chair. With the contractions coming as frequently as they were—only a matter of minutes apart by this time—my "lunges" were almost indiscernible. Carolina said lunging encouraged rotation of an occiput posterior fetus.

"Is that what I've got?" I asked.

"No," Carolina admitted.

"Okay, then," I said. "Then maybe we could move on?" It was between contractions, and I felt momentarily confident.

The last position was "semi-sitting." This was the one Adam and I had already practiced. He sat behind me on the bed, and I tried to relax into his arms, practicing slow breathing.

After a minute or two, I found myself wanting to do something else: my breathing sounded tense and labored; I found it very easy to speed up, and very hard to slow down.

"Tune into your contractions," Adam advised from behind me. "Try to adapt your breathing patterns as needed; that way, you'll continue getting enough oxygen while you calm yourself with the rhythm of your breathing."

"I'd rather calm myself with the rhythm of *your* breathing," I told him.

He laughed; the sound of his laughing, and the jiggling of his body as he did so made me feel a little less nervous.

"Good," said Carolina, from somewhere far off, way down between my legs. "She's more than 90 per cent effaced," I heard her say.

"I suppose you want me completely effaced," I murmured. And Adam laughed again.

I wanted to ask them to take off the diamond music and put on a comedy tape. I wanted to say that Adam's laughing was the only thing that seemed to relax me. But I was too busy battling contractions to say much of anything.

I was swimming now in a rough sea. I had fallen off the cruise ship: I could see it disappearing into the distance without me. I was afraid of drowning.

I was busy. I was going through postures and breathing patterns. I was offered water and juice and flat ginger ale. I was given Popsicles and ice chips to suck on.

"She's fully dilated," someone said. It was Dr. O. —or a mirage that looked like her.

"The baby is beginning to descend," said a deeper voice.

Someone was hiccupping. The hiccups turned to belches. I was embarrassed at first, but when someone asked if I felt like throwing up, I realized the belches for what they were, and was grateful they weren't worse.

I felt aching in my back and thighs. My legs began to tremble, and the rest of my body seemed to want to follow suit. I clamped down against this tendency and felt a gushing between my legs.

"Don't worry," someone said. "It's just more bloody show."

"What does a bloody show *show* though," I asked, apparently aloud, because someone laughed. That was when I realized I was on my back again, and Adam was gone.

"Adam? Why aren't you behind me?"

"Because I'm beside you," a voice said.

Someone took my hand.

I opened my eyes to see. I was in a different room. "Somebody moved the room," I said.

Adam smiled. "You dozed off," he said. "You're in a birthing room now. See? The end of this bed comes off."

"I need to go to the bathroom," I said.

"Don't worry," someone told me.

I stopped holding a breath I hadn't known I was holding.

"Good," someone said. It sounded like Raitlin.

"Raitlin—are you here?"

"Present and accounted for, Susie-Q."

"This is really scary," I said.

"Everything is fine. You're doing really well," someone said.

"Is the baby okay?" I asked. "Don't let them do anything bad to the baby," I said.

"Everybody here loves you and wants to help," someone said.

"This is taking forever," I said. "I can't take any more."

There was a big silence—a big, yawning, cavernous silence.
I was alone.
I was walking on the edge of a cliff.
I had swallowed a grenade. I was about to explode. I would fall to my death.
I was alone.
"When you can't take any more, there's no more to take," someone said.
I thought I knew who it was. "Dr. Oh No?" I asked.
"Here," someone said. And then, "You can push now."
I pushed.
I was pushed.
I felt a buildup.
I gave in.
It happened.
I pushed.
"You're almost there," said someone.
"Good," said someone.
"You're doing great," said someone.
It was the three bears.
I saw a dish of porridge.
Too cold.
I pushed it away.
Another dish.
Too hot.
I pushed it away.
A third dish.
Just right, but not mine.
I pushed for the last time, again.
"One more time," someone said.
I wanted to say I couldn't.
Speech was beyond me.

I pushed again.

"The baby is crowning," someone said.

I visualized her—my princess, wearing a crown, mistress of all she surveyed.

I was her mother.

I was about to meet her, to hold her in my arms.

My baby.

I would call her Lucy, as the angel had told me.

Lucy Elizabeth Manderley.

I pushed again.

Someone cheered.

"The head is out!" someone said.

The waves were starting to subside.

I pushed again.

"One last time."

"Congratulations!" someone crowed.

I looked down.

They were putting a baby in my arms. She was red and wrinkly, and her head was bulging at the top, but her face was perfect. She had a little dwarf face and slate-colored, worried eyes. She had lots of dark hair. Her hands were unbelievably tiny. Her fingers were thin; she had long fingernails.

My baby. She looked at me. My books had said that new-borns experienced the world as a symphony of shapes and colors. But she was looking at me. Her expression reminded me of someone at a party who recognizes you, and can't remember your name, or where they've met you before. She looked focused and perplexed.

"A girl," Adam said.

"I know," I told him. "Her name is Lucy. Lucy Elizabeth Manderley, don't ask me why."

"She looks like you," he said.

"Red and squirmy?" Raitlin asked. He kept running his hand through his hair, and smiling an 'I can't help it' kind of smile. He looked about twelve years old.

"Here," Carolina said. "Make sure her head is slightly lower than her body, so if there's any mucus still in her nose and mouth, it will drain out." She put the baby on my belly, which seemed awfully far away. Adam draped a soft blue baby blanket over most of the baby. I could feel her warmth and her weight.

Carolina smiled. "I wiped away most of the mucus and dried her off to help keep her warm. She'll stay warmest with her skin next to yours, but you might want to cover her head to prevent further heat loss."

"Wait a second." Raitlin pushed forwardly and shyly offered me a soft pink stocking cap. "They give these out," he said, beaming.

"Go ahead," I said. "You can put it on her." He bent over her, but almost immediately straightened up. "I can't," he said. "Her scalp is really soft. I'm afraid I'll hurt her."

"That's just a soft spot," I told him. "A fontanelle."

"I'm still afraid," said Raitlin.

"Please?" I said.

Raitlin reached out with both hands and slowly put the little pink cap on Lucy Elizabeth's head; as if in response, my contractions resumed. "Am I having twins?" I asked.

Carolina smiled a tired co-conspirator smile, and shook her head 'no'. "The contractions now will make sure the placenta separates from the uterine wall and into the vagina. If you bear down, you should be able to deliver it."

I did as instructed but nothing happened. "Give it a little time," said Adam.

"See that salmon-colored patch between the baby's eyebrows?" Raitlin asked. "They call that an 'angel kiss'. Don't you just love it? Those pregnancy books seem like nothing but horror at first, but if you keep looking...."

I couldn't take my eyes off my baby. It was impossible to realize, or even imagine, that she had been inside me only moments ago. I searched around in my mind, trying to bring a half-remembered Bible quote into focus. "Breath of my breath. Bone of my bone"—How did that go, anyway?

I stroked the top of the baby's head. It hurt my arm to have to hold it so lightly, but I was afraid if I let the full weight of my arm rest on her head, I might crush it. "I'm going to pull her up closer," I said, to no one in particular. I put my hands under the tiny, chicken-bone arms, lifted, and pulled her up toward me. She looked adorable sliding naked up toward me.

I hooked my thumbs under her tiny armpits and lifted the back of her head with my fingerprints. Then I moved her around, positioning her in the curve of my left arm. The noises in the room, the other people, subsided to a comforting roar.

Her belly button had a short cord sticking up out of it; it was colored dark blue. "The blue is from the antiseptic," Carolina said. "Within two to three weeks, the stub will turn black and fall off."

I felt another contraction, and then a kind of wet sliding. "It's out," Carolina said.

There was some conferring, then Raitlin came around to my side and put a plastic bowl down on top of the monitor. There was a red, bloody, meaty thing that I eventually identified as my placenta. "How did that get there?" I wondered aloud.

"They give placenta bowls away free here, too," Raitlin said.

"Are you kidding?" I asked him.

He giggled. "Absolutely," he said.

"So where did the bowl come from?"

"I brought it last week," Adam said.

"You can start breastfeeding, if you want," Carolina told me. "Breast feeding will help your uterus contract and reduce bleeding. You're kind of a mess down there, you know, and there's not much point in housecleaning until you stop bleeding."

"I'm not sure I know what to do," I said. I started to lift Lucy into position. "Try to keep her head supported," Adam told me.

I put Lucy down on my left breast. Adam and Carolina exchanged one of their "meaningful" smiles.

"What?" I asked at large.

"The heart breast," Carolina said. "It's a good sign."

The whole idea of signs made me uncomfortable. "Well," I said after a minute, "I don't think the ba—I don't think Lucy agrees with my choice of breast. She's not really sucking or anything."

"That's okay," Carolina said. "Just her nuzzling will probably help your uterus to contract." She started rubbing my abdomen. The massage felt good at first, but Carolina's touch was a little too definite to be comfortable, and the motion of her hands on my belly kept me from focusing on the baby at my breast. After a minute or two, I asked Carolina to stop.

"Okay," she said. "Your uterus is still a little soft, but I'll stop now."

Raitlin started to leave the room.

Suddenly, I very much didn't want him to leave. "Don't go, Rait," I said. "Stay here and be part of the family." Suddenly I knew what he'd had in mind. "You're thinking of David, aren't you?" I asked.

He nodded.

"Well, let's go to him, shall we, all of us?" I asked. "Look, I'll get myself decent and Carolina will help me mop up a bit. You call David and ask if he's up for a visit now. Say we want to all come up. Don't tell him about the baby. Okay? Please?"

Lucy had fallen asleep on my breast. I pulled her over toward my face again. "I know it's not very exciting," I told her, "but I'm afraid it's the best I've got to offer."

I looked around the room. "Where's Dr. O.?" I asked.

"She left a while ago," Carolina said. "Do you want me to get her back?"

"If you think we need her, yes. Otherwise, absolutely not!" I told her, a little more forcefully than I had intended.

Then Adam and Carolina and Raitlin and I laughed. Lucy squirmed a bit. "Don't worry," I told her. "You'll learn how to laugh in a few months."

Adam and Carolina exchanged another of their looks.

"What now?" I asked, knowing I had done something right again.

Adam smiled. "You're talking to the baby," he said. "That's a good sign, too."

"I've been talking to her for months now," I told him. "I see no reason to stop now that's she's born."

Raitlin called David from the bedside phone and got his permission to come up "as a group."

I could hear David, on the other end, asking who exactly was in this group.

"Wait and see," Raitlin said, making an exaggerated grimace to show me how hard he was trying not to giggle. "We'll be right up," he said, and hung up.

Carolina had me in as close to ship-shape as I was likely to get for a while. I had to get up and use the bathroom. That struck me as bizarre. I had just given birth. It had been a miracle. The baby was beautiful. Everything had gone perfectly. And now I had to go to the bathroom. I asked for the basket Raitlin had given me. Raitlin produced it with a magician's fanfare, and I put Lucy in it. I tucked in some of a small stack of rainbow-colored receiving blankets— "More free stuff!"— Raitlin announced gleefully, then I put the basket on the bed, and waddled off to the bathroom.

Before coming out of the bathroom, I tried to fix up my face a little, with modest success. When I got back to the bed, I found the sheets had been changed. The bed looked pristine again, as though I had never lain there, and sweated there, and leaked amniotic fluid there, and given birth there.

The bowl with the placenta in it was still on the monitor. "Do you want to use this?" Adam asked me.

"Use it how?"

Carolina shrugged. "It's full of nutrients," she told me, smiling. "In some so-called primitive cultures, a woman who has just given birth has a sort of placenta stew as her first meal. She offers some to those who have helped her. Not that I'm asking." She made a funny face.

"Well," I said. "The idea of eating anything that looks like that makes me want to vomit. But you all are free to go ahead."

As it turned out, no one was up for placenta snacking. "I'll take care of it," Carolina said.

I climbed into bed and reclaimed Lucy, who still appeared to be sleeping soundly. I tugged her hat down a little more snuggly over her ears and admired her again. She really was beautiful. And so tiny!

"Here," Carolina said, "you probably should sign this before we go up."

She showed me the form she had filled out. It stated that a female infant named "Lucy Elizabeth Manderley" had been born to Susan Manderley at "University Hospital, Ann Arbor, Michigan," at 5:47 p.m. on September 2000. She weighed in at 6 pounds 11 ounces. She was 21 centimeters long. Next to father, it said, "Unknown."

Adam held the form on a clipboard while I signed. I couldn't stop staring at the "Unknown."

"Thank you," I said.

"You might want to try nursing again," Carolina said in a soft drawl.

I stroked Lucy's cheek with my finger, and she woke up. She stared at me, as if wondering why I'd disturbed her. And when I nudged my breast in her mouth, she opened her tiny rosebud mouth in an enormous yawn.

"She's not ready yet," Adam said. "It'll come."

It dawned on me that I could go up on my own power. "I don't have to stay in this bed, you know, Adam," I said. "I can walk up there to see David."

No one seemed to think this was a good idea. Even Raitlin expressed opposition.

"Well, at least let me go in a wheelchair," I said, trying not to sound like a kid, begging for an extra dessert. "I've been in this bed for eons. At least let me sit up for a while."

There was some deliberation about this, but eventually even the authorities agreed. I promised to return to the floor for a final check-up of myself and the baby before we left for good.

Never had the phrase "for good" rung so truly.

I started with Lucy in her basket sideways on my lap, her head pointing toward me. But while we were waiting for the elevator, I extracted her, being careful to support her head the way Adam had showed me. Raitlin carried the empty basket with evident and endearing pride.

But in the elevator, I began to wonder if visiting David with the baby was a good idea.

"I haven't seen David for weeks," I said to no one in particular. And this is—such a happy time for me, and it must be such a horrible time for him.... He might feel—I don't know—like we're saying he doesn't matter, or something."

Raitlin patted me on the shoulder. "It'll be okay, Susie. Trust me."

The warmth of his hand made me feel good. "I do trust you," I said. "I do."

Everybody laughed.

"Where's Adam?" I said. All at once, I wanted him where I could see him, where I could watch his face, where I could watch him watching the baby. It struck me that for the last— what had it been? an hour? a decade?— I had lost track of him. I didn't want to do that, ever again.

I looked down at the baby in my arms. She looked content, at home. The books had scared me: *Don't be nervous*, they had said. *Nervous mothers communicate their nervousness to the newborn.* Apparently I had communicated something else.

"I'm right here," Adam said from behind me. "You did the pushing before. Now it's my turn."

The elevator stopped at the eighth floor, and we got out.

"Carolina," I said. "Would you mind pushing me to the room? I'd really like Adam next to me."

"Of course," Carolina said.

In a moment, Adam was by my right side, smiling down at me. I looked down at Lucy. She was beautiful. I looked up at Adam. He was beautiful, too.

Adam grinned at me. I grinned back. He put his hand on my shoulder while Carolina pushed me down the corridor. Raitlin came up on the left side and put his hand on that shoulder. The two hands felt very different—Adam's definite and big, Raitlin's tentative and small. They both felt good on my shoulders.

Scurrying nurses and doctors saw us, and faded back, smiling. We were like some triumphant convoy. Carolina bent down and whispered next to my ear, "We're the happiest thing they've seen all month." She stopped the wheelchair. "Do you know what day it is?"

"Lucy's birthday," I said.

"Yes," Carolina said. "She was born on Labor Day!"

We were all joking and laughing about that when we reached the door to David's room. Instantly, a kind of chill fell over us. I began to wish I'd taken the time to put on street clothes. My thin little hospital gown, decorated with teddy bears, and my thin little hospital robe were no match for the cold of the hospital corridor.

Raitlin took a few steps into the room. There was an old guy lying in the bed nearest the door. He was scrawny and had a rather long and pointy beard: he looked both skeletal and cheerful, like an anemic Santa Clause or a cartoon version of Death. He had stacks of books piled on his bedside table, and a Polaroid camera perched on top of these like a square plastic blackbird. He greeted us jovially. "Welcome to our humble abode, folks," he said. "Come on in."

Raitlin stepped aside, and Carolina wheeled me forward. The room was so bright it took me a moment to make out David. He was lying in bed, semi-reclined. He looked thinner and paler.

He was wearing a baseball cap.

All he had on his bedside table was a half-full glass of water, but a page had been torn out of a magazine and taped to the edge of the table, so it hung down where David and— if they looked closely enough, his visitors—could see it. The picture was of blocks of snow that had been made into a wall. The blocks had been hollowed out in the centers so you could see sunlight shining through them. The caption under the photo read, "out early to work the cold— Andy Goldsworthy, 2000. MOMA Lecture Series, Sunday 1-5." Under the printed caption was a black ink signature, hard to read against the gray background of the picture: "I'll never stop loving you— R."

I looked down at Lucy. She still had her eyes closed. She was too little to smile, the books said, too little for facial expressions at all. That was nonsense. Expression after expression kept drifting across her tiny face like even tinier clouds. Her silence was more expressive than anything anyone would ever say.

I looked at Carolina. "She hasn't made a peep," I said.

Carolina nodded. "It's okay, honey," she said. "She made several little peeps right after she was born. We were just making so much noise, you didn't hear them."

"Well, she's not making any peeps now," I said.

"That's because she's happy."

I looked back down at Lucy for confirmation. At the moment, she had soared far beyond "happy" in her expression register: she looked blissful. She appeared to be asleep. She was making nose noises.

"What do you think of our Yul Brynner?" Raitlin asked the room at large, his voice breaking. "He couldn't wait, so he made me do it. All that beautiful hair."

David had taken off his "Seattle Mariners" cap.

He was bald. He looked beautiful in a strange way. His eyebrows were gone, too.

"Let it alone, Rait," David said. His voice was mild. He was looking at me.

David smiled. He looked both exhausted and clarified, somehow. It seemed to cost him a big effort to smile, but when he did, his whole face smiled.

"May I hold the baby, please?" David asked.

The simple request caught me off guard. No one else had asked that. It would be the first time someone else held her. I didn't really want to let Lucy out of my arms. I also didn't want to refuse.

"Do you want to me to do the transfer?" Adam asked, bending toward me a little.

"Okay," I said. And it was okay. Somehow, I didn't mind so much giving her to Adam.

Adam took Lucy gently from my arms. Just as he was reaching to lift her, she opened her eyes, and looked up at me. She had the most beautiful eyes in the world. They were a strange and mystical color, a color I had never seen before, cerulean and opalescent.

"Be careful, Adam," I said.

He smiled, too. With infinite care, Adam rewrapped Lucy in her blue blanket, and handed her as a kind of bundled packet to David.

I suddenly felt very tired. I had had enough of sitting up, but my bed was stranded somewhere eight floors below us. "David," I said. "Do you mind if I climb up there with you two?"

"I'd like that, if no one else minds," David said, not raising his eyes for a moment.

Almost automatically, I started to look at Adam.

But then I realized: I didn't need to ask his permission. I needed to get in the habit of trusting myself, my instincts. I was a mother now. I needed to get used to being in charge.

I got clumsily out of the wheelchair, and Adam helped me climb into bed next to David. David was so thin. I was worried I might accidentally push him off the bed. He already had a blanket over him, but Adam got another blanket from the chair at the foot of the bed and put that over the two of us. I took Lucy back from David.

Carolina and Raitlin moved around to stand by David at the far side of the bed. Adam stood next to me and began giving me a gentle one-handed shoulder rub. The muscles in my shoulders seemed to drink in the attention; they were as sore as if I'd been carrying a cross somewhere.

The guy in the next bed began to chortle. "Freeze!" he said. He got out of bed, (grabbed his Polaroid and started taking pictures. "The flash doesn't seem to be working," he said. "But there's enough daylight for something to develop."

He clicked a total of seven pictures. Then he laid all seven out for us on David's bedside table. "Choose on your way out," he said. "I'll take whatever's left. They're all pretty dark."

I was wondering about the "seven." The photographer smiled as if reading my thoughts. "One for me, one for the baby when she grows up," he said. "It is a girl, isn't it? In the old days, you could tell by the blankets. Now they've got the hats."

"This is Lucy," I told him. "Lucy Elizabeth Manderley."

"Well, she's a lucky girl, to have a mom, a dad, two grandpas and a grandma to take care of her."

"You're right," I said. "Not many people have this kind of loving family."

And Adam and Carolina and Raitlin and David and I and the photographer exchanged smiles as if we were sköling.

Lucy was sleeping. I weaseled my little finger into her curled fist.

When I glanced up, Adam was still smiling at me—one of his wide open, sunny, *no matter what happens next, this is wonderful* smiles.

I remembered how, eons ago, Adam had reached out and touched my belly. I thought of blocks of snow, radiant with sunlight, their fragility, their beauty. The moment was so radical in its deep, brief blessing, I could hardly breathe.

"Adam," I said. "She's holding on to me."

"Freeze!" came from another world

The man who looked like a cartoon version of Death was beaming at us. He reached for his camera again.

"You know what?" he said. "This right here is the real ticket!"

This time, the camera flashed.

Lucy turned toward me, eyes closed, rooting blindly.

"I'm right here where you need me," I told her softly, positioning her a little better. "Let me know if I'm holding you too tight."

For answer, Lucy began to nurse.

Epilogue

Not long ago, Adam and I were sitting in our breakfast nook and Adam was watching me nurse Lucy. "You yelled in your sleep again," he said, looking down at his plate of fried egg and toast, as though he weren't addressing me at all.

"I'm sorry, sweetheart," I said.

"You still having that ghost-skeleton nightmare?" he said. He was drawing figure eights on the tablecloth with his fork.

"Yes," I said.

Ghost or skeleton, it's him. I'm still afraid that, somehow, he'll find out where we live and— come after us."

Adam frowned. "Don't say that, Susan. You know he can't do that."

"No, I don't," I said. "I can't be sure of that and neither can you."

The words were hanging in the air.

Adam looked me straight in the eyes. Slowly and quietly, he said, "You can be sure. He's never coming after you. Never."

I looked at him. "Oh, my god," I said. "What happened? What did you—"

"Susan," Adam said. "You can ask me many things, but don't ask me that. I am not going to tell you. Ever."

"But you- You did something, right? You—"

He got up and took his plate to the sink. He began rinsing it in hot water. But when he took it out, there were still remnants of food on it. "I'll say it once more and that's the end of it. I took care of the situation, Susan. You don't have to worry now."

"Oh, Adam, what did you do? You killed him?"

Adam turned. He looked not angry but very, very serious. "You're not listening. I shouldn't have said anything, but it's been hard to see you suffering."

"When?" I said. "When did you take care of things?"

"Please don't," Adam told me. "Just do me a favor and don't have any more nightmares."

He left for a walk soon after that and the walk took several hours. I kept going back over in my mind the months Adam and I had been together. I couldn't remember a time when he had been gone for long enough to– Of course, I knew he had killed people in his line of work, but this was different. This was— murder. For my sake. Our sake. And I had told him to do it. I had said that's what I wanted.

When Adam came back, it was at first a little hard to look at him. If there was fault here– and there was, of course, there had to be– I was part of it. I was a swirl of emotions– guilt and relief among them– but my emotional state didn't seem important somehow. My heart went out to this man, who had gone through so much to keep me and Lucy safe. And conflicted as I was, I was glad Lucy wouldn't have to worry.

"Adam," I said. "I want you to know that I'm really glad and really sorry you had to go through this, that you felt pushed or driven to do what I won't mention." Adam took me by the arms and he looked straight into my eyes. "Do you believe there's an end to it?" he asked.

"Yes," I said. He nodded. After a moment, he said in a voice so soft I almost couldn't hear him– "If you believe me, I've said enough."

"Okay," I said.

The other night, Lucy was fussy and sometimes when she's fussy, Adam can hold her in a way that calms her, a way I can't. "Little Miss Lucy, do you want your daddy now?" I asked her. Adam was across the room and he looked up, a question in his eyes.

"It's true," I said. "That's what you are."

Adam smiled.

Lucy quieted the moment I put her in Adam's large, capable hands. "I love you," Adam said. "And I love Lucy. That's all that matters."

"I know," I said. "You're right. I'm wrong. I'm sorry. I'll change."

We both laughed.

"I mean it," I said.

"I believe you," he said.

We both laughed again.

Tomorrow night, we're gathering together at Raitlin's: Carolina, David, Raitlin himself, Adam, Lucy and I are having a family get-together to celebrate the miracle of David's current remission.

The more I think about it, the surer I am– whatever happens, we're a family now, and we can handle it. We're going to be okay." Whatever it is, we can handle it together. We're going to be okay.

About the Author

Lyn Coffin (b. 1943) is an award-winning fiction writer, poet, playwright, translator. More than 30 of her books have been published by Doubleday, Ithaca House, Abattoir Editions and others. One of her short fictions ("Falling Off the Scaffold" was first published in the Michigan Quarterly Review (1978) and included by Joyce Carol Oates in Best American Short Stories, 1979. *The First Honeymoon, New and Selected Stories*, was published by IronTwine Press in 2015. Her short fictions have been published in Catholic Digest, The Bridge, Rackham Review, Ball State Forum, and Golden Handcuffs Review, among other publications. When a student at the University of Michigan, she won Major Hopwood Writing Awards in every category. She was Associate Editor of the Michigan Quarterly Review for several years, and has taught English and Creative Writing at the University of Michigan, the University of Wisconsin (Milwaukee), the Milwaukee Institute of Art and Design, and the University of Detroit. She has given readings with (Nobel Prize winning poet) Joseph Brodsky, Czeslaw Milosz and Phillip Levine.

Her poems have won many awards and been published in more than a hundred literary reviews and magazines. Her plays have been performed in several cities worldwide, including Singapore, New York (Off Off Broadway) and Detroit. She was a recipient of a Michigan Council for the Arts grant and a National Endowment for the Humanities Award. She lives in Seattle.

To the Reader: The specifics of The Aftermath are not autobiographical. But I was raped many years ago, and that rape still lives somewhere inside me. I believe the telling of our stories helps us to survive. I hope you will write me through the publisher if you have stories of your own to share. Warm best wishes,

Lyn